Shadows of the Past

by

Lannie Sheridan

Copyright © 2015 by Lannie Sheridan

All rights reserved.

This book or any portion thereof may not be reproduced or used in any manner whatsoever without the express written permission of the publisher except for the use of brief quotations in a book review.

Printed in the United States of America

First Printing, 2015

ISBN: 978-1-62217-412-6

This book is dedicated to Linda.
Thanks for being part of my adopted family and helping me find my path. Rest in peace, dear cousin.

Chapter One

Long ago, in our solar system, things were very different than they are today. The ten planets that orbited our sun were inhabitable, thanks to the vast magic of each of the great founders who first claimed the planets as their own. Lady Mercuria, Lord Venusian, Lady Terriana, Lady Marsia, Lady Juna, Lord Saturine, Lady Nephetunia, Lord Urano, Lady Plutonia, Lord Daerus, and Lady Damia used the last of their life forces to fill each world with vast plants and living creatures.

Soon the children of these founders made rich and unique kingdoms that thrived on the worlds named for their creators. In the beginning, these kingdoms had little to do with one another, other than going to war against each other. Eventually eight of the ten kingdoms united under the rule of one woman, Galactica, who created an Intergalactic Court, which she ruled over as the empress. While she was the supreme leader of the court, she was far from being a dictator. Each kingdom was free to rule their subjects as they saw fit and could retain their own governments, just as they had before the court was formed. All she required was that they work together, follow certain ethical policies that they all agreed upon, and that the eldest son or daughter of each family serve as her personal guards, who would represent their homes at meetings of the court. It was a time of peace and prosperity for the kingdoms, but nothing lasts forever. Thus our story begins at the beginning of the end.

* * *

On the closest planet to the sun, named Mercury after the great Lady Mercuria, who blessed the planet with her magical healing waters, the royal family was about to receive two visitors. One was a messenger from the empress, and the other was an old soul who would see the last days of the mighty kingdoms.

As the royal messenger exited the carriage just inside the ornate golden castle gates, he raised his white gloved hand to his orange eyes to shield them from the brightness of the afternoon sun that was reflecting off the blue crystalline walls of the palace. He was greeted by two palace guards in dark-blue Mercurian uniforms whom he knew well. Grabbing his small yellow bag with the symbol of the empress, he made his way through the usual security procedures.

Inside the towering castle the royal family of Mercury was busy with their own tasks. His Royal Highness, King Arkanthius, was in the war room with his generals, going over the latest reports of raider attacks in the outer rim of the system. While Mercury was in the inner part of the system, Arkanthius was the empress's most trusted strategist. Even though he had retired years ago from the court, she still went to him for battle plans and suggestions on defending the system. Her Majesty, Queen Amirilla V, was running around the grand hall giving orders to the servants on how things should be prepared for that night's grand feast. At least eight servants were following behind her, taking notes of every command. They all knew the queen normally wasn't big on making everything perfect for a feast of this size, but, while this was the smallest dinner party they'd given in a long time, the guest of honor was a person of great importance. He was an old friend of the queen's, who had been away for many years. While Amirilla was throwing the dinner party to celebrate his return, only she and the king were aware of that fact.

Meanwhile the princesses, who were home for the Creation Day holiday, were off doing their own things. The sixteen-year-old princess, Tora, was locked in her room, busy with her studies. She would be graduating from the academy this year, and she wanted nothing more than to beat her eldest sister's scores. The eldest daughter, Amirilla VI, who had graduated at the top of her class from the Intergalactic Academy and was about to assume her new position in the Intergalactic Court, was outside with her cousins and close friends.

Amirilla, known as Rilla to her close friends and family, was, as usual, in the courtyard, busy practicing her fencing. Rilla's late older brother, Amdis, had started teaching her to fence at an early age, but very few knew that fact. Rilla's current duel partner was Rukia, the eldest daughter of the Uranus family and the fiancée of Rilla's older cousin Michael of Neptune.

"Hey, Saedi! Watch as I kick the Mercury's ass," Rukia called to her little sister, who was sitting off to the side with the others. She brushed her light brown bangs away from her green eyes and smiled.

Running his fingers through his light blue hair, the eldest Neptune prince grinned. "This should be interesting," Michael stated as he sat by his brother Triston and his cousin Nathaniel. Michael was one of the few who knew of Rilla's skill with a sword.

"Oh?" Nathaniel asked curiously as he leaned against the blue stone table they were sitting at.

"Mmm-hmm…it should be fun," Saedi said cheerfully as she pulled her blonde hair to the side and started to braid it. "Rukia has only ever lost to one person."

"And who was that?" Triston inquired as he played with his thick black mustache.

"My brother," Rilla said with a smile.

Amdis had been the best duelist in the system and often competed against Rukia at tournaments. While he'd taught Rilla all that he knew, he'd asked her to focus on her studies, instead of dueling. So she never dueled with anyone, other than family and close friends.

"And the only person to ever beat Di-chan was me." She grinned at Rukia. "Sure you don't want to take back that previous statement?" Rilla teased the older princess as she lunged back and forth, stretching her legs.

"Now why would I do a silly thing like that? Amdis always let you win, so stop your yapping, and let's get to it," Rukia demanded as she took her fighting stance, golden rapier in her left hand.

"Very well then." Rilla took her stance and glanced at the others, who were sitting at a table by the giant mercurite statue of Lady Mercuria. "Saedi, give the signal, and then we'll see the same result as the last time your big sister claimed she was going to kick a Mercury's ass," Rilla said as she pulled her brother's silver rapier, which was adorned with sapphires and mercurite crystals, from its sheath.

Saedi stood and pulled off her yellow silk scarf.

"Ready?"

"Ready," the two said in unison.

Saedi lifted the scarf up and, as she brought it down, exclaimed, "Then begin!"

At her signal, the two went at each other. For the most part, they seemed evenly matched. They met each other blow for blow and lunge for lunge, but Rukia had one slight advantage. Rilla quickly realized the difference in strength between the two and made up for it by increasing her speed. When Rukia matched her speed, she knew it was time to stop relying on speed and strength. As Rukia lunged at her, Rilla sidestepped and attacked. Rukia barely moved in time to avoid the blow. She lunged again, and this time Rilla sidestepped, moved behind her, and literally kicked Rukia's ass, sending her stumbling forward, causing her to drop her sword and nearly fall flat on her face.

Rukia regained her footing and turned to glare at Rilla. "Why, you little…"

Rilla laughed. "So who kicked whose ass?"

Saedi laughed and retrieved Rukia's sword for her. "That's just how it happened last time."

"Well, almost the same result. If I was a little stronger, you would have fallen flat on your face, just like you did the last time you fought my brother," Rilla stated as she sheathed the sword she had inherited from Amdis.

"So has anyone ever beaten you, Ami?" Nathaniel asked casually as he stood to stretch his long legs.

"Of course, Di-chan kicked my ass all the time. I had to work hard to beat him, and I only did that three times. And my name is Amirilla, not Ami," she said with a slight glare in Nathaniel's direction.

Nathaniel and Triston had attended the academy with Rilla, and while she considered them friends, she wasn't as close with them as she was with Michael and Rukia, who were the same age as Amdis.

"Touchy, touchy," Nathaniel said with a smirk. He knew Rilla well enough to know not to call her Ami, but he enjoyed pushing buttons, just to see what reaction he got.

Shadows of the Past

"Little Mi-chan is picky about her name," Michael stated as he stood and handed Rukia a towel.

While Michael was Rilla's cousin, he and Rukia had also been Amdis's best friends, which meant she saw them a lot because she was never very far from the big brother she adored, when he was actually home.

"Mi-chan?" Triston asked, looking around, confused. He didn't recognize the nickname, but then again he was usually too busy watching and chasing pretty girls to pay attention to little details.

"There are only four people alive who can call me that," Rilla said firmly. "My parents, Michael, and Rukia."

"Mi-chan is the nickname Amdis gave her," Saedi explained.

When Rilla was little, she had trouble pronouncing Amdis, so she had called him Di-chan, Di because it was the only part of his name she could say easily and Chan because he was her dear brother. Chan was an ancient Mercurian word and was used after the name of someone dear to signify a close relationship. Amdis and her mother had often called her Rilla-chan, so she picked up on it, and thus Amdis became her Di-chan. The nickname stuck, and in return, he started affectionately calling her Mi-chan. Everyone else called her Rilla, but her brother only called her by her full name or his personal nickname for her. While she didn't care if Michael and Rukia called her by her brother's nickname, it was rare for them to actually do so, mostly out of respect for their late friend.

Rilla picked up a towel and wiped her face. "Well, I guess it's time to call it a day since it's obvious there is still no one who can beat me," she teased.

Rukia was about to protest when the royal messenger entered the courtyard.

"Excuse me, Your Majesties. I'm sorry to interrupt, but I have messages for all of you."

Rilla sat down and nodded. "Good to see you again, Ramon."

He bowed and took several letters out of his bag. "I bring letters from Central Palace."

Ramon glanced at the group and nodded his head respectfully as he handed each envelope to the appropriate person. The first was handed to Michael. Ramon took a moment to observe the differences between the two Neptune princes. While they were both fairly tall, Michael was slightly taller than Triston, and while various shades of blue were the most common hair color in both the Neptune and Mercury bloodlines, Triston had been born with hair that was as black as a starless night sky. Handing the next envelope to Nathaniel, Ramon thought to himself how Nathaniel and his cousin looked more alike than the brothers. Nathaniel also had black hair, but his had a slight bluish tint to it in certain light. Giving a letter to Rukia, he took notice of the fact that she and the blonde, who he assumed to be her sister, were the only ones with a tan complexion. The Neptune boys and Princess Rilla all had olive skin.

Michael, who had received his letter first, opened it and smiled, "Huh! Looks likes there's a grand ball at Central Palace next week."

"Central Palace?" Saedi asked excitedly. "Wow! I've never been to Central Palace before!"

"And you still won't get to see it, little sister," Rukia said. "This says by invitation only. So unless Ramon has one for you…"

Saedi looked to Ramon with hopeful eyes, but he just shook his head as he handed the last envelope to Rilla.

"No fair!" she pouted.

Rilla laughed. "Don't worry, Saedi. You'll get to go one day."

Ramon nodded and bowed to each of them politely.

"Good day, Your Majesties."

"Good day, Ramon," Rilla said as he turned and left.

"Formal attire? Great! That means I have to wear a stupid frilly dress," Rukia said with disgust.

"Oh, stop complaining. It won't kill you to be girly once in a while," Michael said as he wrapped his arms around her.

"Besides, how often do we get invited to Central Palace?" Triston asked.

"What's this 'we'? As far as I know, you've never been there, cousin," Nathaniel stated.

"He was there in spirit. Just like Saedi will be there in spirit this time," Rilla said as she placed her invitation on the table. "I'll have to find an escort, though. Jacob won't be home from the Sirius Sector until after the ball." She tried not to sound happy about the fact that her husband was away.

"Needs to be someone that husband of yours won't be jealous of," Rukia added. "Don't want him trying to kill the poor fellow just for dancing with you." She chuckled.

Rukia had said it jokingly, but they all knew it wasn't far from the truth. Jacob was very possessive of Rilla, usually too possessive for her liking. She felt he treated her more like property than a wife.

"Nathaniel can be your escort," Saedi suggested happily.

"Why him?" Triston asked. He had been about to offer to be her escort.

"That's obvious, dear brother," Michael started. "Nathaniel has more class than you and is a better dancer. We can't have Mi-chan escorted by anyone who's not a gentleman."

"I'm a gentleman," protested Triston.

"Sure…that's not what that Mars girl was saying after you took her for a walk in the gardens," Rukia teased.

Triston shrugged and stood up to stretch. "Some people just don't appreciate the outdoors."

"Besides, since he's family, Jacob can't object," Michael added.

"Well, not really family," Nathaniel corrected. "I'm your cousin by marriage, so I'm not as close as you are to Rilla."

Shadows of the Past

"Who cares? You're escorting her to a ball, not marrying her," Rukia said, not even noticing how her comment made the two blush slightly.

"Well, anyway, we should be heading home before we miss our ship," Triston said, grabbing his bag.

"Oh, must you leave so soon?" Rilla asked. "Surely you can stay for dinner and catch a flight in the morning?"

"Wish we could, Rilla, but we've got a long trip, and we promised to have Saedi home in time for her lessons," Rukia stated.

"Plus, if we're not home for the Creation Day festival, Mother will have our heads," Michael added.

The Creation Day celebration was different on every planet, but the point of the holiday was the same. It was a celebration of the creation of the kingdoms, in which each planet honored their founder. For Mercury, it was a day of prayer and reflection, usually done by a body of water with hundreds of gallons of Mercurian ale used to honor Lady Mercuria. Neptune, on the other hand, had a three-day festival with parades and shows. Because he was a member of the royal family, Michael was expected to lead most of the events.

Rilla nodded. "All right. Have a safe trip, and I'll see you four at the ball. Saedi, I'll see you in three weeks."

"Three weeks?" Saedi asked.

"I'll be staying with Michael before the ceremony. You'll be on Neptune with Rukia, right?"

"Oh! Right. I forgot about that."

Rilla smiled and shook her head. Saedi apologized and gathered her belongings.

"Won't you at least let me find Mother, so she can say good-bye as well?" Rilla asked.

"Auntie is busy with plans for tonight's feast. We shouldn't bother her," Michael stated.

"Yeah, just give her our regards," Rukia added.

Rilla nodded, walked the group to their coach, and they said their good-byes. Nathaniel stood back from the others and waited for her to finish the hugs and kisses.

"I guess I'll see you next week then." He took her hand and placed a kiss on it while slipping a note into her hand. He climbed into the coach, and as it started to move, he waved and gave her a wink before sitting back in his seat.

As the coach went out the main gate, one of the servants approached her. "Your Highness, your mother wishes to see you."

Rilla nodded, placing the note from Nathaniel in her pocket to read later, and followed the servant to her mother.

"You wished to see me, Mother?"

Her mother turned to face Rilla, a smile on her face and her bright blue eyes almost sparkling. "Yes, we're having a very special guest join us for dinner this evening. I'd like it very much if you wore your formal gown, the blue one with the silk bow."

Shadows of the Past

Lowering her head, Rilla took a deep breath and said, "I'm sorry, Mother. I can't."

"But, Rilla-chan," her mother said, giving her daughter her best set of pleading eyes, "you look beautiful in that gown, and I've already had the seamstress alter it because you've grown since the last time you wore it."

The princess shook her head. "That's the last gown Di-chan gave me. I haven't worn that since his…" She stopped as her eyes began to fill with tears. Amdis had given the dress to his sister for her formal ball at the academy. He was supposed to be her escort, but the day of the ball, Rilla's father returned from a patrol mission with devastating news. Prince Amdis had been killed in a raider attack. That was five years ago, but for Rilla, the pain of losing him hadn't decreased much.

The queen stood and hugged her daughter. "Is that why you never wear it?" Rilla nodded, and her mother sighed. "What about the crystal Amdis gave you?"

"I never take it off," she said as she reached her hand up to grab the dark blue mercurite crystal around her neck. The crystal had been a gift from her brother. He had given it to her when she was three. Rilla was always upset when Amdis left for the academy, so he gave her the enchanted crystal to help make the separation easier on her. "It's all I have left of big brother."

Her mother shook her head. "No, you have his sword, your memories, and all the gifts he gave you, including that dress." She wiped the tears from her daughter's eyes. "Rilla, did you know Amdis spent a month picking out that dress for you?"

Looking up at her mother, she shook her head. "He did?"

Queen Amirilla nodded. "Yes, he had fashion designers from all over bring sketches and samples. He even dragged Rukia and Saedi to various shops to look."

"Really?"

"Yes. So if your brother took such time and care to find you the perfect dress, don't you think he'd be a little upset if you never wore it?"

Rilla took a minute to consider what her mother said. "I guess you're right, Mother. Di-chan only got to see me wear it once. I'll wear it tonight, and I'll wear it to the ball at Central Palace next week."

Smiling, the queen hugged her daughter. "I'm glad. You know Amdis was always extremely proud of you. Oh, if only he could see you now. The youngest Mercurian to assume a position on the Intergalactic Court."

As Rilla smiled, she shook her head. "Almost, Mother. Di-chan was younger."

"No, your brother wasn't inducted into the court until he was twenty-one. He started training with your father after he graduated the academy at the age of sixteen."

"Oh!" Rilla nodded and followed her mother to the kitchen to talk to Maurice about the menu for the banquet.

Chapter Two

Later, in her room, Rilla took the blue formal gown out of her closet, which was where it had been for the last five years. If not for the seamstress altering it, the dress would have still been hidden in the very back. Rilla's eyes filled with tears as she touched the soft, silky fabric. "I swore I would never wear this dress again." She wiped her eyes and placed the gown on the bed.

"*You look beautiful, Mi-chan.*" Her brother's voice echoed in her head. She could still remember the night he gave her the dress, as if it were just yesterday.

"We were so happy that day. You were getting a promotion. Father announced he had decided to retire from the court, and I was about to graduate the academy," she said, talking to herself out loud. "And then everything changed." Sitting on the bed, she closed her eyes and sighed.

Hearing voices come from the princess's room, Rilla's loyal friend and guardian, Vixie, walked in. Seeing she was upset, she hopped on the bed beside her. "Rilla-chan," she said, placing her paw on her hand.

Rilla wiped her eyes. "You always know when to come and find me, don't you, Vixie?"

"Of course. What kind of guardian would I be if I didn't?" Rilla smiled as she picked up the red fox and placed her on her lap. "So what's bothering you, Rilla-chan?"

"Memories."

"Amdis?"

"Yes. Mother asked me to wear the dress Di-chan gave me to the banquet tonight."

"Wow! Must be a big event if Her Majesty asked you to wear that," Vixie stated.

Nodding, Rilla sighed. "I said I would, but I don't know if I can, Vixie. I mean, the last time I wore that dress was at big brother's ceremony of passing. I swore then that I would never wear this dress again."

"I'm sure, if you told your mother, she'd understand."

"I did. And she told me how Di-chan had spent a month picking out this dress. And as much as it saddens me to remember the last time I wore this dress, Mother had a point. Di-chan put so much time and care into making sure he found the perfect dress that he would be disappointed if I never wear it. So no matter how much it hurts, I will wear this dress for Di-chan."

Vixie sat up, putting her paws on Rilla's chest. "I know that would have made Amdis very happy," she said as she nuzzled Rilla.

Shadows of the Past

Rilla nodded and hugged Vixie. As she was about to stand, she heard dogs barking outside. After placing Vixie on the bed, she stood and walked to the window. "I wonder what has them all worked up?" She looked and saw three of the royal hounds jumping around and barking at a boy by the lake. "Now who could that be?" she asked as she turned to run downstairs.

"Wait for me! Rilla!" Vixie called, chasing after her.

Racing down the stairs, Rilla flew out the door to the courtyard. She ran through the garden toward the lake. Most would have run around the large hedge labyrinth, but she knew it so well she dashed in and out and made it through in no time at all. As she reached the lake, she looked around. "I…know…I…saw… someone…here," she said, between deep gasps for breath.

As Vixie finally caught up, she jumped on Rilla's shoulders to avoid the hounds, who rushed over to greet them. "I really hate those hounds," she commented as they sniffed and whimpered at her.

"It's all right, Vixie. They just want to play with you," she replied as she petted each of the three hounds in turn.

"But must they slobber all over me and…everything?"

Rilla laughed as she bent down and hugged the three large blue hounds, who took the chance to knock her down and try to sit on her lap, all of them at the same time.

"Hey! Easy, boys," she said, laughing harder.

Vixie jumped down when Jarod grabbed her tail. "That is not a chew toy, you mutt!" she yelled as she raced to the nearest tree and climbed up to the safety of its branches.

Jarod chased her, barking the whole time while Marcus and Maxwell continued trying to sit on the princess. "That's enough, boys," she said, still laughing as they licked her, wagging their tails. Once she finally calmed them down enough so that she was able to get up, she walked over to the tree where Jarod was still barking at Vixie. "That's enough, Jarod. Vixie doesn't want to play."

He whimpered and rubbed his head against her leg. She patted his head and then reached up for Vixie, who jumped to her waiting arms. "Come on, boys. Let's head back to the palace, unless there's someone else here you want to play with?"

The hounds sat at her feet, wagging their tails, but didn't make a sound. Vixie shook her head. "These mutts couldn't lead you to an intruder if he had a steak tied around his neck."

"Vixie, that's not nice," Rilla scolded.

"It's the truth, though."

Rilla tapped her gently on the nose. "That's enough, missy. Come on, boys. I'll get you some bones." They barked and followed her happily to the palace.

* * *

As the princess and the hounds walked back to the palace, he watched from the shadows. "Silly pups," he said to himself. Grabbing his cloak, he headed back to the palace. He had promised the queen he would behave and try to be on time for dinner.

* * *

Shadows of the Past

Meanwhile, inside the palace, the queen and her servants were running around, making the final preparations for dinner. The table was being set, the cooks were busy in the kitchen, the musicians were tuning their instruments, and the king and Princess Tora were hiding in the study, playing a game of chess. Tora studied the board and made her move. "Check."

King Arkanthius laughed and rubbed his bearded chin. "I see you've gotten a lot better since we last played. Pretty soon your old dad is going to be the worst player in the castle." He made his move and motioned to her. It was her turn.

"You just have to practice more, Father," Tora replied, making her next move. "Check, and, I believe, mate."

"Again, I lose." He sighed. "It seems I shall have to convince your mother to practice with me as you and Rilla-chan are away so much these days."

Entering the room, the queen walked over to her husband and wrapped her arms around his neck. "Don't worry, dear. I'll be sure to let you win now and then," she teased as she kissed his cheek. "Now come on, both of you. It's time to clean up and dress for dinner."

"Yes, dear," Arkanthius said as he stood. "Perhaps we'll play another game after dinner, Tora-chan."

"Gladly, Father," she replied before heading up to her room.

The king smiled and took his wife's hand. "They grow up so fast, don't they, my dear?"

Queen Amirilla nodded and walked with him to their chambers. "Yes, they do. Seems like only yesterday they were running around fighting with sticks in the gardens, and now look at them. Rilla's about to join the Court, and Tora will soon be graduating from the academy. I just wish Amdis could be here to see them. I know he'd be so proud of both of them."

"Yes, he would," Arkanthius agreed. He turned and embraced his wife. "I miss him, too."

Amirilla laid her head on his shoulder and sighed. "I hope Rilla will be all right. I hit a nerve earlier." When the king looked at her with a questioning expression, she continued, "I asked her to wear the blue dress that Amdis got for her to dinner tonight."

He nodded and slowly led her the rest of the way to their room. "You explained to her all the trouble he went through in order to find that dress, I presume?"

"Yes, and she seemed to cheer up a bit. Said she'd wear it tonight and to the ball at Central Palace next week. I just hope asking her to do so wasn't too demanding on my part."

"Nonsense, my dear. Rilla looks beautiful in that dress, and I know Amdis would be very upset if she never wore it." Queen Amirilla nodded and walked into her chambers with her husband, closing the door behind them.

* * *

As they dressed for dinner, young Rilla snuck three bones from the kitchen and gave them to the hounds.

Shadows of the Past

"There you go, boys," she said, handing the last one to Maxwell. "Enjoy. I have to get cleaned up before dinner." Rilla and Vixie walked slowly up the stairs, hoping to avoid being seen.

"Out romping with the hounds again, sister?" Tora asked from her doorway. It was obvious that Rilla had been tackled to the ground from all the dirt on her clothes.

Rilla stopped and looked over her shoulder. "Shh! Not so loud, Tora. You know Mother doesn't like it when I have a bit of fun with them."

"I know, and she'll be even more upset if you're not dressed and ready in time for dinner. So you'd better hurry up," Tora replied as she turned and entered her room.

"Right!" Rilla said before hurrying to her room.

Closing the door, she rushed over to her bathroom and quickly stripped. As the clothes landed on the floor, Vixie followed behind, picking them up and tossing them on her back. Rilla quickly washed as Vixie took the clothes to the hamper for the maid to collect later. She grabbed a towel and dragged it to the bathroom and then made sure that Rilla's underthings were on the bed, waiting for her. Hopping out of the shower, the princess grabbed the blue towel and quickly dried off. "Thanks, Vixie!" she exclaimed, finding her clothes all laid out on the bed.

"Welcome," Vixie said in a muffled voice. She was busy opening Rilla's jewelry box and collecting all the accessories. By the time Rilla was dressed, Vixie had everything on the vanity waiting. "Tiara?"

"Yes, please," Rilla replied as she sat and brushed her short dark blue hair. She put on the sapphire earrings that had been a gift from one of her best friends, Mahogany, who was also her roommate at the academy. The bracelet Vixie had chosen was a silver band with ancient Mercurian runes on it. It had been given to Rilla by her good friend Rena, who was also Rilla's husband Jacob's cousin. Vixie hadn't bothered with a necklace because there was only one that Rilla ever wore, the mercurite crystal on a silver chain that was given to her by her older brother. Rilla looked at herself in the mirror and noticed a small bruise on her neck, probably from her duel with Rukia earlier. Closing her eyes, she cast a spell called a glamour, and hid the bruise. When she opened her eyes, the bruise was no longer visible. A glamour was a type of illusion magic that was often used to hide or change the appearance of something. Rilla had studied illusion magic at the academy, and, as in all her other classes, she'd received the highest marks.

As Rilla stood up, Vixie jumped up on her hind legs to give her the silver tiara adorned with mercurite and sapphires. "Thanks."

"You look beautiful, Rilla-chan," Vixie said as she jumped up on Rilla's bed and admired her princess.

Rilla spun around to give her a better look. The dress was bright blue and sparkled in the light. The wide straps sat loosely on her shoulders and the material flowed eloquently down her sides. The back was open just past her shoulder blades, where the ends of a dark blue ribbon, which wrapped around her waist like a belt, were tied into a bow.

"How's the bow?"

"Needs a little work," Vixie told her as she motioned for her to back up. Vixie did her best to straighten the bow with her teeth and paws. When she was done, she smiled. "Amdis would be very happy if he could see you now."

Rilla smiled and adjusted the tiara on her head. "Well, I'd better hurry downstairs before Mother comes looking for me." She patted Vixie on the head and hurried downstairs after slipping on her silver slippers, which were waiting by the door.

As she made her way down the stairs, her mother and father were waiting for her.

"There she is," the queen said.

"Beautiful as always, Rilla-chan," her father said, smiling.

"Thank you, Father," she said as she hugged him once she reached the bottom of the stairs. "You look gorgeous, Mother," she stated before hugging the queen in her full-length gown. The queen had her teal hair pulled back into a bun with her crown resting on top of her head.

"Thank you, my dear," the queen replied, smiling.

"Shall we?" Arkanthius asked, extending his arms to the ladies. The queen took his right arm, and Rilla took his left. When they walked together, it was quite obvious the three were related. Rilla's hair was the same dark shade as her father's had been in his younger days.

While King Arkanthius now had mostly grayish-blue hair, here and there he still had a few dark strands left. Queen Amirilla's teal hair was much lighter than her husband and daughter's, but Rilla had inherited her deep blue eyes, while her father's violet eyes had been passed to the late Prince Amdis.

"Where's Tora?" Rilla asked.

"She'll be along shortly. She said she has a surprise for us and went to attend to the last details," Arkanthius explained.

"A surprise? I wonder what it could be," Rilla pondered out loud.

"We will just have to wait and see," the king said with a smile as he escorted the ladies to the dining hall.

As they entered the large room filled with paintings of the ocean, the few guests that were invited were waiting, and they all bowed to the royal family as they entered. They nodded to everyone, and Arkanthius took his place at the head of the large dining table. "Please, everyone, be seated."

Everyone took a moment to find their assigned seats while the queen sat to the king's right and Rilla sat in the second seat to his left. The seat to the queen's right was saved for Tora, and the seat between the king and Rilla would forever remain empty. It was left empty in memory of the prince who was only twenty-four when he lost his life.

Shadows of the Past

Once everyone had taken their seats, the servants began filling their glasses with water and Mercurian ale. While it wasn't the strongest or best-tasting ale in the system, it was the only one with healing properties. It was made with water from the spring that Lady Mercuria had created centuries ago. The spring was what gave life to the once-barren world. The planet was now completely covered in water, except for the one large land mass where the inhabitants of the planet lived. The giant ocean of Mercury provided a variety of fish and other seafood, most of which was exported off world. Mercury's healing waters were known throughout the galaxy, and many traveled from other systems just to see the spring.

When all the glasses were filled, Arkanthius picked up his ale. "A toast. To absent loved ones and to the continued health and happiness of everyone here."

Everyone raised their glasses and bowed their heads. "To the health and happiness of the royal family," everyone said in unison before drinking their ale.

Arkanthius looked around the table and sighed. Leaning over to his wife, he whispered. "Where is he?"

"I don't know. He promised he'd be here," the queen replied before calling a servant over. While the servant went to find the guest of honor, the king and queen joined in polite conversation with the others.

"Your Highness, where is Princess Tora tonight?" asked an older man with white curly hair. The man was one of the many dukes on the Mercurian court. Unlike most, Duke Louis was invited to almost every large dinner at the palace and was very involved in helping with the affairs of the planet.

"She'll be along shortly," the queen replied.

"Apparently my sister has a surprise for us," Rilla stated.

As they continued chatting about random things, everyone was suddenly startled into silence as shouts were heard from the kitchen: "I won't stand for this! No one tells me how to run my kitchen!"

The queen excused herself to see what the issue was.

"Oh, dear," Arkanthius said, faking a smile. "Sounds like Maurice is having trouble with his new assistant. I'm sure it's nothing to worry about," he assured his guests.

As the queen entered the kitchen, a large man in white chef's clothing with dark hair furiously stormed over to her. "I cannot work like this, Your Majesty. He can cook his own meal," Maurice informed her before marching off.

Amirilla was sure she knew exactly who he was. Sure enough. She found a tall boy who looked to be about sixteen with short brown hair, busy at work by the stove.

"Must you always upset poor Maurice so?"

"Not my fault. He refuses to listen," the boy replied.

The queen sighed and watched him chop some vegetables. "What did he do wrong this time?"

"Well, first you really have to stop having him try to prepare exotic dishes. He can barely prepare traditional Mercurian dishes properly," the boy explained as he added the vegetables to the large pot of boiling water. "Second, he uses way too much cinnamon in his dishes. How you eat his cooking every day, I'll never know."

Queen Amirilla shook her head. "Well, not everyone has your talents." She took the spoon he held out to her and tasted the soup. "Mmmm…what is this?"

"I don't know. I just started throwing things into a pot," he replied sheepishly.

"Well, don't let Maurice hear you say that," the queen chuckled.

The boy shrugged. "If he was smart, he would have stayed and learned a few things, instead of storming off in a huff."

"So I take it you intend to cook tonight's dinner?"

"If you want decent food, I'll have to," he commented as he tossed the fish on the fire.

"Very well then. Just make sure you also join us to eat this feast," the queen reminded him as she headed for the door. She found the other cooks waiting by the door. "Take tonight off. Our guest is going to prepare tonight's meal himself." Looking to the serving crew, she told them to do whatever the young lord asked of them, and once dinner was done, they were free to take the rest of the night off as well.

"Yes, Your Majesty," they all replied as they bowed.

When the queen rejoined everyone in the dining hall, Tora was standing by her father, wearing her thick black winter cloak wrapped completely around her. "There you are, Mother."

"What's going on, Tora? Did I miss the surprise?" Queen Amirilla asked as she took her seat.

"Not at all, Mother," Tora replied. "We were waiting for you."

"Is everything all right, my dear?" Arkanthius whispered to his wife.

"Yes, everything is fine. He just wanted to cook his own feast," Amirilla explained quietly to her husband. "But anyway, Tora, what is the big surprise?"

Tora smiled and took her cloak off. "Once I graduate the academy, I'll be training with the Hellacian Army as a sharpshooter."

The room was silent as everyone stared at Tora, who was wearing a Hellacian uniform. The dark blue and black cloth made her red hair seem brighter. Almost reading everyone's minds, she pulled out a black hat and tucked her hair in into it.

"Well? Mother? Father? Say something," Tora demanded.

Rilla looked at her parents. Their expressions were of anger, hurt, and disappointment. "Tora, are you serious about this?" she asked, hoping this was all some horrible joke. The Hellacian Army was known throughout the system as the toughest and most efficient force. It was a great honor to be accepted into the army, but it wasn't the life expected of a member of a royal family.

"Of course I am. I received a letter of welcome and this uniform from Queen Hellenia herself," Tora said as she spun to show off the uniform. The army was led by Queen Hellenia, who was originally a princess of Earth. She had married the king of a kingdom outside of the system and found herself as the new ruler when her husband was killed months later. Many believed she was building the largest army she could to attempt to take back her home planet, which was now under the control of a man named Lucydion. His father had led a revolt and killed Hellenia's sister and niece. It was a touchy issue since Earth wasn't a formal member of the Intergalactic Court and Hellenia was an ally of the Empress. Numerous times, Hellenia had sent troops and supplies to help Galactica and her forces when they were in need.

"I don't believe this," Arkanthius said before downing his glass of ale.

Tora's smile dropped to an instant frown, and her green eyes lost their sparkle when she saw that her parents were anything but pleased by her surprise. Even the dukes, earls, and their wives didn't seem to approve. "I thought you'd be proud of me. Out of the hundreds who applied to join the Hellacian army, I got accepted."

"We understand that, Tora, dear. Trust me. We do. But what about your duties to your own kingdom?" her mother asked.

"My duties? You mean attending formal parties, dancing the night away, sitting at boring council meetings, arguing about the same old bullshit day after day? I think big sister has that covered."

"Now wait a minute, young lady!" the king yelled, jumping up.

"No, Father, you wait! I'm not done. All my life, I've been in Amirilla's shadow. 'Study harder, Tora, if you want to be like Rilla. Tora, don't play in the dirt. Follow Rilla's example.' Nothing I did was right unless I was being like Amirilla!"

"Tora…"

"Rilla, don't even," Tora spat, cutting her sister off. "You spent your whole life trying to impress Amdis, and now that he's gone, you just do what is expected of you with no argument. You married a man you barely knew for political reasons, gave him a child that you have little to do with, and now you're going to take your place in the Intergalactic Court. I'm not you, Amirilla, nor do I want to be."

"Tora, that's enough!" Queen Amirilla said firmly. "We will discuss this later. Now go and change and join us for dinner."

Tora stormed out in a huff, and the queen turned to her guests and apologized.

Rilla stood. "Mother, Father, please excuse me for a little while. I'll be back in time to eat with all of you."

The king started to object, but the queen stopped him. "Very well, my dear. Take your time."

She knew Tora's words had stung, and she didn't blame Rilla for wanting a little space. Rilla bowed to the guests and then to her parents before making her way out to the courtyard.

Chapter Three

Rilla walked silently through the massive labyrinth, turning this way and that. She soon found herself at the center of the maze, facing a large bronze statue of the empress, sitting in the center of an ornate fountain. As she sat in front of the statue, she sighed and looked up at the stars that filled the night sky. *"You spent your whole life trying to impress Amdis, and now that he's gone, you just do what is expected of you with no argument...I'm not you, Amirilla, nor do I want to be."* Tora's words echoed in her head.

"How did things end up like this?" Rilla asked herself out loud.

"Take good care of Tora for me, Mi-chan. I'm counting on you to be a good big sister. I love you, Mi-chan." A tear made its way down her cheek as she remembered the words her brother said to her every time he was about to leave, which were also the last words she would ever hear him say. She had looked up to Amdis all her life and always

did as he asked. Rilla tried so hard to care for Tora the way Amdis had cared for her, but Tora never made it easy. They fought all the time, and Tora refused to let Rilla help with her lessons.

"Why? Why does she hate me so?" Rilla pondered out loud. "Am I really that horrible of a sister to her?" She thought back to all the times she had tried to help Tora and all the times that she had seen her sister happy. She soon realized that the last time she had seen Tora truly happy was before Amdis died. "Was Tora ever happy just spending time with me?" Rilla tried to remember a time when they had sat and talked or done anything that didn't end in a fight.

"All my life, I've been in Amirilla's shadow. 'Study harder, Tora, if you want to be like Rilla. Tora, don't play in the dirt. Follow Rilla's example.' Nothing I did was right unless I was being like Amirilla!" Rilla suddenly knew the answer. She and everyone else were so set on Tora following in her older sister's footsteps that they didn't let her be herself, and for that she resented Rilla.

Heading back to the castle, Rilla was determined to do all she could to fix things. She might be too late to change Tora's mind about the Hellacian Army, but she owed her sister an apology and wanted to better understand the little sister she hadn't really gotten to know at all.

* * *

Meanwhile, in the kitchen, the young boy was busy making dessert. The servants had already taken the soups and salads out to the dining hall. The main course was almost done, and the side dishes were on the fire, staying warm. "All right, everyone. Start making plates," he said as he took the fish off the fire. He placed it by the other dishes, and the servants hurriedly made plates and set them on rolling carts.

As the servers took the food out, a young servant approached the boy whom had taken over the kitchen. "Excuse me, my lord," he said, bowing.

"Yes?" the boy asked, not even bothering to turn around.

"Her Majesty asked me to remind you that you are also to eat this feast and not to hide in the kitchen all night," the servant boy stated calmly.

The boy sighed. "Very well. Take a soup, salad, and plate out to my seat and tell her I'll be right there. I just need to finish dessert."

"Yes, my lord," he said, bowing. Grabbing a tray, he gathered the food and took it out to the dining hall.

The boy added the last ingredient to the bowl and mixed it thoroughly. "There. All done. You there," he called to a blonde maid who had been cleaning dishes.

"Me, sir?" the maid questioned.

"Yes, come here," the boy said, motioning for the young lady to come over. "When it's time for dessert, take this out of the ice chest and put a scoop on each plate with a slice of cake. Understood?"

"Yes, my lord."

"Good. Now I'd better get out there before Ami sends the guards to fetch me." He grabbed his jacket and headed out.

* * *

When he entered the dining hall, he nodded to Queen Amirilla. "Ah, there he is. Our guest of honor, Lord…"

"Abraxis," the boy said, cutting Queen Amirilla off. "Abraxis is fine. No need for the 'Lord.' After all, I trust these are all friends of yours, Queen Amirilla?"

"Very well, Abraxis. Normally tardiness is shunned, but we'll forgive him since he was busy preparing this marvelous feast for us," Arkanthius said with a hint of scolding in his tone.

Everyone clapped for him as he took his seat. "This soup is divine, lad," Duke Louis said, rubbing his rather large stomach. "You must give the recipe to my cooks."

"Afraid I can't," Abraxis stated before starting to eat his salad.

"Yes, our young lord doesn't use a recipe," Queen Amirilla explained. "He simply throws things in a pot and goes by taste."

"You mean, there's another way to do it?" Abraxis asked innocently.

Everyone laughed, and the ladies commented on how cute and charming he was for someone his age. Then Princess Amirilla returned and took her seat. "Please forgive my absence."

"It's quite all right, Rilla-chan," King Arkanthius assured her.

"Yes, Rilla dear, don't worry about it. Enjoy the meal," her mother added.

"You must try the soup," Duke Louis suggested cheerfully.

Rilla smiled. "Very well, Uncle Louis." She picked up her spoon and gave the soup a try. "Mmm…this is wonderful and oddly familiar. Has Maurice made this before?"

The duke busted out laughing, and Queen Amirilla explained that Maurice hadn't prepared anything she saw on the table.

"I'm glad the soup pleases you, my dear," Abraxis said with a smile.

Rilla nodded and looked at the boy. "Have we met before?"

The queen and king exchanged glances, but Abraxis spoke before they could. "Not to my knowledge, and surely I would remember such a beautiful princess. Perhaps in another life?"

"Perhaps," Rilla replied as she continued eating.

"Abraxis, this is my eldest daughter Amirilla. Rilla-chan, this is our guest of honor and a dear old friend of mine, Lord Abraxis," the queen said, introducing them to one another.

"It's a pleasure to meet you, Lord Abraxis," Rilla said with a smile.

"Please, Abraxis is fine, and I assure you the pleasure is all mine. It's clear that you inherited your mother's beauty, and I hear you've got your father's gift of strategy."

Rilla blushed slightly at his kind words and started to speak but was cut off by Lord Erial. "Careful, Abraxis. Rilla's hand is spoken for."

"That's right. Don't want you ending up like the last fellow that flirted with our Rilla," Duke Louis's wife Inez said seriously.

"Oh?" Abraxis inquired with a raised eyebrow.

Lord Erial nodded. "Jacob didn't hesitate to put a stop to that. I believe the lad had a black eye for weeks."

"That was nothing compared to what my Rilla did to Jacob." Arkanthius chuckled. "Now that was a sight to see."

"Really?" Duke Louis looked up excitedly. "Why hadn't we heard of this, Rilla? Come now. How could you keep this from your dear uncle?" The duke wasn't related by blood, but since she was little, Duke Louis had always treated her as family, so she affectionately called him "uncle."

"It was an unfortunate incident that was dealt with privately," the queen cut in. "And that is all that needs to be said on the matter," she said, giving her husband a glare for bringing it up in the first place. "Even if it was amusing to see Jacob with a broken nose." She smirked as she lifted a forkful of salad to her lips.

The rest of dinner went smoothly. The conversations were mainly about the upcoming events for the Creation Day celebration and the happenings in the local villages. When it was time, the servants brought dessert, as instructed, and not a single plate had food remaining on it. All the guests went home full and happy.

Shadows of the Past

Princess Tora remained in her room the entire time, not even bothering to respond to the servants sent to check on her. Once all the guests had left, Rilla tried to get Tora to talk to her, but she refused to open the door. Deciding to give her sister a little time to calm down, Rilla went in search of Lord Abraxis. She wished to talk to him some more, but he had vanished.

"I'm sure he's around here somewhere," her mother had told her. "He's famous for disappearing."

Rilla continued to search for him and soon found herself in the rose garden near her favorite hiding spot. Hearing voices, she rushed over to the silver fountain, only to find it was deserted.

"That's odd," she said, looking around. "I could have sworn I heard voices coming from here." Shrugging, she walked to the giant willow tree surrounded by blue roses and sat down, leaning against its massive trunk.

As she sat, deep in thought, Abraxis walked by with a smirk on his face. He returned to the castle to find Queen Amirilla, waiting for him by the door. "I knew you'd wander back this way eventually."

"And what if I didn't?"

"Still a lovely evening to admire the stars," she replied with a smile. "Haven't heard you go by the name Abraxis since the day we first met."

Abraxis shrugged. "Sounded better than Merlonas. I must have been drunk when I came up with that one," he said almost jokingly.

The queen wasn't sure if he was joking or not. "Rilla was looking for you. She seems quite intrigued by you."

"She's in the gardens by the old willow…where she always hides." As soon as the words were out of his mouth, he looked to the queen, confused. "Or was that your hiding spot?"

Queen Amirilla laughed, "No, that's Rilla's spot. She loves the blue roses. Amdis always gave them to her when he returned home." Sighing, she asked, "You really don't remember her, do you?"

"Ami, I barely remember you at the moment. Like I said, when I'm waking up, my memory is weird. What I remember today, I might forget tomorrow, and that's how it is until I'm fully awake." Abraxis sat on the stairs and looked up at the stars. "Though there is something familiar about her. I feel like I know her, but the memories just won't come forward. I take it we were close?"

The queen nodded. "She adored you almost as much as her brother. She waited desperately, wishing for you to come back. Since you can't remember her, it's best that Rilla never finds out your true identity. She was heartbroken when you didn't returned. Last thing she ever said about you was when she was five. You didn't show up for her birthday, and she said that, if you ever showed up again, she was going to have you arrested for abandoning her."

Abraxis chuckled a little and nodded. "I sensed at dinner that she was troubled by something."

The queen nodded. "Tora, my youngest, told us tonight of her intentions to join the Hellacian Army. She said some things that hit Rilla pretty hard."

"What is so bad about her joining the army?" Abraxis asked.

"She'd be forsaking all her royal duties and abandoning her people. She's needed here, not off fighting for another kingdom."

"Rilla is next in line for the throne, am I correct?" Abraxis asked. Amirilla nodded. "And does Rilla have an heir?"

"My granddaughter Marisa."

"So she's not going to inherit the throne, unless something happens to Rilla and her child, and she's not a member of the Intergalactic Court. So forgive me, but I think it's something else."

The queen sighed. "I've already lost one child in battle; I don't want to lose another. Rilla is going to be risking her life in service to the empress. I guess I just expected Tora to be a diplomat like I was until I married Arkanthius."

Abraxis nodded and sat on the stairs. "You can't protect them forever, Ami. Sooner or later, you have to let them go."

"I know. I'd just prefer it to be later rather than so soon."

Chapter Four

Princess Tora was busy in her room, packing her things. "'Why don't you act more like Rilla? Rilla's so perfect.' Ha! What would they say if they knew her secret? Maybe I should tell them before I leave and see how Rilla likes that," Tora mumbled angrily to herself as she shoved clothes into a bag. She ignored the mumbled cries of her guardian, Xhavior, from the closet, where she had him tied up and gagged. "Sorry, but if you're not going with me, I can't have you running off telling Mother or Father that I'm planning to leave tonight," Tora told the small ferret before closing the closet door.

Sighing, she looked around the room to see what else she wanted to take with her. Walking over to her desk, she picked up a photo. It was of her, Amdis, and Rilla. She debated taking it with her. It was the only photo she had of her brother, but then Rilla was also in it. "Oh, well, I guess you can come, too." She packed it safely into her bag and hurried to the window.

Shadows of the Past

Tora looked out to make sure no one was around to see her leave. Tossing her bags down, she quickly climbed down to the courtyard. She picked up her things and hurried to the stables. As she saddled a horse, she stopped when she heard footsteps coming from outside the stables. Drawing her sword, she peered around the building and quickly ducked back when she saw Rilla coming closer.

While she was looking for Lord Abraxis, Rilla had spotted Tora rushing into the stables; her red hair had given her away. "Tora, are you in there?" Rilla called as she stopped in front of the open door.

Suddenly Tora charged out on the back of a black stallion, with sword in hand. "Not a word of this to anyone, Rilla, unless you want Mother, Father, and everyone else to know about your secret."

"What?" She honestly wasn't sure as to what her sister was referring.

"Oh? Did you forget I was on Neptune with you last year?" Tora laughed. "Did you think no one saw you? Wonder what Mother and Father would say if they knew."

Rilla stood there for a moment, unsure of how to respond. "Do you really hate me that much, Tora? All I've ever tried to do was look after you, like I promised Di-chan. I'm sorry if I failed and made you feel insignificant."

"Whatever. You're a spoiled brat who gets everything handed to you on a silver platter, and I'm tired of being compared to you," she spat angrily. "I'm going to show you, Mother, and Father that I'm better than you. One day the entire system will know my name, and I'll be remembered as something other than the youngest daughter of the Mercury family." Tora sheathed her sword and took off and didn't look back.

Rilla didn't even call after her. She simply shook her head, sighed, and got her horse, Star, from her stall. "I wouldn't if I were you," a voice came from behind her.

"Who's there?" Rilla asked, looking around.

Abraxis stepped out of the shadows and bowed his head. "It's only me, Princess."

"Lord Abraxis? What are you doing here?"

"Merely taking a walk. After all, it is a lovely evening, isn't it?" He slowly walked over to Rilla and extended his hand. "Care to walk with me?"

"I have to stop Tora," Rilla responded as she continued to saddle her horse.

"Like I said, I wouldn't bother. Her mind is made up, so no point in trying to change it. Now come on. Let's head back to the castle and inform your mother that she's gone."

"No, I can't. I—"

"Relax," Abraxis said reassuringly. "I'll tell your mother I saw her ride off and then met up with you on the way back to the castle. That way your secret is safe."

"What?" Rilla questioned nervously.

"Didn't Tora threaten to reveal your secret to everyone if you told anyone she left?"

Shadows of the Past

"Yes, but—"

"Don't worry. Your secret, whatever it may be, is safe with me," Abraxis stated cheerfully. "Now come on. It's getting late. We should head back before they start searching for us. Otherwise someone might think we're having a secret rendezvous," he said with a grin.

Rilla couldn't help but chuckle, and after she locked the golden mare back in her stall, she walked with Abraxis back to the castle. "Tell me something, Lord Abraxis."

"Please, just call me Abraxis," he requested with a smile on his face.

"Very well, Abraxis. Mother claims you're an old friend, but you don't look like you're any older than I am. How old are you, if you don't mind me asking."

"Older than I look. That much I can say."

"Surely you're not that old. You don't look much older than sixteen," Rilla stated as she studied the young boy, who stood just a hair taller than herself. "So how can you be an old friend, if you're not old?"

Abraxis laughed and replied. "Not everything is as it seems, Princess."

"Meaning?"

"Meaning everyone is entitled to have secrets, even your mother."

"I'm not sure I like what you're implying," Rilla said, glaring slightly.

"Forgive me. I didn't mean to suggest your mother had done something inappropriate. I just meant that there are things you don't know about everyone you know, including your mother."

"Oh, I see," Rilla replied, nodding.

"You yourself have a secret, right?" Abraxis inquired. Rilla opened her mouth to speak, but he raised his hand and stopped her. "I need not know what it is. I'm just making my point. Not everything is black and white. Many things and people reside hidden in the shadows."

Thinking about his statement, Rilla smiled slightly and shook her head. "It's funny. You say we've never met, but for some reason, I feel like we have. You remind me very much of someone, though I can't think of who it might be."

Chuckling, Abraxis smiled as well. "Well, perhaps tonight is just the beginning of a wonderful friendship, and don't worry, I promise to keep my distance from that jealous husband of yours."

Rilla's smile dropped, and she sighed. "I don't know why I'm going to tell you this, but…I'm not in love with my husband. In fact, sometimes I wish we weren't married at all."

"Arranged marriage, I take it?" he inquired.

Nodding, Rilla ran her fingers through her hair. "He treats me more like property than a wife. I guess I had hoped things would work out like they did with Mother and Father. Their marriage was arranged, but they eventually fell in love and are happy now. It's been three years, and I still have no love for Jacob. Sometimes I even think I hate the man." Rilla sighed. "I'm sorry. I don't know what came over me. I shouldn't be bothering you with my problems."

"No need to apologize, Princess. I'm a very good listener, and I assure you, anything you tell me will stay between us."

Rilla's smile returned. "Thank you."

"Princess, I do have a question. If I'm out of line, feel free to say so, but your sister…" Abraxis paused, thinking on how to best word his question. "Well, I noticed that she doesn't look very much like you or your parents."

Rilla nodded. She'd heard these similar comments many times over the years. "You're wondering if she is adopted or if she is, in fact, my father's daughter."

Abraxis nodded. "Again, I apologize if I'm being too personal."

"It's all right," Rilla replied. "You're not the first to wonder that. Truth is Tora has been picked on and looked down on by many for her appearance. Many believe Mother had an affair, but that's not the case. My grandmother on Father's side was from Venus. Tora was unlucky enough to inherit her red hair and green eyes from her, but everyone likes to forget my grandmother was a redhead. They would rather assume the worst about my mother." Running her fingers though her dark hair, Rilla sighed. "Thank you for asking and for not just making assumptions."

"You're welcome, and for what it's worth, I never thought your mother had an affair. My thought was that she may have been adopted. I know how kind-hearted your mother is, and taking a needy child in would be something she would do without hesitation," Abraxis stated. Rilla smiled at him. It warmed her heart to know that her mother had those who thought so well of her.

They walked in silence the rest of the way back to the castle and found Queen Amirilla waiting for them at the door. "There you are. I see you found him at last, Rilla."

"Yes, Mother. Although we have some bad news for you."

"That is, I have bad news for you," Abraxis said, staying true to his word that he would be the one to tell the queen. "I'm afraid your youngest daughter has run away. I saw her saddle a horse and ride out. Right after that, I ran into Princess Amirilla here, and she graciously escorted me back to the castle."

"What? Tora? How could she?" Queen Amirilla started to run past them, but Abraxis stopped her. "Let me go, Shadow," she whispered, trying to get by him.

"You know I can't do that, Ami," he whispered. "And it's Abraxis now, remember?" As he turned her back toward the castle, he said, "Let's go inside and talk to your husband, and we'll figure this all out."

Rilla watched as Abraxis grabbed her mother's arm and led her back inside. She had heard them whispering but couldn't make out what they had said. "Mother, I'll…"

"No, Rilla. It's all right. Your father and I will handle this. It's late. You should head to bed. I'll see you in the morning, dear," the queen said, pulling free from Abraxis.

"Very well, Mother," Rilla replied, before kissing her mother good night. "If you go after her, please take care and be safe. She's hurting and didn't mean all those things she said earlier. I know that, and I know I wasn't as supportive of her as I should have been." Rilla lowered her head, staring at the blue marble floor. "I just want her to be safe and happy."

The queen raised Rilla's head, forcing her daughter to look at her. "I know, darling. I'll do all I can to see that she's safe. I love you both more than you know." She embraced Rilla tightly and whispered, "You two are the world to me." Releasing her daughter, she sighed and forced a smile. "Now off to bed, young lady. I'll see you in the morning for breakfast."

"Of course, Mother." Rilla watched as her mother walked away with Abraxis and turned to make her way upstairs to her room. She found Vixie asleep on the bed with a wrinkled paper under her paws. She gently pulled it from under Vixie and looked at it. Her eyes grew wide in horror as she realized what it was. It was the note Nathaniel had slipped her before leaving. She had placed it in her pocket and forgotten all about it. Rilla quickly woke Vixie up and asked, "Did you read it?"

Vixie stretched and gave a big yawn. "Come now, Rilla. How long have you known me? Have I ever read something without your permission?"

"No, but…"

"But nothing. I didn't read your silly love letter. I did see who gave it to you though. I saw from the window, so be warned that the others might have seen Nathaniel give it to you as well," Vixie informed her as she hopped onto the window sill. "And not a word will reach that idiot husband of yours. Just be more careful. I almost didn't get it out of your pocket before the maid took the laundry."

Rilla smiled and picked Vixie up, hugging her tightly. "What would I do without you?"

Vixie licked Rilla's cheek and shrugged. "Get in even more trouble than you already do." The two laughed as Rilla sat on the bed, still holding Vixie. "Now go on and read your love letter," Vixie said, hopping off her lap and curling up on Rillas's pillow. "I'm here if you want to talk."

"Thanks, Vixie," Rilla said as she opened the letter.

My Dearest Rilla,

I know you said that you wanted to pretend that week at the Neptune palace months ago never happened, but I can't. I've thought of you every day since you left and missed you more as time went by. You can't tell me you felt nothing and that it was a mistake that never should have happened. It did happen, and it happened for a reason, Rilla. I told you then, and I'll say it again — I love you. I have ever since the academy. I know you're married and our relationship can never go as far as I would like, but I can't stand the thought of not seeing you, not being able to hold you in my arms, or kiss your sweet lips. Please, Rilla, I need you in my life. Even if we have to hide it. Please don't deny what we both felt then. I await your answer.

With Love,

Nathaniel

Rilla read the letter over and over and finally gave a heavy sigh. Nathaniel was right; she had felt something back then. Something she had longed to feel and wanted to feel again. She had felt what it was like to be loved and wanted as a woman, not as someone's property or because she was a princess. Nathaniel hadn't seen her as his, nor did he want her in hopes of getting the kingdom. He had loved her simply for who she was. She had refused his advances so many times during her stay with her cousins on Neptune, but finally she'd given in. And what a wonderful night it was. She felt her cheeks get warm at the memory of that night. While part of her knew it was wrong, she couldn't help herself. It had been years since Jacob had held her, and even then, it wasn't like this. Jacob was rough and possessive and treated her like property. Rilla thought that she was doing the right thing by marrying him at the time, but was it right for her to be so unhappy? Amdis had objected to the engagement of his little sister to the Venusian, but her parents said it was for the good of the kingdom. And surely the cousin of her dear friend Rena couldn't have been that bad? Rilla had always heard Venusians were wonderful lovers, but that certainly wasn't true of Jacob. "Maybe Tora was right."

Vixie lifted her head to look at Rilla. "About what?"

"She said, since Di-chan was killed, I've done what I was told with no argument. Am I doing the right thing? Should I do as I'm told even if it makes me so unhappy?"

"Referring to that idiot husband of yours?"

Rilla sighed. "He's not an idiot, Vixie. He's just...I don't know. He's not what I imagined. I mean, I expected things to be like Mother and Father have it. Their marriage was arranged, but they're so much in love now. I figured, over time, things would get better. Instead they've gotten worse." She ran her fingers through her short dark blue hair. "And really, is there anything I can do now?"

"Want me to get rid of him?" Vixie asked with a smirk.

"Vixie!"

"Kidding, kidding. Sheesh! Just relax, Rilla." Vixie sat on Rilla's lap and nuzzled her neck. "Rilla, I was against it from the start. So was your brother. Amdis always said he would never allow any man to touch his sister unless they could beat him in a duel."

"What?" Rilla asked, chuckling.

"It's true. In fact, did you know he held a tournament for your hand when you were just a little baby?"

"Really?"

"Yes," Vixie said, smiling. "Anyone who thought themselves worthy had to fight him. There were hundreds who came to participate as your brother said anyone from any family was welcome to try. I believe your idiot husband was even there."

"You must be joking. He isn't much of a fighter now; I doubt he could even hold a sword when I was little," Rilla stated as she sat Vixie on the pillow and started getting ready for bed.

As Rilla sat at her vanity taking off her jewelry, Vixie continued with her story. "No, it's true. He was barely able to pick up a sword, but try he did. The tournament went on for days. No one was able to beat Amdis. Then on the last day of the tournament, a stranger appeared in the castle. Amdis challenged him to fight. The man claimed he had no interest in your hand and wished to be left alone, but your brother was a stubborn and proud boy. He took the refusal as an attack on the honor of his precious baby sister and demanded the man fight him."

"Who was this man?" inquired Rilla as she took off her dress.

"I only ever heard him referred to by a name once, and that was one of the maids gossiping. Claimed his name was Mist, Cloud, Shadow, or something like that. Your brother really didn't like him, but as he was a friend of your mother's, Amdis was forced to behave. Eventually he started getting along with the stranger and was even all right with you playing with him."

"I played with him?" came Rilla's muffled voice as she pulled her nightgown over her head.

"Yes, you were quite fond of the man. You followed him around everywhere he went. Always hanging on his cloak." Vixie stopped her story just long enough to pull the covers back for Rilla. "I wonder what ever happened to him."

"What do you mean?" Rilla asked as she climbed into bed.

"He left one day and promised you he'd be back but was never heard from again. You were so sad when he left, almost as sad as you got when Amdis left. Your brother was the only one that was able to cheer you up."

Vixie sighed. "Seems all the good ones disappear, but enough of that. You should get to sleep, my dear. We can talk more in the morning." Vixie pulled the covers over Rilla and started to leave. "Sweet dreams, Rilla-chan."

"Hey, Vixie."

"Yes?" Vixie stopped at the door to hear what Rilla had to say.

"Tell me…" Rilla paused uncertain if she really wanted the answer to her question, "did that man ever fight my brother?"

"Why, yes. He did."

"And who won?"

"Your brother would never admit it, but that man was the first person who ever beat him. Now good night, Rilla." Vixie walked out, pushing the door closed behind her.

"Good night," Rilla called after her. "So big brother was beaten in a duel…" Rilla closed her eyes as thoughts of this mysterious man plagued her mind.

Chapter Five

The queen paced nervously around the room. "Dear, you're going to wear a hole in the floor," Arkanthius told her calmly.

"We should be going after her, not just sitting here!" Amirilla shouted. "What's so funny?" she demanded when her husband chuckled.

"Oh, just the role reversal. Usually if he tells you it'll be okay and to wait here, you're calm and patient while I pace the floor. Is there a reason you don't trust him this time?" Arkanthius asked as he stood.

Amirilla continued pacing and shook her head. "I don't know. I'm just worried, I guess. Oh, Arkanthius, did we screw up with Tora? Were we too hard on her? Is that why she ran away?"

The king walked over and hugged his wife, kissing her forehead gently. "Don't blame yourself, dear. We did our best to do what's right for all of our children, and we taught each of them to be his or her own person. If this is what Tora wants, then we need to honor that. The only thing we're guilty of is how we reacted to her telling us about it. She worked hard, and she was right — it is an honor to be accepted into the Hellacian army, especially as a sharpshooter. We had no right to be upset with her." Arkanthius sighed as he hugged her tight. "I just wish I had realized that before she ran off." Letting go of the queen, he smiled. "We'll find her and straighten things out. You'll see."

"Glad to hear you're in such good spirits about this. Saves me the trouble of talking to you and trying to get you to see reason," Abraxis said as he walked into the room.

Chuckling, the king nodded. "Guess you don't get to argue with me or knock sense into me like you usually do, Shadow."

Abraxis looked at him, extremely confused. "If you say so, Your Highness, and please call me Abraxis while I'm in this form. As Amirilla pointed out to me earlier, it's best to keep my real identity a secret from your daughter. I still have no memories of her, and if she was as upset about my leaving as the queen claims, then my being here with no memory of her would only hurt her further, and I have no desire to do that." Abraxis sat and leaned back. "Besides, I think she's hurting enough over the words her sister said before she departed."

The king and queen nodded and sat on the couch across from Abraxis. "So what do we do now?" Amirilla asked.

"We wait until morning," Abraxis answered. "I've sent Shade and Shyy to look for her. They left word at all the shuttle stations not to let Princess Tora leave. I'm guessing she's headed for the Hellacian training camp, but I sent the twins to the academy to be safe. We'll head out first thing in the morning. If she's still on Mercury, we'll find her." Abraxis stood and stretched his arms over his head and yawned. "Well, I'm off to bed, and I suggest you two do the same." He headed for the door and waved as he called "good night" over his shoulder.

* * *

The next morning, the king, queen, and Abraxis left before dawn to search for Tora. Meanwhile Rilla was left to continue sleeping and dreaming.

"Mi-chan," Amdis called as he walked into her room.

Rilla turned around and almost tipped her chair over as she jumped up. "Di-chan! You back! Did you bring me present?" the excited three-year-old asked.

Laughing, he knelt beside her and wrapped his arms around her, and she clung tightly to his neck. "Maybe. Tell me, have you done your studies for the day?"

"Almost."

"Almost?" he asked.

"Have trouble with math," Rilla explained.

"Well, I might be able to help with that." Amdis stood.

"Stay there for a moment." He stepped outside and returned with a large box in his hands. Placing the box down, he knelt beside it. "I have someone who can help with your studies and who will keep you company while I'm away."

"And they in box?" Rilla asked curiously.

Amdis laughed. "Actually, yes, she is." He lifted the lid, and Rilla looked inside to see a small red fox. "She may look small at the moment, but she can change her size. She can shrink smaller to fit in your pocket, or grow large enough so you can ride her like a pony, though I don't suggest trying that one. Her name is Vixcianie, and she is your guardian."

"What a guardian?" Rilla asked as she stared at the sleeping fox.

"A guardian is a kind of mentor or protector. When you get into higher magic at the academy, you can learn to summon one. I had a friend help make this one for you. She's able to talk and can teach you basic things. Until you get into higher studies at the academy, she'll be able to tutor you. She'll also play with you. Consider her your new best friend."

"But you my best friend!" Rilla protested.

Chuckling, he scooped up his baby sister. "And you're mine. But we can have more than one best friend. I have several. You've met Michael and Rukia. It's nice to have lots of friends."

"Fine," Rilla said defiantly. "But you always be my bestest best friend."

Amdis smiled. "Deal." He kissed her forehead as he sat her down. "So how about we wake up this silly fox?"

"Okay!" Rilla exclaimed excitedly. "Vixie, wake up!"

Rilla woke to the sunlight pouring in through the window. Rubbing her eyes, she thought about her dream.

"It's been a long time since I dreamed of Di-chan," she said to herself. Sitting up, she looked around. The castle was quiet, and something felt out of place. She looked for Vixie, who usually acted as her wake-up call. "Vixie?"

She wasn't there, though. Shrugging, Rilla got up and dressed in her casual riding clothes and packed her bag, which was a very special bag that she carried with her all the time. She intended to go for a ride after breakfast, maybe even talk Lord Abraxis into accompanying her. Hurrying downstairs, she was surprised to find that no one was in the dining hall.

"That's odd."

Checking her father's study, she found it empty as well. Her parents' room, the grand hall, and the throne room were the same. Finally she found one of the servants busy cleaning.

"Where is everyone?" Rilla asked.

The young maid bowed. "Your mother and father left early this morning with Lord Abraxis. Her Highness instructed us to let you sleep and inform you when you awoke to expect them home later this afternoon."

"I see. Thank you," Rilla said before heading to the courtyard. She was certain she would find Vixie in her usual napping spot under the willow tree. Sure enough, Rilla found her there, just as expected. She sat beside her sleeping guardian and petted her gently. Vixie slowly woke and stood, stretching as she did. "Morning, Vixie."

"Afternoon, Rilla-chan," she replied. "I hope you slept well."

"Afternoon?"

"Well, yeah, just look at the sun and the shadows. It's well past noon. I was—"

"I know, told by Mother to let me sleep," Rilla interrupted. "So Mother and Father left early with Lord Abraxis?"

"Yes, before sun-up. They went after Tora. Oh, Rilla, how could you forget to tell me that?" Vixie put her paws on Rilla's shoulders. Shaking her head, she continued, "I was so worried. I went to say 'good night' to Tora and found Xhavior locked in her closet. Why didn't you tell me she'd left?"

"Sorry, Vixie, I was distracted, and Mother said she and Father would handle it," Rilla explained as she leaned back against the willow tree.

"Poor Xhavior was panicking."

"She left him here?"

"Yes," Vixie growled, a little annoyed that Rilla was only half-listening to her. "Like I said, I found him in her closet. She'd locked him in there." Vixie hopped onto Rilla's shoulders and sighed. "Where did we go wrong? Even Xhavior didn't know about this whole Hellacian Army thing."

"Why didn't she take her guardian with her?" Rilla wondered out loud.

"According to Xhavior, he told her to wait and talk to your parents, and when he refused to leave with her immediately, she tied and gagged him. She locked him in the closet before she left and said she couldn't have him telling anyone that she was leaving," Vixie explained as she shook her head. "If I hadn't gone to say 'good night,' who knows how long he would have been locked in there?"

"Where is Xhavior now?"

Shadows of the Past

"In Tora's room, moping probably."

"We should go check on him," Rilla said as she stood. Vixie held on tight as Rilla made her way up to Tora's room. Opening the door, Rilla found Xhavior asleep on her sister's bed. Picking up the small white ferret, she headed to her room.

As she opened the door, Xhavior yawned and looked around. "Tora?"

"Sorry, Xhavior. She's not here. I just didn't want you to be all by yourself," Rilla explained, placing the ferret on her bed.

Vixie jumped down and lay next to him. "Don't worry. The king and queen will find her." She gently licked his furry cheek and looked at Rilla. "So what are you going to do, Rilla-chan?"

"Think I'll go grab something to eat and then go for a ride," Rilla answered. "Do you mind staying with Xhavior?"

"Not at all. I can stay here with him."

"Thanks, Vixie," Rilla said, smiling. She hurried downstairs to find Maurice griping to the kitchen staff about the events of the night before. "Now is this any way for our head chef to be behaving?" Rilla asked jokingly, causing Maurice and the others to jump.

"Princess," Maurice said, bowing. "Forgive me. I wasn't aware you were up. What can we prepare for you?"

"Surprise me," Rilla said happily. "You know you've always pleased us with your dishes. So why so upset that one person, who isn't your employer, complained?"

"Sorry, Your Highness. I guess he just rubbed me the wrong way. He reminds me of that other guy that managed to kick me out of my own kitchen many years ago," he explained, his face red from just thinking about it.

"Other guy? Who was that?"

"I never learned his name. He visited for a while and was a friend of your mother's. He left and never came back," Maurice answered.

Rilla rubbed her chin, thinking. "Was I always hanging on his cloak?"

"Why yes," Maurice said, chuckling lightly. "You were so adorable at that age. Now that you mention it, I remember you used to call him Mister."

"Mister?"

"Yes, you followed him all over the palace." Maurice sighed. "Those were happier days for all of us."

Rilla lowered her head, cursing herself for bringing up things of the past. "Sorry, Maurice. I didn't mean to bring up painful memories," she said, placing a hand on his shoulder.

"Don't worry, my dear," he said, smiling, though his eyes were moist. "Little Alexander wouldn't want me to be sad. Just like Prince Amdis wouldn't want you to be sad." He wiped his eyes and sighed. "Enough of this chitchat. I have a surprise to make for you, and I know you're going to love it."

Rilla smiled. "I'll be waiting in the dining hall." She hugged Maurice and went to sit at the table to wait for her meal. As she sat waiting, her mind wandered. She thought of Alexander, the kitchen boy she had played with and called friend when she was five. Maurice had intended to train the boy to be a chef like him and had hoped that one day he would take over as head chef, but those dreams vanished the day the boy became sick with a mysterious illness. Nothing the royal healers tried worked, and the boy got sicker and sicker. Even Queen Amirilla, who was the greatest healer in the kingdom, was unable to help Alexander. Then one day he simply didn't open his eyes. Rilla was eight at the time. After Alexander's death, Rilla asked her mother to teach her to heal. She never wanted to watch a friend suffer and not be able to help him or her again.

That was also when she learned to cook and became close with Maurice. Queen Amirilla had given Maurice leave for as long as he desired when his son died. After a week of bland food, Rilla decided to sneak into the kitchen and fix her own meal. Luckily Maurice saw her and followed her, curious to see what the young princess was up to. Seeing her trying to make her favorite dish brought a smile to his face, as it was a dish he had invented just for her. So he taught her how to make it. It was a mix of white grain, four types of fish, chopped vegetables, and sweet cream all made into a roll and dipped into a batter of water, wheat, egg, and various spices. The roll was then fried in oil for a few seconds to cook the batter and melt the cream, and then a sweet sauce was drizzled over it, Maurice called it a Rilla Roll, in honor of the princess.

Rilla was so lost in her memories that she didn't hear or see Maurice enter the room. She jumped slightly when he suddenly appeared beside her, placing a tray on the table. "One Rilla Roll for the sweet princess," he said, placing the plate in front of her. "And one tall glass of Mercurian Ale."

"It's a little early for ale, isn't it, Maurice?" she teased. She knew why he had served the ale but loved hearing him rant about mixing certain flavors.

"How many times must I tell you…this particular blend requires…" he continued on about mixing tastes and which ones complemented or killed the taste of others. Rilla ate slowly, savoring the flavor as she listened intently to Maurice. "And furthermore…" He stopped and sighed. "You know all that, though. You just wanted to make me rant, didn't you?"

Nodding happily, Rilla said, "Of course. You always seem to be so happy and full of life when you talk about food, and I'd rather see you happy than sad or depressed."

Maurice smiled and picked up the empty tray. "You're too sweet to an old man, Princess. You and your family have always taken such good care of me. Makes me feel almost like I am family." He looked around and almost jumped as he realized something. "Oh, dear! I forgot your dessert."

Rilla smiled as he dashed off to the kitchen. While awaiting his return, she sat quietly and drank her ale and finished her Rilla Roll.

"You're spoiling me today." Rilla beamed when Maurice returned. He brought a large piece of fried sweet cream cake, another recipe he had created, although this one was on accident.

Shadows of the Past

One day, while making dinner for Rilla, he'd dropped the slice of sweet cream cake into the batter he used for the Rilla Roll. It was the last slice of cake, and he didn't want to disappoint the waiting nine year old. So he fried the cake and presented it as *his latest creation*.

"And what's wrong with that? After all, you're not home very often. So I have to spoil you when I can," Maurice replied as he placed the cake in front of her.

Rilla nodded and ate her cake quietly. Maurice refilled her glass and excused himself to return to work, preparing for that night's dinner. When she was done eating, she thanked the servant who took her dishes and asked him to thank Maurice again for her.

She made her way to the stables to take a relaxing ride. After saddling her golden mare, Star, she rode around the palace, deep in thought. So many things were on her mind that day that she didn't know where to start trying to organize her thoughts. She thought of Tora and what she had said, wondered if her big brother Amdis would be proud of her, pondered many things about her marriage to Jacob and her affair with Nathaniel, and lastly she thought of the mysterious Mister that she'd been hearing a lot about lately. Who was he? What had happened to him? And why couldn't Rilla remember him?

All these thoughts and more plagued her mind as she rode out the gates. She nodded to the guards and assured them she'd be back shortly and that no escort was needed. As she rode across the open fields that surrounded the castle, the tall grass tickled her legs, and Star moved side to side, indicating she wanted to run full out. Smiling Rilla guided her to the path that ran through the woods. "All right, Star. We'll have a nice run through the forest."

Giving Star a gentle kick with her heel, Rilla let her horse run as fast as she wanted. Star knew to stay on the path, so guiding her through the thick forest was extremely easy. Racing down the path, the two startled birds and other wildlife as they passed. Nearing the end of the forest that led to one of the small villages, Star started to slow down, but Rilla nudged her again with her heel, encouraging her to keep going. "Don't stop, Star!" she called.

Star whinnied and took off, once more, at full speed. Villagers waved and bowed to the princess as she raced by. Everyone knew her and her mare on sight, as she rode through often and usually stopped to visit or do a little shopping. Today she had other plans, though. Guiding her horse down yet another path, Rilla made her way toward the beach. The sound of the ocean waves always helped calm her mind, and that was exactly what she needed to do. As Star's hooves hit the sand, her rider pulled gently on the reins, instructing her to slow down. Nodding, the mare trotted down to the water's edge and slowly walked down the beach, letting the cold water of the waves miss her legs by mere inches.

Closing her eyes, Rilla took a deep breath, savoring the salty, yet almost sweet smell of the ocean. Smiling, she looked out across the vast teal waves that were rushing to meet the gray sands of the beach. "We should have packed a picnic, Star." The horse whinnied and nodded in agreement. Laughing, the princess rubbed her loyal

Shadows of the Past

friend's neck. "I'll make sure you get lots of your favorite vegetables tonight."

Hopping down, Rilla tied the reins to the saddle horn and allowed Star to wander. Taking a deep breath, the princess drew in the sand and carefully made a casting circle. The outside was surrounded by symbols of protection, peace, and healing. Inside she drew the royal seal, upon which she sat with her legs crossed. Closing her eyes, she focused on the sounds of the ocean and took deep breaths, slowly clearing her mind of all thoughts. Just as she was calm and had cleared her mind, she fell backward as a vision hit her.

Everything was dark, and Rilla was filled with feelings of fear and anger. Looking around, she spotted a path as red as blood. Slowly she followed it, each step filling her with more dread. Then suddenly she heard voices from all around her.

"Can anyone save us?"

"Why is this happening?"

"Where are the soldiers?"

The voices came more and more and all spoke at once until Rilla was surrounded by noise and couldn't stand it. She screamed, closed her eyes, and covered her ears until the noise suddenly stopped. Slowly opening her eyes, she was suddenly in front of a dark figure with glowing red eyes.

"How can you see me?" the voice was dark and almost like a growl. "How can you see me?" the shadowy man demanded.

Rilla tried to back away, but the figure had her. It kept asking the same things over and over again, demanding that she answer. As she felt its claws wrap around her throat, she screamed.

Rilla jolted upright as she felt something wet against her face. She was screaming and panting as if she was out of breath. Star gently nudged her rider, causing the princess to jump.

"Star?"

As she said the name, she remembered where she was and what she had been doing. "I had a vision…though I don't really remember it."

Rilla stood and hugged the mare. Rilla had been having visions since she was little, so it was nothing new to her. Over the years, she had learned to control them, to a point, at least. She never knew when one was going to happen or what it would be about, but she didn't thrash about or hurt herself like she had when she was little. Her mother had helped her through it all. Queen Amirilla also had visions. She and Rilla had what was known as *oracle blood*. It was something found only in the Neptune bloodline, and it gave most that had it visions or premonitions of the future. Sometimes it was just feelings or blurred images; other times, it was full-color, detailed scenes that played out in their heads. For Rilla, full-color scenes were rare. Usually she saw black and white images with only certain details in bright colors.

Rilla tried to focus on the details of the vision, as they might be important later. "I know it was terrifying, and that something wasn't right, but I can't remember the vision." She was so focused on remembering that she never noticed the crystal around her neck was glowing; at least, it was until she reached up and touched it. Letting out a whinny, Star knelt, indicating that she should climb on. Nodding, Rilla smiled. "I think you're right. We should head home."

Climbing back up on the golden mare, Rilla was barely seated when the horse stood and took off at a dead run, heading back for the castle. Rilla let Star take her home; it was obvious that the horse was also spooked. In the hurried exit from the beach, Rilla never saw the odd marks on the sand by her casting circle, nor did she see the dark shape that left the circle and entered the ocean.

* * *

Once inside the safety of the castle gates, Star slowed to a walk and wandered around the trees and grassy yards around the castle. Rilla continued riding until the sun started setting, stopping occasionally to let her horse rest. She had been sitting by a willow tree, thinking, when she heard trumpets announcing the return of the king and the queen. Jumping up, Rilla mounted her horse and rode as fast as she could back to the castle. She arrived just in time to see her parents approaching the main staircase.

"Mother! Father!" Rilla cried as she jumped off her horse, handed the reins to a servant, and ran to greet them.

The queen and the king stopped and turned to see Rilla running toward them with a hopeful expression.

"Rilla, my dear," the king said with heavy heart. "I'm afraid we have some bad news."

Rilla stopped and stared at her father. "Tora? Is she all right?"

"We don't know. We were unable to find her," the queen replied. "Lord Abraxis is doing all he can to try and locate her for us, but I doubt if we'll see her again anytime soon."

Rilla stared at the ground, unsure of what to say. "Oh, I see" was all she managed.

"Don't worry, Rilla. I'm sure she'll be all right," the queen said, trying to comfort her daughter.

"Yes, you taught her how to take care of herself, and she was able to get into the Hellacian Army after all. If she makes it there safely, I know Queen Hellenia will take good care of her," Arkanthius added.

The queen nodded in agreement. "Your father's right. Come on. Let's head inside." Rilla nodded and followed her mother and father inside and cleaned up for dinner, which she could smell the minute she walked in the castle.

Chapter Six

The rest of the week flew by in a flash. No one had heard from Tora, but they had received word from Lord Abraxis that she had arrived safely at the Hellacian training camp, where she would remain until classes started again at the academy. The queen and king agreed that they would try to go see her and try talking to her while she was at the academy. Rilla never remembered her vision, but upon mentioning it to her mother, she was told to just ignore it. Her mother suspected it was simply Rilla's nerves and emotions getting the better of her.

The princess had spent most of the week relaxing at home and doing some serious thinking on the choices she had made in the past, wondering whether or not they were the correct ones. As the week ended, she was both excited and nervous about the party, Nathaniel had made it quite clear in his letter that he wanted to continue their affair, but should Rilla allow herself this pleasure, knowing it could cause embarrassment for three kingdoms, ruin any political influence she currently had in the court, and even go so far as to cause a war? These were the thoughts that plagued Rilla the most the day before her departure from her home planet.

* * *

After dinner that night, she decided the best person to ask for help was her mother, whom she found in the study, playing chess with the king.

"Check," the queen said with a smile.

Arkanthius rubbed his chin, thinking hard about his next move. Glancing up, he smiled when he saw Rilla walk in. "Rilla-chan, come in and have a seat. Maybe you can play the winner and show your old man a new trick or two."

Smiling, Rilla nodded. "Love to, Father, but I need to speak with Mother for a moment first."

Arkanthius made his move. "Go on, my dear. I'll wait."

The queen stood, moved her rook, and with a smirk said, "Checkmate." She turned and walked out to the courtyard with Rilla. "What's wrong, Rilla-chan? You seem troubled."

"Mother, have you ever questioned the choices you've made in your life?"

"A few times, but we must live with our choices, dear. That's why I want you to think long and hard before making decisions, especially really important ones," the queen stated as she brushed the hair from Rilla's face.

"What about things I didn't choose? Was I right to just go along with it, even if it means unhappiness for me?"

"Sounds like you've got a specific thing in mind," the queen noted. "Rilla, which decision are you talking about?"

"I'm wondering if marrying Jacob was the right thing to do."

"Oh, I see," the queen said as she sat on the bench.

"Mother, were you and Father always in love like you are now?"

"No, it was a year or so after we were wed before he said he loved me. Oh, Rilla, I'm sorry if you're unhappy. I told your father to let you choose your husband, but he felt Jacob was a good man. He hasn't hurt you, has he?"

"No, no, nothing like that. He's tried a few times, when he's been really drunk, but he's not much of a fighter when sober, so handling him drunk isn't hard. It's just…well, there's no emotion there. I don't feel anything for him. It's been three years, and I've given him a child, but I have no love for him. He hasn't held me since Marisa was born, and even then, it wasn't like…" Rilla paused not quite ready to tell her mother about Nathaniel.

"Wasn't like what, Rilla?" Queen Amirilla stood and put her hands on her daughter's shoulders, looking into her eyes. "Who, Rilla? It wasn't Lord Abraxis, was it?"

"What?" Rilla was caught off guard by the question.

"No, no, I just met him last week. It was someone from the academy."

The queen gave a silent sigh of relief and nodded.

"What happened, Rilla?" She sat back down and patted the bench beside her, inviting her daughter to sit with her.

Rilla sighed and sat by her mother. "It was last year when I was staying with Michael." She paused a little, afraid of telling her mother the complete truth. "Nathaniel confessed his love for me. He said he's loved me since the academy. At first, I refused him, but then one night, I gave in," Rilla said with her head down.

"And you fell in love yourself," the queen said more as a statement than a question.

"Yes. No. I don't know, Mother. I felt horrible about it, but at the same time, it felt so wonderful. I felt like I was more than a possession."

"You felt needed, wanted, and loved," Amirilla said, wrapping her arms around her daughter. "And I take it the affair has gone on since?"

"No. I ended it before I left Neptune last year. I told him it was a mistake that never should have happened," Rilla explained. "Before he left last week, he gave me this." Rilla pulled the note from her pocket and handed it to her mother before turning her head.

Shadows of the Past

Queen Amirilla read the note and looked at her daughter. "I see, so now you're wondering which is right and which is the bigger sin—being faithful to an unloving husband you barely see or being true to your own heart. I faced the same dilemma once."

"What?" Rilla turned to look at her mother, unbelieving. "But you and Father—"

"Are very much in love at this moment, but the first year was rough. Also, my heart belonged to another before we were wed."

"So you cheated on Father?"

"No, never. My love was unrequited. I loved a man I could never have, but then lots of women are guilty of that. But I don't want you to think this was right, Rilla. Loving someone from a far and having an affair are two completely different things. You know what's at stake if this gets out."

"Yes, I do, which is why I ended it back then. There's too much at risk to give in, but I slipped once. I admit it, but was I right?"

"Morally, yes, ending an affair before it goes too far is always best, but in your case, I see your issue. Tell me, Rilla, do you love Nathaniel?"

"I don't know. I loved the way he made me feel, but I can't honestly say I love him. I guess I just loved being treated as a person and not property."

Queen Amirilla nodded. "Then my advice to you is not to continue the affair. As you said, there's too much at risk, but if you're honestly unhappy and want out of your marriage, I may know of a way."

"Really?"

Nodding, the queen replied, "Yes, but it won't be easy, especially if we want to avoid incident. I'll do what I can, Rilla. I've never been thrilled with the idea of arranged marriages. I should have done more to stop yours. Now, I'll do all I can to fix this, but your affair must never come to light; otherwise my plan will fail."

"I understand." Rilla hugged the queen. "Thank you, Mother."

The queen stood and held her hand out to her daughter. "Come on. You promised your father a game of chess. Shouldn't make him wait too long. You know how impatient he is."

Rilla nodded and took her mother's hand and stood with a slight sigh. She walked in silence back to the study with her mother. After three short games of chess, Rilla retired to her room for the night. Talking things over with her mother had helped to calm her nerves. She was now certain of what to tell Nathaniel when she saw him again.

* * *

The next morning, Rilla woke up feeling calm and well rested. She had a nice breakfast with her parents

Shadows of the Past

and packed the last of her things. As always, she packed her special bag with her valuables and weapons. Her brother encouraged her to never go anywhere without a sword if she could help it; that included Central Palace. While only ceremonial swords were allowed at the palace, Rilla's bag got her around that. The bag had been in her possession since she was a little girl, and while she didn't even remember where it came from, she knew that she wasn't supposed to tell anyone about it. There was a very strong glamour spell on it that prevented those not trained in illusion magic from seeing it, and even then, it was difficult. Rilla often misplaced it if she took it off and set it down, but luckily she had been taught a retrieval spell that allowed her to summon it to her hand at any time. The bag itself was enchanted to be practically bottomless. No matter how much she put into the bag, it never seemed to get full, yet it didn't have the weight of the items in it either. The best part was, if someone could see it and looked inside, all they would see was an empty bag. You had to physically reach in below the visible bottom to find anything. She always kept a couple daggers, throwing knives, a spare rapier, rope, crystals, and other items that came in handy during emergencies in the bag, which were always on her. There were also a few very special items she kept in it for safekeeping. Once she had packed all her bags, Rilla was off to the station.

Her mother and Vixie accompanied her, and after saying her good-byes, Rilla boarded the shuttle for Neptune, leaving Vixie to look after her mother and father.

* * *

Rilla had made arrangements to meet Nathaniel on Neptune and then leave for Central Palace with him, Triston, Michael, and Rukia. The trip was pleasant, and she used the time to catch up on some reading she had been meaning to do for a while. Halfway there, another vision hit Rilla.

She was surrounded by tall white trees that were bare of leaves. The branches reached out to her like gnarled, wrinkled fingers. All around her was the sound of footsteps. Frantically she looked around. All she saw were the trees, but she couldn't shake the feeling she was being watched. Taking a step forward, she suddenly tripped and fell. The ground was black and cold, and something was wrapped around her ankle. Looking down, she saw a white hand that looked deformed. Pulling away, she jumped up and ran. As she ran through the thick forest of white trees, she heard a laugh that made her skin crawl. "Run, run, little girl. You can't escape," the voice called before laughing again.

"Miss, are you all right?"

Rilla opened her eyes to see several people staring at her, including the shuttle attendant with orange hair.

"What happened?" Rilla asked as she rubbed her head, trying to remember the details of what she had just seen.

"You were sleeping, and then suddenly you started thrashing about and screaming," the attendant said, sounding very concerned.

"Was it a vision, Your Highness?"

Rilla looked to her right to see one of the villagers. He, too, looked extremely concerned.

Nodding, the Mercury Princess closed her eyes for a moment. "There were strange white trees and a voice that was laughing at me…" Opening her eyes, she gripped the arm of the chair tightly. "That's all I remember."

The attendant handed her a glass of water, and the young man offered to sit with her for a while. Rilla thanked them both as she took the glass and tried to focus her thoughts. The more she tried to remember the vision, the more her head hurt.

For the rest of the trip, she sat in silence and stared at her book. No matter how much she tried, she couldn't focus on it. The vision had her shaken, especially the fact that she couldn't remember it clearly. She hadn't thrashed about or forgotten a vision since she was little, so why was it happening now? As her thoughts played through all the reasons and scenarios that could be causing her visions to be blurred and forgotten, Rilla couldn't help but wonder if there was something vital going on that these visions were trying to warn her about. Closing her book, she decided to talk with Michael about it.

* * *

When she arrived on Neptune, the others were waiting for her, along with Saedi, who had accompanied them to the station. After nearly being tackled by an excited Saedi, Rilla hugged the others, and they talked quietly about the events of the past week while they waited for their shuttle. Rilla did her best to avoid eye contact with Nathaniel. She knew what she was going to tell him, but she didn't want to have to deal with him just yet. She also made sure to let Michael know that she needed to talk to him about a private matter later. While it was an open secret that Rilla and Michael had oracle blood, Rilla didn't like talking about it in front of everyone else.

When they announced the shuttle was arriving, Michael handed out the tickets. "Sorry, Mi-chan, but the shuttle was almost sold out, so we're not all seated together, but Nathaniel volunteered to sit in the back with you."

While it didn't surprise her, it did create a knot in Rilla's stomach. "That's fine, Michael. We'll see each other when we get there," she said, trying to sound understanding.

"True, and we will be sitting together on the return trip," Rukia added.

"Shuttle 563 to Central Planet now boarding."

"That's us," Nathaniel said as he picked up his bag, along with Rilla's.

Rilla said a quiet "thank you," and they boarded after a quick good-bye to Saedi. When Rilla saw how far back their seats were, she wondered if Nathaniel had somehow arranged it. The others were seated in row three, while she and Nathaniel were in the very last row, which was usually reserved for important diplomats who wanted to travel in peace. While Rilla was royalty, she wasn't usually considered important enough for the diplomatic seats. The shuttle system was run by the Stellar Court, which the empress was a part of. The shuttles offered transport to all the planets in thirty different systems. Each kingdom in the system used the shuttles provided by the Stellar Court for traveling, while the shuttles and ships of each planet were reserved for trading and planetary defense. The diplomatic seats on the shuttles were normally reserved for people like Galactica, Lady Orion, Lord Draco, and other system leaders. The seats were larger, covered in a soft velvety fabric, and there was even a curtain that could be pulled closed. Rilla seriously hoped that he didn't plan on closing it. Once they were seated and the shuttle had left the planet, Rilla finally glanced over at Nathaniel. She expected to find him staring at her; instead he was busy scribbling on a piece of paper. Leaning over, she studied it carefully, as he always wrote very small and not always neatly. "Is that…"

"A silencing barrier? Yes," he replied as he closed the curtain and placed the paper on it, saying the words needed to activate the spell. "There. Now we can talk in private," he said, turning to Rilla, giving her a devilish grin.

"Talk. Right. We do need to talk," Rilla said, trying to keep her composure, which wasn't easy with Nathaniel holding her hand and gently stroking the back of it with his thumb.

"I've missed you so much, Rilla," Nathaniel said gently as he leaned closer. As he leaned in to kiss her, Rilla turned her head, so his lips landed on her cheek, but that didn't discourage him. He scooted closer, wrapped one arm around her waist, and pulled her to him as he kissed down her cheek to her neck. He nuzzled her, inhaling deeply as he kissed and nibbled her neck. "You smell so good, Rilla. I could just eat you up."

It took all of her self-control not to give in and let him do as he wished with her. Gathering all her willpower, she pushed him away and put some space between them. "This isn't talking, Nathaniel, and you need to stop. The affair is over. We can't do that again."

"What?" Nathaniel was suddenly pissed. "So you're going to continue with the games? Why? Tell me why!" he shouted.

"As long as I'm married to Jacob, there's too much at risk."

"So what? I don't care about that idiot, politics, or anything else. I'll fight him for you if need be. Rilla, all I want is you. I'm not even asking you to get rid of him. I just want to be able to have you all to myself whenever possible. We can keep it a secret. That's fine with me. Just please don't refuse me."

"No, Nathaniel. I can't do that," Rilla replied.

"You're serious?"

"Yes, Nathaniel, I am. I told you it was a mistake and it wouldn't happen again. I'm sorry, but that's how it has to be for now."

"Fine. So be it," Nathaniel said in a huff as he sat back, crossing his arms. "Enjoy the party tonight and get used to it. I may be your escort for the night, but you're on your own. I won't dance with you and play nice in front of others, and no one else will dance with you because of your jealous husband, so I hope you are looking forward to sitting all night."

"Nathaniel, don't be like that. Mother said that—"

"Mother? You told your mother?" Nathaniel shouted, not believing what he'd just heard.

"I wasn't going to at first, but—"

"I don't believe it. Of all the people to ask for advice, you asked your mother? I'm sure that was a conversation she was proud to have with you."

"No, but—"

"Oh, yes, I can see it now," Nathaniel went on ranting, not letting Rilla speak. "I won't be able to show my face on Mercury now. I'll be shot on sight."

"Nathaniel…"

"Next, you'll tell Michael, Rukia, and the others."

"No. If you would just—"

"No, I'm done, Rilla. You don't want my company. That's fine. I'll leave you alone," he said as he stood and opened the curtain, breaking the barrier.

"Where are you going?"

"Away from you," he answered before storming off.

Chapter Seven

Hours later, Rilla sat alone in the back of the shuttle. Nathaniel hadn't come back, and she was beginning to think he wouldn't.

"Approaching Central Planet. Please take your seats and prepare for landing."

A moment later, Nathaniel returned and took his seat without saying a word or even looking at Rilla.

She watched him silently as he stared out the window, his head resting on his hand. Rilla could barely make out the smell of alcohol on him. She sighed and started to reach over and touch his shoulder. She needed him to listen and hear her out.

"Don't." His voice was cold and harsh. "Don't touch me. I only came back because we're landing. Other than when we enter the castle, don't expect any contact from me."

"Nathaniel, please listen to me," Rilla pleaded.

"Why should I? You've said enough already, and I grew tired of the chitchat."

Rilla sighed. "Fine. I won't talk to you."

"Good. And don't forget your bag. I won't be carrying it when we get off the shuttle," Nathaniel stated plainly.

Rilla nodded and turned to look out the window on her side. Mother was right when she told me not to continue the affair, she thought. I guess he doesn't love me after all. Otherwise he'd listen to me, wouldn't he? She was even more confused than she had been a few days ago.

Once the shuttle landed, Nathaniel hurried away with his bag, leaving Rilla alone. She grabbed her bag and made her way off the shuttle. The others were waiting for her outside.

"Where's Nathaniel?" Triston asked.

"He left already."

"What?" Rukia exclaimed.

"He left you alone? Why?" Michael asked.

"We had a fight."

"What did he do?" Rukia demanded. "If he hurt you, I'll…"

"No, no. It was a verbal fight. I'm fine," Rilla insisted, trying to calm her friend down.

"I'll go look for him. I think I know where to find him," Triston offered.

"Go ahead," Michael said as he took Rilla's bag from her. "We'll meet you at the palace."

Triston nodded, and Rilla could have sworn he glared at her before walking away.

* * *

Rilla went with Rukia and Michael to the palace. No matter how many times Rilla saw Central Palace, she was always amazed by it. The tall golden walls towered over everything. Every stone was carved with exquisite detail and seemed to glow even at night. The courtyards around the palace had the largest and most beautiful collection of trees and flowers she had ever seen, and nothing ever seemed to be out of place.

Once they stepped inside, they were escorted to rooms they could use to freshen up and prepare for the party. Walking down the halls, Rilla looked around, admiring the many portraits hanging on the wall. She recognized most of them as the works of Loth and Tsuna, the famous artists from the Vega System. It was often said that if they ever painted your portrait, you had become one of the most important people in the universe.

Once in the provided room, Rukia and Rilla helped one another get dressed. Afterward, they met Michael outside. Michael, as usual, was rather dashing in his dark blue tux with a teal vest and white bow tie. Taking off his top hat, he bowed to the ladies as they approached. "And here come the two most beautiful ladies at the ball," he said with a grin. "Even if one of them is dressed rather manly."

His joke earned him a slap on the arm from Rukia, as it was her dress pants he was referring to.

"You know I hate dresses," Rukia reminded him as she tucked a strand of hair behind her ear. While she was in pants, she was far from looking manly. Her dress pants were billowy, and if she stood still, they almost looked like a straight black skirt. Her yellow top, while formal, was also unpretentious and comfortable. What gave her attire its serious business appearance was the ceremonial rapier on her belt. Weapons were prohibited in the palace unless they were ceremonial, but rarely was that enforced, as the guards, and most of the guests attending the balls were skilled fighters and quick to end any sign of physical conflict. Michael also wore a ceremonial sword at his side. Rilla preferred keeping hers safe and hidden in her bag.

"No sign of Triston and Nathaniel?" he said as Rilla looked around. "Oh, well! Guess I'll be the lucky guy to have two beautiful ladies on his arm," he said, grinning as he extended each arm to the girls.

"Afraid not, cousin," Nathaniel called as he walked up with Triston and a tall girl with raven hair that hung to her waist. The pale-skinned, green-eyed beauty that was Triston's date for the ball was Princess Mahogany of Jupiter.

"Mahogany!" Rilla shouted as she rushed over to greet her dear friend and former roommate.

The first year at the academy, students were paired up based on the request of the parents or by class ranks. After that the students could choose whom they wished to room with. Rilla and Mahogany had chosen to stay roommates for their entire time there. Quickly becoming the best of friends with Mahogany, Rilla spent almost as much time with her as she did with her cousin Michael and Rukia.

"Rilla, how are you?" Mahogany asked as she embraced the Mercury.

"Better now that you're here. I have so much to tell you," Rilla whispered.

"We'll talk inside," Mahogany responded.

Rilla nodded, and they walked over to join the others. "Shall we, ladies?" Michael asked as he extended his arm to Rukia. She took his arm and headed up the stairs to the main door. Rilla looked the others over and felt a bit better after seeing that Mahogany wasn't wearing a sword at her side either. While seeing the boys with swords was normal, their attire was a bit unusual for them. Triston, who looked surprisingly different in his light-blue tux with dark-blue bow tie and white vest and shirt, extended his arm to Mahogany, which she took, and they followed behind.

Rilla looked at Nathaniel in his teal tux with white tie and blue shirt and vest. He glanced over at her and sighed. "Come on." He extended his arm to her, and she took it gently; she was almost afraid to touch him.

As they walked up the stairs, Rilla noticed that the smell of alcohol was gone, but his eyes were red and puffy looking. "Were you crying?" she asked barely above a whisper. If he heard her, he didn't answer.

They stopped at the door and waited to be announced. "Presenting Princess Rukia of Uranus escorted by Prince Michael of Neptune," the herald called. Michael and Rukia walked in slowly, waving at people they knew. "Presenting Princess Mahogany of Jupiter escorted by Prince Triston of Neptune." Once announced, they followed Michael and Rukia in. Mahogany released his arm once they stopped walking. "Presenting Princess Amirilla VI of Mercury escorted by Lord Nathaniel of Neptune." Rilla and Nathaniel walked in, but as soon as they were inside, he pulled his arm away and walked away.

Rilla sighed and walked over to join the others.

"Excuse me," Triston said. "I'll go see about Nathaniel." This time Rilla was certain he glared at her before walking away.

"Wonder what his problem is," Mahogany said, watching him leave.

"Who knows," Rukia said, shrugging.

"Oh, well, we'll catch you two later," Mahogany said as she grabbed Rilla's arm. "We're going to go scout out all the cute single guys." Michael and Rukia laughed as Mahogany pulled poor Rilla away.

"Mahogany," Rilla whined. "You know…"

"Yes, I know. It was an excuse for us to get away from the others, so we could talk," Mahogany explained as she grabbed two glasses of ale and handed one to Rilla. "Now come on. Let's step outside and chat."

Rilla nodded and followed Mahogany out to the balcony. She leaned against the railing and began to fill her friend in on everything — from Tora leaving to her affair with Nathaniel and their fight on the shuttle. When she was done, she sighed and finished her third glass of ale, which was quickly refilled by a servant. "So now I don't know what to do."

"Wow" was all Mahogany could say. She stared up at the night sky as she tried to absorb and process all Rilla had just told her. "You know what I think?"

"What?"

"I think you should forget about that stuck-up Neptune. Let him sulk and pout. We came here to have fun. So have fun. You don't need him for that," Mahogany said, smiling. "It'll piss him off even more to see you having fun." She held out her hand to Rilla. "Come on, Rilla. Let's go party."

"There's one more thing. I've had a couple visions," Rilla said calmly.

"Uh-oh, I don't think I like the sound of that," Mahogany said as she sat down to listen.

"I don't really remember them. I know the one I had on the shuttle was dark and something was after me."

"The shuttle here?" Mahogany inquired.

Rilla shook her head. "No, the one to Neptune. I blanked out, and apparently I was thrashing and screaming. I think I scared most of the passengers."

"Thrashing?" Mahogany's eyes got wide. "You haven't done that since you were little, right?" Living with Rilla at the academy for years, Mahogany had seen Rilla have many visions, but she'd never experienced the violent ones her friend had had as a child. Rilla had warned her about them though, so she'd be prepared if it ever happened.

"Exactly, and it's rare that I can't remember vivid details of the vision."

"Have you talked to your mother or Michael?" the Jupiter asked in a very concerned tone as she took her friend's hand.

"Not yet. I haven't had a chance," Rilla explained.

"What about the first one? When did you have it? What was it? Did you remember it in detail?" Mahogany flooded Rilla with questions in an almost panic.

"Mahogany, calm down. The first was almost a week ago on the beach by Aturia Lighthouse. I don't remember it at all. I told Mother about it, and she told me to ignore it, that it was just my nerves with all that was going on with Tora. But—"

"But now that you've had the second one, you don't believe that, do you?" Mahogany asked.

"No, I don't," Rilla responded. "I plan to talk to Michael as soon as I can before I rush to any conclusions."

"Good plan." Mahogany stood and gave Rilla a big smile. "So in the meantime, stop worrying about it and let's go have some fun. I'm sure we can find some cute available guys," Mahogany teased.

Rilla smiled. Mahogany was always able to switch from one emotion to another at the drop of a hat, and she was an expert at cheering Rilla up. "You go on. I'll catch up. I want to enjoy the stars for a bit longer."

Shadows of the Past

Mahogany put her hands on her hips and sighed. "All right, but if you take too long, I'll be back to drag your ass around with me. One way or another, you're having fun tonight."

Rilla chuckled and watched her walk back in. She sighed and drank her fourth glass of ale.

Chapter Eight

Rilla stood on the balcony, overlooking over the garden. Hearing the crowd inside, she sighed. Everyone was having a thrilling time. Everyone but her. *"No one else will dance with you because of your jealous husband."* His voice echoed in her head.

"Mahogany's right. I can't let him ruin a good party, and I'll prove that to him," she muttered to herself as she turned back to the party. Looking around, she searched for a single man. No, not him. He's too short…she mentally commented to herself as she went through the crowd, looking for the perfect man. Then she saw him—tall, extremely handsome, and he looked lost and alone. Smiling, she looked around for Nathaniel. Rilla wanted to make sure that he was watching. Sure enough, she spotted him leaning against a wall, talking to Triston, his eyes on her. He smirked, seeing her look at him, obviously mistaking her looking for him as a sign she had changed her mind. She glared at him and turned her attention back to the handsome stranger.

Walking over, she studied the young man. He was slightly taller than her, dark brown hair, and his eyes appeared to be brown, but something looked off to her, almost as if he had glamoured them. Ignoring it, she continued walking over, not paying attention to the stares and whispers. Stopping in front of him, she curtsied and gave him a smile.

He returned her smile and bowed. "Good evening, Miss..." He chuckled a bit. "Please forgive me. I'm new to the system. I'm sure you're a lady of great importance, just as you're a lady of great beauty. So please tell me who you might be." Honestly, he couldn't have cared less. The people of this system mattered little to him, but Galactica insisted on throwing him a party for his sixteenth birthday.

Blushing slightly, she ducked her head and replied, "I'm Amirilla, daughter of Arkanthius and Amirilla, rulers of the Mercury Kingdom."

"Mercury princess..." he mumbled. For some reason, that sounded familiar to him.

"Did you say something?"

"Oh, no, no. Sorry. I was repeating your name and title. It helps me remember names," he fibbed.

Rilla nodded and started swaying back and forth to the beat of the music. "I don't suppose you'd care to dance, would you?"

"No, I...uh, that is..." He sighed and gave in. He was supposed to be enjoying himself, and he wasn't going to do that standing in a corner. Plus, there was something about this girl that had piqued his interest. "All right," he said with a smile as he held his hand out to her. Rilla took his hand, and they walked out to the dance floor. Bowing before her, he looked to see the crowd dancing a traditional waltz from Mars called the Canta. As he took her hand again, he noticed several sets of eyes focus on them.

Rilla saw the insanely jealous look from Nathaniel as she twirled in the stranger's arms. She also saw the look of disgust on Triston's face. Smiling, she ignored them and focused her attention on her dance partner. "You said you're new to the system. So where are you from?"

"Oh, no place in particular. I travel a lot." He tried to relax and enjoy the dance, but something told him this princess was trouble.

As the dance ended, Rilla found herself starting to feel slightly light-headed. The four glasses of ale she'd had before rejoining the party while she was talking with Mahogany were the cause, no doubt. She nearly fell as she curtsied.

Seeing her legs become wobbly, he grabbed her arms to steady her. "Are you all right?"

"Yes, I'm fine. I just need to sit down for a minute." He nodded and helped her to an empty chair by the window. Once she was seated, the room seemed to stop spinning. She looked up at the handsome stranger. "Thank you, Mr.…." Then it dawned on her that he had never given his name. "You never told me your name."

He chuckled. Only took you a whole twenty minutes to notice that, he thought. "Just call me Shadow."

"Oh! A mysterious one you are," Rilla replied, smiling.

"If you say so, Princess."

"Please drop the 'princess' thing. My name is Amirilla, but my close personal friends call me Rilla." The second part of her statement came out sounding a lot more seductive than she had intended for it to.

"So what should I call you?"

"Well, what do you want to call me?" Rilla asked with a mischievous grin.

"Hmm…" he thought a moment. "You sure you want to know?"

"Yes, yes. I insist."

He smiled. "All right." He stepped away and grabbed an empty chair and pulled it over. As he sat down, he looked her in the eyes and said, "Trouble."

Before she had a chance to reply, Triston and Nathaniel came charging over. "There you are, Mi-chan." Nathaniel said purposely, trying to upset her.

"I've told you not to call me that!" Rilla yelled as she stood up.

"Mi-chan," Shadow mumbled. *I know that name*, he thought to himself.

"I think you've upset the princess, cousin," Triston said as he pulled the chair that Rilla had been sitting in to the side and sat down.

"Poor little Mi-chan," Nathaniel said mockingly. "Her hero died a cowardly death and left her all alone."

SLAP! BAM!

Before he could react, Rilla slapped him as hard as she could and a boot collided with his gut. Nathaniel then found himself on the ground in excruciating pain. The minute his cousin hit the ground, Triston jumped to his feet, hand on the hilt of his sword. "I wouldn't do that if I were you," a stern voice said.

Triston turned to see Rukia standing behind him. "Stay out of this. It doesn't concern you."

Rukia smiled. "You might want to rethink that, unless you want to be a eunuch." She gently tapped his leg with her sword, which was in position to carry out her threat. "And this is my concern. You and your cousin were harassing Mi-chan and spreading lies about Amdis. He was my best friend, and even if I wasn't fond of Rilla, I'd protect her because she's family, and I know Michael would never forgive me if I didn't defend his favorite little cousin."

Triston glared at Rukia, and after she moved her sword from between his legs, he helped Nathaniel to his feet. "I won't forget this, Rukia."

"Good. Maybe by the next time you'll have learned some manners." She watched them leave and turned to Rilla. "Are you all right?"

Rilla nodded. "Yeah. Thanks, Rukia."

"Those two can be quite nasty when drunk," Rukia replied as she sheathed her sword. "If they give you any more trouble, feel free to call me, Mi-chan. I'll gladly beat the crap out of them, or you can do so yourself. Just be sure to call me, so I can watch."

"That's all right, Rukia. I think they'll behave for a while." Nodding, the brunette princess gave Rilla a wink and walked over to the food table.

"You certainly do have interesting friends, Rilla," Shadow said once Rukia was out of site.

"Rukia and Michael are the closest family I have other than my mother and father." Sighing, she sat back down. "Please forgive me for getting the others mad at you."

"Forgive you?" Shadow sat down and gave her a confused look. "One was clearly trying to upset you, and the other was ready to pull a sword. There's nothing for me to be upset at you about."

"Nathaniel may cause you more problems later."

"Let him try. I have no quarrel with him, but if he wishes to start one, I'll show him who the real coward is."

Rilla sighed. She could handle Nathaniel, but she worried about what he and Triston might do to Shadow. With luck he'd ignore it, and after tonight, no more would be said about the issue. "Did you have to kick him so hard though?"

Shadow chuckled. "I kicked no harder than you slapped." He glanced around and spotted the two Neptunes in a corner. Turning back to Rilla, he extended his hand to her. "How about another dance?"

Looking around, she shook her head. "I'm not that good at the—"

"Actually," Shadow said, cutting her off, "I had something a little more robust in mind." He took Rilla's hand and helped her to her feet. "Unless you don't think you can keep up."

Rilla laughed. "Just try to lose me."

Smiling, Shadow nodded and walked to the stage, where the famous trio from the Orion sector, the Lights of Starfire, were performing. He motioned to the guitarist, and when he came over, he told him what to play. The lead singer nodded and told the other two the requested song.

As Shadow rejoined Rilla, she asked him, "What did you tell them to play?"

Taking his jacket off and folding it neatly, he looked to the princess. "Are you familiar with the Jonetsu?

"Of course, it's an old dance on Venus. My husband taught it to me."

"Husband? Wait! He wasn't one of those two, was he?" Shadow panicked. Last thing he wanted to do was get in the middle of a lovers' quarrel.

"No, no, Jacob isn't here. Nathaniel and Triston are distant relatives of mine. Both from the Neptune family."

"Ah, good," Shadow replied as he led Rilla to the dance floor. "This will be a slightly different version of the Jonetsu. Just follow my lead, okay?"

She gave him a curious look, shrugged, and took his hand. "All right."

As the band finished the previous song, they looked to Shadow. When he signaled them, they nodded and started playing the song he had requested. Shadow took Rilla's hand and led her in the dance. True to her word, she kept in perfect time with him and the music. Slightly impressed by her, Shadow had to smile. She was intoxicated, and not even five minutes earlier, she'd looked as if she were going to pass out, and now she was dancing as gracefully as any professional dancer.

Meanwhile, as expected, Triston and Nathaniel were watching the two and plotting revenge. As the pair danced slowly closer and closer to their location, Triston handed his dagger to Nathaniel. "He's an outsider and a stranger to everyone here. No one will care if he's killed, and since no one will miss him, there won't be an investigation."

"Don't be so sure about that, cousin," Nathaniel said as he tried to hand the dagger back to him. "Don't forget who he's dancing with."

"You really think she'd turn you in for killing him?" Triston asked as he pushed the dagger back at his cousin.

"I know she would. She's just like her brother. Always following the rules and defending the weak, even if it's not a politically wise thing to do. When we were at the academy, she even scolded me once for breaking a classmate's arm in a duel." Nathaniel shook his head. "No, Rilla would insure justice for the stranger, even if she had to do it herself." He pulled a small vile of liquid from his pocket. "That's where this comes in."

"Poison?"

"The best kind. It's odorless, tasteless, and completely untraceable," Nathaniel explained.

"How do you plan on giving it to him?" Triston asked. "Slipping it in his food or drink?"

"Too risky. I have a better idea." Placing his hand on the hilt of his sword, he continued. "I'll challenge him to a duel. My blade will be lined with the poison. So all I have to do is give him a tiny cut."

"But won't that look suspicious; you cut him and he dies?" Triston questioned.

"No, no. It's a slow-working poison. It will be hours or days even before it kills him. All depends on his metabolism."

"Still it's too risky to challenge him to a duel," Triston replied.

"You worry too much," Nathaniel stated. "Just leave everything to me." He handed the dagger back to his cousin and smiled. "Trust me. Nothing will interfere with my plan."

While Nathaniel started to put his plan into action, the princess was completely unaware of the danger she would soon be in. Unhappy with his cousin's plan, Triston decided to take matters into his own hands. As the dance neared its end, he positioned himself behind the couple with dagger in hand. Seeing an opening, he lunged for the stranger, but things didn't go as planned.

Just as Triston lunged to stab Shadow, the couple twirled. The dagger missed Shadow completely and cut the bow of Rilla's dress. Before he could react, Triston found a hand colliding with his nose. While the force was great enough to break his nose, Rilla only felt a slight brush against the back of her hand, even though it was her hand that collided with his nose.

As the dance ended, Shadow dipped Rilla and tried not to smile at the sight of Triston clenching his nose with both hands. He lifted her up and bowed to her. "Thank you for the wonderful dance. Now if you'll excuse me, I have a few things I must attend to."

Rilla nodded and smiled. "Perhaps we'll meet again."

"Perhaps." He nodded and walked away. As he made his way across the ballroom, a tall woman in a white dress followed him. Once they were on the other side of the room, he acknowledged the woman's presence. "So you decided to show up after all."

She stopped behind him and smiled. "Well, I couldn't let you and Shade have all the fun."

"Fun?" Shadow questioned. "Shyy, you know this isn't my idea of fun."

"Oh, I don't know," Shyy replied. "Looked like you were enjoying yourself to me."

"I have no idea what you're talking about," Shadow stated.

"Uh-huh. Sure. Keep telling yourself that, but you're enjoying this. Just don't get too crazy without me," she stated as she turned to walk away.

Shadow shook his head as he watched her leave. Shrugging he turned and continued on his way outside. As he walked out the door, a dark figure ran into him. "Excuse me," he said as he tried to continue out the door.

"Watch where you're going!" the man said as he shoved Shadow.

As he stepped into the light, Shadow saw it was Nathaniel. "I said excuse me. Now step aside and let me go on about my business. I have no quarrel with you."

"But I have one with you," Nathaniel said as he removed his glove. "I challenge you to a duel," he stated as he slapped Shadow with his glove.

Sighing, he asked, "Are you sure you wish to go through with this?"

"What? Of course. Do you accept, or are you a coward as well?"

Shaking his head, Shadow removed his glove. "I accept," he said as he slapped Nathaniel back. "Though it won't take long for you to regret this."

Glaring, Nathaniel put his glove back on. "We'll meet in the courtyard in an hour." Nathaniel made his way back inside to make preparations for the duel.

"Very well." Shadow shook his head and stepped outside. "The Mercury Princess was right; those two are troublesome."

"Want me to get rid of him?" a voice said from above.

Shadow chuckled, "No, old friend. He's an arrogant fool, but not worth the time. Besides, he's no threat to me."

Shadows of the Past

"Are you sure? I can take care of him easily."

"Tell you what, Shade…have a little fun with him, if you wish, but don't harm him. Bother, annoy, and mess with him all you want but leave him in one piece."

"Fine, fine. Be that way. Ruin all my fun."

Shadow laughed. "You can have fun later. I have a job for you. I'll tell you all about it when it's time. For now, go find the other three. I'll need all of you. Shyy is inside, but I'm not sure about the twins."

"Very well." There was a gust of wind, as though two large wings had spread and taken flight.

* * *

Back inside, Rilla was still feeling a little tipsy, but that didn't stop her from grabbing another glass of ale. She found Michael and Rukia sitting near the stage where the Lights of Starfire were performing.

"Ah, there you are, Mi-chan," Michael greeted her with a smile. "Come, have a seat, and enjoy the show. Toya should be singing his solo soon."

"Actually, Michael, I was wondering if I could speak with you for a moment," Rilla said softly. "In private."

"Of course, cousin." He quickly stood and told Rukia he'd be back shortly. He walked with Rilla to a secluded corner of the ballroom. "What's going on, Rilla? Is this about Tristan and Nathaniel? Rukia told me what happened."

"No, no, this is something private." Rilla stared at the floor. "Michael, I've been having weird visions and dreams lately."

"Weird in what way?"

"Weird in the fact that my dreams are all about Di-chan. They're more like memories than dreams though. I haven't dreamt of big brother in years, and now he's all I see in my dreams. My visions are dark and unnerving, especially since I can't recall them clearly, and I've been thrashing about when I have them again."

Michael lifted her chin and made her look him in the eyes. "What did you see, Rilla?"

"I don't know. The first one was the day after Tora ran away. I was on the beach. I know I had one, and it bothered me, but I don't remember any of what it actually was. The second was on the way to Neptune. I was being chased by someone or something through a forest of weirdly shaped white trees. That's all I remember. I have no clue what it means, and it bothers me," Rilla explained. "My visions haven't been this unclear since I was little, but I learned to control them and ended the thrashing long ago. Why is this happening, Michael?"

Michael sighed. "I have no idea, Mi-chan, but you're right. Something is off. If your visions are hazy, I fear for the worst. You've always been stronger than me when it came to that. Mother says that Auntie was the strongest between them as well. Did you ask your mother about the dreams and the first vision?"

Rilla nodded. "She told me it was stress over Tora and to ignore it." Michael nodded and rubbed his chin, staring at the wall, deep in thought. "What should I do?"

"For now, nothing. When you get home talk to Auntie. See what she says. But if you have another vision between now and then, be sure to let me know."

Rilla nodded and hugged her cousin. "Thank you."

"Anytime, Mi-chan," Michael said as he hugged her tight, his head resting on top of hers. "Anytime." Michael told her to go enjoy herself, and he returned to Rukia.

"Everything all right?" Rukia questioned when he was seated.

"She's having hazy visions," Michael said in a serious tone. "And she's thrashing about again like when she was little."

"Did she see the same thing as what you saw?" Rukia inquired, sounding deeply concerned by what Michael had just told her.

Shaking his head, the Neptune prince sighed. "I don't think so. From what she remembers, no, but who knows what she doesn't remember from her visions."

"Did you tell her about the black arrow?"

"No. She's got enough on her mind at the moment. But mark my word, I won't let that arrow find its mark." Michael downed his ale and turned to watch Rilla, who was across the room drinking and talking with Mahogany. "One way or another, I will prevent it."

* * *

After talking with Mahogany and downing another three glasses of ale, Rilla headed out to the balcony for some air. She smiled when she saw who else had stepped outside for some night air. Shadow paced around outside, deep in thought. "Why does trouble always find me?"

"Well, with a name like Shadow, you attract the odd and mysterious."

He turned around to see Rilla stagger out, quite drunk. "Are you all right?"

"Of course!" She exclaimed as she nearly tripped. "Never better."

"You're drunk."

"Am not!" she shouted as she stepped toward him. "A lady, especially a princess, never drinks too much."

"Uh-huh, and there's no such thing as too much to drink, right?" Shadow reached for her arm. "Come on. Let's get you back inside."

As his hand reached for hers, she slapped it away. "Oh, no, you don't. I…hic…am a married…hic…woman. You, sir, are a…a…"

"Good Samaritan?"

"A scoundrel."

Shadow shrugged. "I've been called worse."

"I know what you're planning."

"Oh?" Shadow leaned against the balcony and waited to hear her drunken ideas.

"You think you can turn on your charm and then take advantage of a defenseless woman."

"Uh-huh, and I planned to leave my own party just to have my way with you," Shadow said sarcastically.

Shadows of the Past

"You fiend!" Rilla lunged at him and missed, nearly going over the balcony. The only thing that stopped her was Shadow grabbing the back of her dress. "Let go of me, you villain!"

"You sure that's what you want?"

"Yes!"

"Okay." Shadow let her go, and she went head first over the balcony. Even though she floated the few feet to the ground, thanks to Shadow's spell, she screamed the whole way down. Luckily the party was loud enough to drown out her screams. As she landed softly, Shadow shook his head and jumped off the balcony, landing on his feet a meter or so from her.

"You're horrible!" Rilla cried.

"Why? Because I made you float rather than fall?"

"You threw me off the balcony!"

"No, you nearly jumped over it. I grabbed you, and you told me to let you go. So I did." Shadow crossed his arms and leaned against the building.

Rilla jumped up and dusted herself off. "You horrible, despicable man!" She reached in the bag at her side and pulled out a dagger and threw it at Shadow.

He turned his head to see a small ornate mercurite dagger stuck in the wall just above his left shoulder. "What is it with everyone and daggers tonight? Although that's not too bad, considering how drunk you are."

"I am not drunk!" she exclaimed, and with that, she threw two small knives at him.

"Okay, who's in charge of security?" Shadow took a step toward her and ducked another knife. "Where in the name of the king of dragons are you hiding all those?"

As she went to throw another, Shadow grabbed her hand. "Unhand me!"

"Only if you promise to stop throwing knives and daggers at me."

"All right."

"I have your word of honor, Princess?"

"Yes, I promise I won't throw any more daggers."

"Good." Shadow released her arm and turned his back to her. "Sheesh. Women. One minute they love you, the next they're trying to kill you."

As he started to walk away, Rilla slowly pulled out a rapier. Before she could swing her sword, he turned around with his own sword in hand. "How did you—"

"I could ask you the same thing. Now please drop the sword and stop trying to kill me," Shadow said as he lowered his blade.

"I'll never surrender to you," Rilla replied as she stood, extremely wobbly but standing nonetheless, ready for battle.

Shadow sighed and mumbled something in a language she had never heard before. She dropped her sword and shook her head as she felt her eyes getting heavy. He slowly walked behind her and mumbled again. She closed her eyes and fell fast asleep. Shadow caught her as she fell backward and gently placed her on the ground.

"Now then, let's see what you're hiding, Princess."

Shadows of the Past

Looking her over, he noticed a small bag by her side. He almost missed it as it was heavily glamoured with magic that he recognized. "Well, well, what do we have here?" He opened the bag and looked inside but saw nothing. "It couldn't be…" Slowly, he reached his hand in and found the bag had no bottom. "I don't believe it," he said as he pulled his hand out with a very special item.

He smiled slightly seeing it, and his memories became very clear on who she was at last. The item was a rose, surrounded by flames and encased in ice. The flames continued to burn, never melting the ice, and he knew for a fact that the ice would never break. Holding the rose in his hand, he stood. "After all these years you still have them." He gathered all her weapons and placed them and the rose back in her bag. "You certainly have grown, little girl. Now I remember you." Shaking his head, he knelt beside her. "I knew you were trouble." He chuckled. "If your mother had reminded me of all the trouble you caused as a child, I would have remembered sooner." He sighed and brushed a strand of blue hair from her face. "Oh, well, as your mother said, 'It's best you never find out who I am.' Forgetting is easier." Placing his hand over her forehead, he mumbled a spell to help prevent her from having too horrible of a hangover. Sighing, he shook his head. "I really am too nice sometimes."

Shadow gently picked her up and carried her in through a side door. He was met by several servants at the door. "The princess became light-headed and passed out. Please take care of her and see that she makes it home safely."

"As you wish, my lord," one of the servants replied as he carried the princess to a room upstairs.

As Shadow rejoined the party, he walked over to two guards who were standing near the refreshment table. "There's going to be a duel in the courtyard in less than an hour."

"What?" the tall chubby guard exclaimed. "I'll put a stop to it."

Shadow put his hand out to stop the man from charging outside. "You'll do nothing to interfere. You will simply ensure that no one other than myself and Nathaniel of Neptune are permitted to enter the courtyard. Is that clear?"

"Yes, my lord," the guards replied in unison.

"Good," Shadow stated as he grabbed a glass of Galactica's famous ale and walked to the ballroom. Shaking his head as he made his way through the people, he sighed.

"Three people trying to kill me in one night. Why does this always happen to me?" he mumbled to himself.

* * *

Meanwhile Nathaniel was preparing for his duel upstairs. "I told you to wait, you idiot," he said to Triston as he polished his blade.

"I don't trust this plan, Nathaniel," Triston replied, sounding rather funny because of his bandaged, broken nose. While it was an easy thing to heal, he wasn't about to ask Rilla, who was the best healer in the group, to do it, and he didn't trust Rukia. He was afraid she'd mend it crooked, and knowing her, it would be on purpose.

"Oh? And your plan was such a brilliant one, wasn't it? Kill him in an extremely crowded ballroom, while dancing with a member of one of the royal houses, no less? Oh, yes, you really are the brains of this operation."

"Well, at least, I was doing something, unlike you, just sitting here polishing your blade. Who cares if your blade is shiny?" Triston asked in a disgusted tone.

Nathaniel sighed. "Dear, simple fool, if my blade is clean and polished, no one will notice the poison. Or would you rather I dye the poison red, then smear it on my blade for everyone to see?" He stood and poured the poison on a rag and wiped his blade thoroughly, coating it completely with the clear liquid.

"I still don't like this."

"Then go home. I'll handle this," Nathaniel replied as he sheathed his sword. "Trust me, Triston. In a little less than an hour this will all be over. We'll have our revenge, and the stranger won't bother anyone ever again."

Unhappy with his cousin's attitude, Triston stood and left the room. "Idiot. What's so special about Rilla anyway?" he mumbled as he walked down the hall. "I should run them both through. That would solve everything. Show her not to mess with a guy's feelings like that." As he turned the corner, he collided with something rather solid that wasn't visible and was knocked back. "What?" Slowly he reached his hand out and felt in front of himself. Not feeling anything in the way, he shrugged and continued to walk.

Suddenly he was knocked back as if he'd been hit squarely in the jaw by a rather large fist. Triston fell to the ground unconscious, his jaw now broken. "That'll teach you to talk bad about Mi-chan," a voice whispered before dragging the Neptune into a room, so he wouldn't be seen.

Chapter Nine

Nathaniel paced around the empty courtyard. I don't like this, he thought. The courtyard was dark and quiet and lights and sounds of the party made it clear things were still in full swing. He wondered, "Where is he? And where is that idiot Triston?"

"The idiot is probably attending to his broken jaw."

Nathaniel jumped, hearing the voice. He turned to see Shadow walking casually toward him. "It's about time! You're almost half an hour late! And what do you mean 'attending to his broken jaw'? Triston has a broken nose, not jaw."

"One, I'm not late. I arrive precisely when I intend to, and two, you're half-right. Yes, he has a broken nose, but apparently the clumsy fool tripped and collided with *something* rather large and broke his jaw," Shadow replied as he leaned against a tree. "Besides, no one is allowed in the courtyard other than the two of us."

"What? Why?"

"I told the guards to see to it. Looks like they actually managed to do something right tonight. I figured I'd spare you the embarrassment of having your ass handed to you in public."

"You cocky bastard!" Nathaniel shouted as he drew his sword. "Looks like I'll have to teach you more of a lesson than I originally thought." He swung his sword and took a fighting pose. "Draw your weapon."

Shadow sighed and walked over to face Nathaniel. "Very well. Let's begin this duel. Attack whenever you like." He stood there, arms crossed, with a slight smirk on his face.

Nathaniel blinked and looked at him, confused. "Aren't you going to draw your weapon?"

"Do you see a sword on me?" Shadow asked as he turned in a circle with his arms held out.

"You arrogant fool! You actually came here without a sword?" Shadow simply smiled and shrugged. "So be it. Die, you pompous son of a bitch!"

As the Neptune lunged at him, Shadow sidestepped and avoided the blade. "Temper, temper. You act like I've committed some serious crime against you," Shadow stated as he dodged twelve more attacks. "What could I have possibly done to you that makes you want to kill me?"

Nathaniel continued swinging his sword wildly at Shadow, letting his anger get the better of him. "You've injured and insulted me and my cousin, and you've acted inappropriately toward a member of a royal family."

Shadows of the Past

Shadow ducked and looked at him with a confused expression. "Okay, to whom, how, when, and where did I do all this? Injure and insult you and your cousin maybe, but you two asked for it."

Nathaniel stopped his assault and glared at Shadow. "Again you insult me!"

Shadow sighed. He was beginning to grow tired of Nathaniel's antics. "So you're telling me you want to kill me for insulting you and protecting a princess?"

"Protecting? She was in more danger from you than us," Nathaniel said before lunging at him once more and, once again, missing.

"Then why is it you hurt her more than I did?"

"I would never harm her!" He dove at Shadow and landed face-first in the dirt, his sword flying out of his hand.

Shadow shook his head. "So says the man who called her brother a coward and whose cousin came close to stabbing her with that dagger of his. Oh, and if you're counting Triston's broken nose as an injury from me, well, you're not completely accurate in that. It was your dear princess's hand that broke his nose." He grabbed Nathaniel's sword as he reached for it and held it behind his back. "Now let's settle this. Either give me your word that you'll stop trying to kill me or suffer the consequences. I don't like people trying to kill me, and you're making me miss a halfway decent party." Shadow extended his hand to Nathaniel. "What will it be?"

Glaring up at him, Nathaniel took his hand. "Fine." Shadow nodded and helped him up. He dusted himself off and looked at Shadow again. "But this isn't over."

"You know you're right." Shadow jumped back and swung Nathaniel's sword in the air. "This isn't over. *You* need to be taught a lesson." He held the sword at his side as if it were in a sheath and bowed his head. Taking a deep breath, he focused his energy and made sure to restrain himself so as not to kill Nathaniel. In the split second that he attacked, which was too fast for most people to see what happened, Shadow drew the sword from its imaginary sheath in an upward swing and brought it down with such force that Nathaniel was knocked back a good four feet.

Nathaniel barely had time to get back on his feet before Shadow was on top of him. He moved with a god-like speed that Nathaniel had never heard of. If not for the fact that Shadow was missing on purpose, Nathaniel would have been hit over one hundred times in a matter of a minute. While the blade never touched him, the power Shadow wielded was enough to knock him around. As the blade passed right in front of his eyes, Nathaniel was knocked back against a tree. Shadow stopped his assault long enough to see the look of fear on his opponent's face. "Please…"

"Now to end this," Shadow said, cutting off Nathaniel's plea for mercy. He spun in a circle, and in the blink of an eye, he slashed and made contact with Nathaniel ten times with the blunt side of the blade. His final move was spinning around and throwing the sword like a spear at him. The blade went in the tree, halfway to the hilt, and cut Nathaniel's upper arm in a straight cut, deep enough that it would leave a nice scar. Shadow turned and started to walk away.

"Please, help me!" Nathaniel called after Shadow had taken a dozen steps, which was how long it took for him to realize the blade he'd poisoned had just cut him.

Shadow turned back and looked at him. He tried hard not to smile at how pathetic he looked. "I spared your life. What more do you want?"

"No. Please. You don't understand…" Nathaniel went on as he tried to stand.

"Oh, I understand perfectly well. You came here with a poisoned blade and the intent of killing me," Shadow stated calmly. Then he turned back toward the castle. "What I don't get is why, but then at this point, does it really matter?"

"Please! You can't let me die! What I did was wrong and I'm sorry!" he called after him. Nathaniel tried to stand, but his body felt as if it had been beaten by a steel beam.

Shadow ignored his pleas and continued walking. He glanced to his right as he felt a large wing brush against his shoulder. "Does that moron really believe he was defending Rilla's honor?"

"Let him think what he wants to, Shade. It matters not to me," Shadow stated.

"So how long are you going to let him think that he's been poisoned?"

"Until he realizes that, if he had been, he would have been dead days ago," Shadow answered.

"Ouch. Feeling a bit vindictive tonight, are we?" Shade asked as he walked Shadow back to the castle door.

"Just giving him a lesson that he won't soon forget."

Shade chuckled and shook his head. "And you said the party would be boring."

"Yeah, yeah. I know. There's no such thing as boring where I'm concerned, right? Although your little stunt with his cousin didn't help."

"I have no clue as to what you are referring," Shade said as he scratched his chin and looked away.

"Uh-huh, and I'm going to eat my hat, too," Shadow said as he went up the steps to the main door.

"Yeah, right…Hey, wait. You don't have a hat."

Shadow laughed. "Exactly. Now go keep an eye on our friend. Don't want him trying to end his own life to avoid the suffering. And feel free to hit him if you believe he's endangering himself."

"My pleasure," Shade replied with a smirk as he turned and flew back to where they'd left the defeated Neptune.

Shadow walked back in the castle, leaving Nathaniel in the courtyard in the capable care of the black dragon. As he entered the ballroom, a tall woman with golden hair with red tips, wearing a gold dress, followed him across the crowded dance floor. He stopped in the back of the room

Shadows of the Past

and waited for her to catch up. "I wondered when you were going to show up."

"Did you think I wouldn't be here? I mean, this is my castle after all," she said as she walked around to face him.

"Of course not. I just expected you to show up sooner," Shadow said as he leaned against a column.

"Well, I figured I would wait until the party was in full swing before I made my grand entrance."

Shadow laughed and shook his head. "You always were one for the dramatic entrance." He looked around at the party. "So was all this really necessary?"

"Of course. It's not every day that someone of your standing turns sixteen," she teased.

He rolled his eyes and stated, "And I've turned sixteen how many times now? Besides, you know I hate being the center of attention, and as far as this being my party, you failed. Nobody knows me or that it's my birthday other than you, your servants, and the guests that came with me."

"I can fix that if you want," she said with a sly grin.

Shadow shook his head. "No, that's okay. You'd enjoy it too much." He looked around at the crowded room. "So tell me, Galactica, how many of these people do you actually know?"

She looked around. "Hmm...on a personal level, none of them other than those in my personal court. I mean, I know who some of them are or, at least, what family they're from, but you know me. I care little for the affairs of others." She looked around and signaled to one of her servants, and he brought over a tray of drinks. She took two glasses and handed one to Shadow. "But they aren't important. So here's to you, old friend. I hope this will be the first of many such parties. "

"How many times must I tell you that I don't like big parties?"

Smiling, Galactica took a drink of her ale, and replied in a sweet voice, "I never said the party had to include anyone other than you and me, now did I?"

Shadow shook his head and sipped his ale. "I get in enough trouble without your help."

Galactica nodded. "I've noticed. You've broken the nose and jaw of one boy, gotten a princess drunk off her ass, and beaten another boy without ever drawing your sword. Oh, yes, I can see you've been very busy causing trouble tonight, my dear Shadow."

"Whoa! Whoa! Wait just a minute. First, I was only partially involved with breaking Triston's nose, and I had absolutely nothing to do with breaking his jaw. Talk to Shade if you want information on that. And why haven't you had one of your healers fix that for him?

Shrugging Galactica smirked. "All he has to do is ask, and it will be done. But I can't help it if he'd rather suffer than ask for aid."

Shaking his head, Shadow continued, "Second, the little princess was tipsy when I first met her. It's not my fault she doesn't know when to stop. And third, you know I wouldn't bring a weapon in here, especially when you've specifically stated that no weapons are allowed. Which reminds me, who is in charge of security?"

Shadows of the Past

Galactica laughed and finished her ale. "Good one, Shadow. You almost had me believing it. You and I both know that you never go anywhere without your sword. And my security is fine. Only ceremonial blades are allowed, and they have to be peace bonded. Besides, most ceremonial swords are so dull they can't cut hot butter."

"Sure it is. That's why three people have tried to kill me with swords, knives, and daggers tonight. And trust me, all those blades were not peace bonded, and they were sharp enough to cut a lot more than butter." Shadow shook his head and finished his glass of ale. "Hate to see what you call poor security."

Shrugging, Galactica handed her empty glass to a servant and grabbed another. "Well, one of the three was your doing." Seeing the look of confusion on Shadow's face, she smiled. "Yes, I know all about your little Mercury princess. Too bad for you, she's already married."

"I haven't got a clue what you're talking about," Shadow stated calmly as he handed his empty glass to the servant.

"Sure, you don't. That's okay. You keep your little secrets. You don't fool me, though."

"There's nothing to hide. I knew her years ago when she was just a little girl, but she doesn't know I'm the stranger she met all those years ago. I doubt that she even remembers me at all."

"Is that a hint of sadness I hear in your voice, Shadow?" she inquired.

Shadow tilted his head and looked at Galactica. "When you have delusions, you really have delusions. What happened to 'the affairs of others don't concern you'?"

"They don't concern me, but I do find *your affairs* to be quite interesting and entertaining," she replied with a smug grin before she turned and walked away.

Chapter Ten

Rilla sat hugging her large, blue stuffed dog with floppy ears. Amdis had given it to her a week earlier for her fifth birthday. The dog was bigger than she was and had already been torn slightly in a fight between Rilla and her younger sister, Tora, who was jealous of the dog.

"What's wrong, Mi-chan?" Amdis asked as he walked into the room.

Rilla looked up to see her brother's smiling face. "Di-chan!" She tossed the dog on the bed and ran to hug him. "You're home!"

Smiling he scooped up his little sister and hugged her as he carried her over to the bed. She giggled as he tossed her on the pile of pillows she always had at the head of the bed, and started tickling her. "So why is my Mi-chan so sad?" he asked when he was done tickling her.

She caught her breath, sat up, looked at her brother, and in a very sad and serious tone said, "No one likes me, Di-chan."

"Now you know that isn't true, Mi-chan," Amdis replied as he picked up the blue dog that Rilla had named Ruu.

"Yes, it is," she said as a tear rolled down her cheek. "None of the kids in the village will play with me. They say I'm just a spoiled, bratty princess. Tora hates me. Mother and Father are too busy to play. You're always at that dumb old academy. Even Mister stopped visiting."

Amdis couldn't help but laugh. "You silly girl, none of that means we don't like you." He tossed Ruu on top of her. "Would I have given you this if I didn't like you?" He grabbed the crystal around his neck and made both his and her crystal start to glow. "Would I have enchanted that crystal for you if I didn't love you?" Before she could answer, he continued, "You know that Mother and Father care. I know Father begged and pleaded with the empress to be able to be here for your birthday, and look at all the work Mother put into that party. Would they do all that for a girl they don't even like?"

Rilla used the dog's large paw to wipe her eyes. "No, but Tora still hates me. She won't play with me, and she tried to steal Ruu! She even..." She stopped in mid-sentence and put her head down.

"She even what?" When she didn't reply, he lifted her head and made her look at him. "Amirilla, what did she do?"

"She hurt Ruu!" She cried as she held the dog's head up to show the torn ear to her brother.

"When did this happen?"

"Yesterday."

Amdis took the dog from her and ran his finger over the tear. "Why didn't you show Mother or one of the servants? They could have easily fixed this."

Ducking her head again, she softly said, "I didn't want anyone to know that I didn't take care of the gift you gave me, Di-chan."

"It was an accident, Mi-chan. Accidents happen." There was a small blue light as he ran his finger over the tear for the third time and then it was gone. "Besides how are you going to learn to fix things, if you never let people know it's broken?"

Rilla sat there wide-eyed. She had looked up just in time to see the tear disappear in the blue light. "You mean, I can learn to do that?"

"Sure, but only if you do your studies like you're supposed to," he replied as he handed Ruu back to her.

"Aww! Do I have to? Can't you just teach me, Di-chan?"

He laughed, "No, silly I can't teach you everything. You have to learn to stand on your own. I won't always be around to fix things for you. Besides, if you do your studies, you'll learn stuff that I don't know."

"Not true. You know everything, big brother!"

Amdis simply laughed, and they both looked to the door as they heard their mother calling. "Amirilla...Rilla...Rilla..."

"Rilla!"

Rilla sat up with a start. "What?" She grabbed her head and lay back down. Her head was throbbing, and she felt sick in her stomach.

"Sheesh, Rilla! Can't you hold your liquor?"

She looked up to see Mahogany. "What are you doing here, Mahogany?"

"I went looking for you and was told you had passed out in the garden and had some lord bring you in. Being the good friend that I am, I had to make sure you were okay."

Rilla smiled. "Thanks, Mah—"

"And I had to find out what fun you were having in the garden without me." Mahogany said, interrupting Rilla.

Rilla sat up, holding her head. "Ha! Ha! Very funny."

"So what happened?" Mahogany asked.

"I'm not sure that I remember everything. Things are fuzzy. I know we talked on the balcony. I wound up dancing with this stranger named Shadow. I had some drinks, talked with Michael, and that's about all I remember."

"Shadow?" Mahogany looked at Rilla with a curious expression.

"Yeah, that's the name he gave me, at least."

"That's the same person who brought you in from the garden. Think, Rilla. He didn't hurt you, did he? If you even think he might have, tell me and I'll kick his ass."

Leave it to a Jupiter to kick ass first and ask questions later.

Rilla laughed. "No, he didn't hurt me, Mahogany. Actually, I know it's going to sound weird, but I think I've met him before."

"Oh?"

"Yeah, something was familiar about him, yet I know I've never seen his face before." She shook her head. "I don't know. It's weird. The dream I had was even weirder."

"Oooh?" Mahogany asked with raised eyebrows.

"Not that kind of dream." Rilla stood and rubbed her neck. "I dreamt of Di-chan. I've been doing that a lot lately."

Mahogany put her hands on Rilla's shoulders. "You want to talk about it?"

She shook her head and turned to look at her friend, with her hand wrapped around the blue crystal around her neck. "It wasn't anything bad. It was more like a memory replaying in my head. I was five and I told Di-chan how no one liked me, and as usual, he made me feel better."

As Rilla let go of her crystal, Mahogany stared at it. "Uh, Rilla…" She pointed at the crystal, which was now glowing bright blue.

Looking down, Rilla grabbed the crystal again, intending to lift it up, to look at it closer, but the moment she touched it, the crystal stopped glowing. "That was weird," Rilla commented as she looked back at Mahogany.

"I haven't seen your crystal glow in years. Didn't you say your brother was buried with his crystal?"

Rilla nodded and sat back on the bed. "Maybe it was because I was thinking of my big brother. I did dream about him just now."

"Think it means anything? The dream and now your crystal? I mean, is it one of your vision things?" Mahogany asked as she sat beside Rilla.

"I don't think so. Like I said, it's more like a memory playing in my head, but something feels terribly out of place. I can't seem to focus my thoughts or power at the moment."

Mahogany laughed. "That could be the alcohol. But then again, it could be your oracle blood being goofy again. I'll never understand how you and Michael can stand all the visions and such. It would drive me nuts."

Nodding, Rilla sighed. "It is a pain at times, but then it comes in handy at times."

"Really? So can you tell me who's going to win the duel between Keggar and Lonwonni next week, so I know who to bet on?"

"Mahogany, you know, as a member of the court, it's forbidden to bet on fights. It's even more illegal for an oracle to use his or her gifts to foresee the outcome for a profit."

"It's only illegal to bet money. I'm not betting money. If I win, Junto has to duel me, and if I win, he has to take me to the Orion Sector next month to see the Lights of Starfire perform."

"So you're finally taking one of your suitors seriously? That's a change. I thought you were never going to get married, unless you could find a guy who could beat you in a fair fight."

"Never said I was serious about him. Besides, guys knocking on the door, wanting to give you gifts, has its advantages, like getting tickets to see the Lights of Starfire."

Rilla laughed. "You're horrible, Mahogany."

"Fine. Be that way. And I was going to see about getting a ticket for you, too. Oh, well, guess I'll go alone."

"You mean you're not getting enough of them tonight?"

Mahogany was about to reply when the door opened, and after seeing who entered, both girls jumped up and stood up straight, their eyes looking down at the floor. "Well, well, it seems our Mercury princess is awake at last. I was beginning to think you were going to sleep right through the party."

"Forgive , Empress. I should have known my limit and stopped drinking long before I reached the point of intoxication," Rilla said, feeling ashamed of herself.

"What is there to forgive? This is a party after all, and I'd be slightly insulted if you didn't enjoy the food and ale. Besides, if you slept through it, the only harm done would be you missing a great party," Galactica replied. She stepped closer to the girls and lifted their heads. "You can look at me, ladies. You're friends in my home tonight, and in two weeks, you'll be official members of my court. So starting tonight, you no longer need have to look at your feet in my presence. After all, you can't be of use to me if you aren't looking around and noticing the important details."

"Details, Empress?" Mahogany asked.

"Yes, details. The smallest things can give you information. For example, your friend's dress is torn. So I can gather she was involved in a bit of a scuffle earlier."

"Torn? Where?" Rilla asked, panicking, thinking that she might have ruined the dress.

"Here," Galactica said, pointing to the bow. "Looks almost like it was cut more so than torn."

Rilla hurried to the mirror to get a better look at the large blue bow on her back. "Oh, no!" She exclaimed. "This is terrible. I knew I should have left this dress in the closet. I can't let Di-chan's gift get ruined."

"Easy, Rilla," Mahogany comforted. "I'm sure the seamstresses can fix it."

"No time for that," Rilla said, rubbing her hand over the cut that was made by Triston's dagger. Suddenly a blue light appeared, and Mahogany watched in surprise as Rilla mended the cut. "Since when could you do that?"

"Since I was six," Rilla replied, a little surprised. "I thought you had seen me do that before."

"No, I hadn't, but it was amazing. Can you fix anything or just cloth?"

"It was a simple mending spell her brother taught her. Am I right, Amirilla?" Galactica asked.

"Yes, Empress," Rilla said, blushing a little, unsure of how to act around the Empress, especially with her acting so familiar toward them.

"Amdis always was very good with his hands. He could fix almost anything and gave one hell of a massage,"

Galactica said with a smile. "I'm sure he passed many such talents onto his precious baby sister."

Rilla blushed even harder, not knowing whether the Empress meant being able to fix things or give a good massage. "He tried to teach me what he could," she said shyly.

"Oh, well, maybe you just need practice," Galactica replied, "but I must get back to the party before Shadow decides to run away."

"Shadow?" Rilla said, nearly jumping.

"Yes, I know him, and I know all about your adventures with him tonight," she said with a smirk. "Though I'm sure your version will be more interesting than his." She chuckled. "He can't say his birthday was boring this year."

"It's his birthday?" Mahogany inquired.

"Why yes, it is. This is his sixteenth birthday party. But anyway I'm off. If you feel you can manage, please rejoin the party," she said as she walked to the door. She stopped and looked back. "Oh, and you might want to go to the courtyard and check on that Neptune boy you came with. The idiot challenged someone way above him to a duel." She turned and left, closing the door behind her.

"Do you think she means Nathaniel or Triston?"

"Probably Nathaniel," Rilla replied. "Though both would be dumb enough to do something like that." She gave a heavy sigh and headed for the door. "Let's go see what trouble the idiot got into."

Mahogany nodded and walked with Rilla back to the ballroom to find the others. Michael, Rukia, and Triston, whose face was heavily bandaged, were sitting together enjoying the food, all but Triston. "Looks like you were wrong, Rilla. Just look at Triston, he's all beat up."

Looking around, Rilla said, "Yeah, but I don't see Nathaniel." She grabbed Mahogany's arm. "Come on. Let's go check out the courtyard." Mahogany let Rilla pull her along, and sure enough they found Nathaniel sitting under a tree with a man with spiky black hair kneeling beside him. Rilla rushed over. "What have you done to him?" she demanded.

The man stood, dusting off his dark-blue suit. "I've patched him up a bit. He took quite a beating, but he'll be all right. Though he's a bit delusional," he informed the ladies as he wiped sweat from his pale face with a handkerchief.

"What are you talking about?" Mahogany asked.

"He keeps claiming he's going to die, that he's been poisoned, but if that were true, the poison would have to have been on his blade as his opponent came unarmed, and it was his own sword that sliced his arm." The man picked up the sword. "I've examined this thoroughly, and there's no poison."

"His opponent was unarmed?" Rilla asked, unbelieving.

"And just who are you?" Mahogany demanded.

"Oh, I'm the doctor. I was here to observe the fight and patch up the loser," he replied with a grin. "I was asked by the winner to watch over him till he was able to stand."

"Who was his opponent?" Mahogany inquired.

"A traveler who has great skill with weapons. He apparently offended the lad somehow, something about a princess."

"Was his name Shadow?" Rilla asked.

The doctor rubbed his chin. "Umm…Well, I've seen him here a lot, but I'm not sure what name he is going by." He stood and grabbed his brown trench coat, which was hanging on a nearby tree branch. "Well, I believe he'll be just fine now, and I'm sure he'd rather have you two lovely ladies looking after him, instead of grumpy old me. There's nothing broken, just badly bruised."

"Thank you, Mr.…." Mahogany paused. "What was your name?"

"Most people just call me Shade," he replied with a smile. "Now, if you'll excuse me, I have other things to attend to."

Rilla and Mahogany thanked Shade and knelt by Nathaniel. "So what do we do with him?" Mahogany asked.

"I guess we try to wake him and get him inside," Rilla answered before attempting to wake Nathaniel. She touched his shoulder and gently shook him. "Nathaniel," she called softly, but he didn't wake up.

"Should I give him a shock?"

"No, Mahogany. I don't think that'll be necessary." Rilla held one hand out and formed a blue orb filled with water. She gently inserted her other hand into the orb and flicked water at Nathaniel's face. "Come on, Nathaniel. Time to wake up."

He twitched at the water hitting his face and slowly opened his eyes. "What? Where am I?"

"The courtyard at Central Palace," Rilla answered.

"Someone beat the crap out of you," Mahogany added with a smirk.

"What?" As he tried to sit up, he quickly remembered his injuries. "Oh, shit! I hurt all over." He groaned as he tried to stand. Rilla and Mahogany grabbed his arms to help him, but he pulled his arm free from Rilla's grasp. "Leave me alone! This is all your fault!"

Mahogany released his other arm, causing him to lose his balance and fall back against the tree. "Rilla isn't to blame for this. Your arrogance and stupidity are."

"I fought to protect her honor," Nathaniel spat.

"From whom?" Rilla questioned. "My honor was never in danger."

"That man, or should I say devil, that you were with. You'd better pray Jacob doesn't find out and take his anger out on you."

SPLASH!

The water orb that Rilla held in one hand suddenly collided with Nathaniel's head and exploded, soaking him with ice-cold water. "Come on, Mahogany," Rilla said as she turned to leave. "I think he can make it back on his own."

Mahogany gave a chuckle at his shocked expression and followed Rilla, leaving Nathaniel alone in the courtyard.

* * *

Once they were back inside, they joined Michael and Rukia and told Triston where he could find his cousin. He quickly headed out to find Nathaniel.

"What happened, Mi-chan?" Rukia asked after Triston dashed off.

"Nathaniel challenged the wrong person to a duel," Rilla explained.

"Supposedly to protect Rilla's honor," Mahogany added.

"From whom?" Michael asked.

"According to Nathaniel, the guy Rilla was with earlier," Mahogany replied quickly. "I think he's just jealous."

"Mahogany." Rilla gave her a scolding look, warning her not to tell them everything.

"Speaking of which, where is this Shadow guy?" Mahogany inquired as she looked around, ignoring Rilla's glares.

"I don't know. The empress did say something about him running off," Rilla replied as she looked around.

"The empress?" Rukia asked unbelievingly. "You have had a busy night."

Rilla shrugged. "Most of it is a blur." She fixed a plate of food for herself and enjoyed a quiet conversation with her dear friends.

The rest of the night went on without incident. Rilla danced once or twice with Michael and kept her eyes out for Shadow, but she never found him. When it was all over, they said their good-byes and made their way to the shuttles after changing into their traveling clothes.

Chapter Eleven

The trip home was surprisingly quiet, even though Rilla was seated by Nathaniel the whole way to Neptune. When they arrived on Michael's home world, Triston and Nathaniel left without a word to anyone, while Rilla said her good-byes to Rukia and Michael.

"What's their problem?" Rukia grumbled, watching them leave.

"I'm sure Mi-chan will tell us all about it later," Michael said with a smirk. Rilla blushed, and before she could respond, Michael changed the subject. "Are you sure you won't stay?"

"Yeah, I mean, you'll be back next week anyway," Rukia added. "Why not just stay with us?"

Rilla smiled. "Wish I could, but Jacob and Marisa are waiting for me."

Rukia sighed. "All right. I won't deny Risa her mommy time. Give her a hug for me."

"Will do." Rilla hugged them both and boarded the shuttle to Mercury.

* * *

The trip was smooth and relaxing as Rilla was one of only six passengers. While the other five slept, Rilla did some quiet reading, though she did doze off at some point.

Rilla sat in her room crying. She hugged her pillow tightly and let it soak up her tears. "Mi-chan," she heard her brother Amdis calling from the doorway, but she didn't look up. "Mi-chan, please don't cry." Amdis sighed and walked over to the three-year-old. "I won't be gone forever. I'll be back before you know it," he said softly as he knelt in front of her.

"I no believe you!" Rilla screamed before burying her face in the pillow.

"Mi-chan, I would never lie to you. I'll be back for the winter holidays, and you'll be so busy helping Mother with Tora that you'll never even know I'm gone."

"Yes, I will," she cried as she looked up. "And Mister promised he be back soon and he lie. He not back, and he no answer his bell now." She cried harder and, once again, buried her head in her pillow.

"Mi-chan." When she didn't look up, he called to her again. "Amirilla." As she looked up at him, Amdis pulled out his handkerchief and wiped her tears away. "I know you miss him, and yes, you're going to miss me when I go to the academy, but you have to be strong. Crying won't make anything better." He reached in his pocket and pulled out a small bag. "I have something for you."

"What?" Rilla asked, perking up a bit at the mention of a present. Amdis handed her the small bag and waited for her to open it. Inside was a small blue crystal on a long silver chain. "Pretty," Rilla said, smiling.

Amdis took it from her hand and placed it around her neck. "It's a magic necklace."

"Magic?" Rilla asked as she looked at the crystal that hung almost to her stomach.

"Yes. Hold it in your hand and close your eyes." Rilla did as Amdis told her. "Now think about me." Rilla giggled but did as he asked. "Open your eyes." Rilla opened her eyes to see a huge smile on her brother's face. "Now look at your crystal."

Slowly she opened her hand and looked down. "Wow!" she exclaimed, amazed to find the crystal glowing bright blue.

"You like that?" Amdis asked, chuckling. Rilla nodded happily. "There's more to the magic." He reached inside his shirt and pulled out the gold chain he wore around his neck. At the end of the chain was a second crystal, which was glowing as bright as Rilla's. "See, Mi-chan. Now I'll always know when you're thinking of me." Amdis touched his crystal, and both stopped glowing. "No matter how far apart we are, these crystals will keep us connected. When we're missing each other, all we have to do is hold our crystal and think of one another, and the crystal will instantly send our love to the other," Amdis explained as he held onto his

crystal and thought of his precious baby sister. Suddenly both crystals started glowing again.

Rilla smiled and touched hers, but frowned when it stopped glowing. "Why it stop?"

Amdis laughed. "So I know you got my message."

"Message?" Rilla asked, confused.

"Yes, when you see that crystal glow, you'll know I'm saying, 'I love you, Mi-chan.'"

Rilla threw her arms around her brother. "I love you, too, Di-chan!"

Smiling, he hugged her tight. "You have to wear your crystal all the time; otherwise, it won't work. Plus I enchanted your crystal with a couple of protection charms to keep you safe while I'm away."

"I neva take it off," Rilla replied with a smile.

By the time the shuttle arrived, it was early morning on Mercury, and Rilla was starting to think her dreams were trying to tell her something. Unsure of what it could be, she decided to talk to her mother about it all when she could — the dreams, the visions, her glowing crystal, and the mysterious Mister.

Queen Amirilla and Marisa were waiting for Rilla at the station. "Mama!" the excited three-year-old cried when she spotted her mother.

Rilla held out her arms and caught the bouncing child. "There's my baby. Did you miss me?"

"Of course, Mama."

Rilla hugged her tight. "I missed you, too." She put her down and took her hand. "Where's your father?"

Shadows of the Past

"Papa no wake up. I tink he sick." Rilla nodded and smiled as her mother walked over. "Grandma was up. She come wit me."

"Well, I couldn't let you come alone," Queen Amirilla stated.

"I not alone. Vixie come wit me," Marisa informed her grandmother.

"Where is Vixie?" Rilla asked.

"Over here," a voice called. Rilla looked to see Vixie stretching on a chair.

"Taking a nap?" Rilla teased.

"I thought I was done chasing rug rats when you went to the academy. She's worse than you ever were about running off," Vixie said as she hopped off the chair and walked over.

Rilla and the queen laughed.

"I doubt that Vixie," the queen said. "Rilla was just easier to find." She ran her fingers through her granddaughter's hair and added, "And sorry to tell you this, but you're going to be looking after Risa a lot more in the future."

"Oh?" Vixie questioned, curious to know the reason for that.

"Yes, Rilla and Marisa will be spending a lot more time at the palace," the queen replied with a smile.

"Mother, did you—"

"Shh…" the queen interrupted Rilla. "We'll talk later. For now, let's go home and have some breakfast. Maurice is preparing a treat to celebrate your return."

Rilla laughed. "I haven't even been gone a week."

"Doesn't matter," her mother said. "Having you home is reason enough to celebrate."

"Yay! Party!" Marisa exclaimed.

Rilla and her mother laughed as the hyper child danced around. "Come on, Risa. Let's head home."

"But I tot we were going to Grandma's?"

Rilla smiled. "That's right, but it's our home, too."

"We have two homes?" Marisa asked, confused.

"Something like that," Rilla said before scooping up her daughter and carrying her to the carriage.

The ride to the palace was filled with question after question from Marisa. She wanted to know everything—where her mother went, who was there, what did they wear, and when could she go.

When they arrived, King Arkanthius was waiting at the gate for them. "There are my girls!"

"Hello, Father," Rilla said, smiling as she put Marisa down, so she could hug her father.

"How was the party?" he asked.

"Delightful. The food and the ale were superb, and the music was marvelous, but then the Lights of Starfire were performing, so that was to be expected," Rilla explained.

"Bah. I will never see what attracts you youngsters to that new stuff they call music," the king complained as he followed them inside.

"I believe the attraction has something to do with the three handsome musicians," the queen said with a smirk.

"Am I right, Rilla?"

Rilla blushed slightly. "I suppose so, Mother."

"Humbug. Looks alone don't make a band," the king griped. "Bet they don't even know the songs of old."

"Actually, Father, they played several of them, including 'The Jonetsu,'" Rilla informed him.

"Really?"

"Yes."

Before Rilla or her father could say anything else, Maurice walked out with open arms. "There you are. What are you doing out here? Your breakfast is in the dining hall getting cold."

Rilla hugged him and headed for the dining hall. "Guess we'd better hurry then. Can't have a cold breakfast, right, Risa?"

"Right, Mama!" the green-eyed girl exclaimed as she followed her mother.

The king and queen followed Rilla and Marisa, and they talked casually over breakfast. When the plates were empty Rilla and Marisa headed upstairs to Rilla's room.

"Mama."

"Yes, Risa?" Rilla said as she started unpacking her things.

"Why can't Papa sweep in your room?"

Rilla chuckled. "He chooses not to. I guess he prefers the guest rooms. And besides, my bed isn't big enough for two people to sleep in."

"Not true!" Marisa cried. "I sweep there wit you all da time."

Laughing, she picked up her daughter and sat her on the bed. "All right. You have a point, but two adults can't fit in the bed. Anyways it's rare for your father to be here for long. I don't think he likes it here."

"Why? I love Grandma's!"

"I know you do," Rilla said, hugging her daughter. "What would you say if we lived here all the time?"

"Really?" Marisa asked excitedly.

"Maybe. We'll have to see. I have to talk to your grandmother."

"Papa, too?"

Rilla hesitated. "We'll talk about it later." She kept her daughter entertained until Vixie came to retrieve her.

"Risa, go with Vixie for a little while. Mama needs a nap."

"Okay, Mama," Marisa said before chasing Vixie down the hall, and Rilla sighed. She lay back on the bed, closed her eyes, and soon drifted off to sleep.

Rilla was surrounded by darkness. The only light that could be seen was far off in the distance. Slowly she walked toward it. As she walked, she looked around nervously. She stopped and started to look back when she heard footsteps behind her.

"Don't look back!" a voice called to her. It came from the direction of the light. "Hurry, Mi-chan!"

She started running to the light. "Big brother?" she asked as she rushed toward the voice, which she thought was her brother. "Di-chan, is that you?"

The light grew bigger and brighter the closer she got. "Hurry, little one. You're in danger. Don't stop and don't look back."

Rilla realized the voice wasn't Amdis as she stepped into the light. In the middle stood a tall man who was like a giant to her. His long silver hair flowed down his back, and he held open his cloak with arms stretched out to her.

"Who are you?" Rilla asked as she stood in front of him.

"No time, child. I must get you home." He bent down and picked her up and suddenly he shrank to her size. Or did she grow to his? She wasn't sure. As he carried her out of the light, Rilla suddenly relaxed, feeling calm and safe. She looked into his eyes, which were almost solid white. There was something familiar about those eyes. When she laid her head on his shoulder, he smiled. "That's my girl." Wrapping his cloak protectively around her, he gently kissed her forehead. "I always knew you were trouble."

Hours later, Rilla woke from her dream to find the room being illuminated by the light of her crystal. Upon being touched gently, the crystal around her neck stopped glowing, and the room was dark once more. Sitting up, Rilla found a small child curled up next to her back. Smiling she carefully got up and pulled a blanket over Marisa. "She's been by your side for the last hour," a voice said from the doorway, which caused Rilla to jump.

Rilla turned to see a tall redhead leaning against the open door. "Hello, Jacob."

"Hello, Rilla," he said, smiling. As he walked over to her, Rilla backed away. "Did you miss me?"

"Not really," Rilla responded.

"That's no way to talk to your husband," he growled as he grabbed her arm.

"Jacob, don't raise your voice. You'll wake up Risa."

"Don't tell me what to do!" he shouted. "And her name is Marisa. I hate it when you and your mother shorten it to that annoying nickname." Hearing Marisa toss on the bed, Rilla turned to check on her. "Look at me when I'm talking to you!" Jacob ordered as he grabbed her chin and made her look at him.

Rilla pulled away from him and moved toward the door. "You've been drinking again."

With that, she headed out the door and walked down the hall, hoping he would follow, so she could get him a safe distance away from Marisa. She didn't want him to wake her up with his shouts.

"Get back here!" he shouted as he chased after her.

Rilla kept going till they were outside on the balcony. Then she turned to face him. "Now if you insist on this, we can fight all you like. But I won't allow you to wake up and upset my daughter," Rilla said firmly.

"Your daughter? Last I checked, she was mine, too!" Jacob went to grab Rilla's arm, but she dodged him. "Or are you saying that I'm not the father?"

"No sadly, you are her father, though most times I wish you weren't. Just like I wish you weren't my husband. But then you already knew that. Question is, do you know how many other children you have bouncing around?"

"How dare you…"

"How dare I? How dare you drag my child all over the system and leave her with a nanny while you go out partying! How dare you disrespect me and my family! And how dare you assume that I will allow you to behave like a drunken fool in front of Risa!" Rilla scolded, purposely using Marisa's nickname.

"Why, you little…" Jacob lunged and went to slap Rilla, but she ducked and he stumbled forward. As he stumbled forward, Rilla kicked his feet out from under him, and he fell forward, landing hard on the crystalline floor with a loud thud.

"Really?" Rilla questioned with her hands on her hips. "You're that drunk?" She almost laughed. "You do realize that if, and that's IF, you manage to lay a hand on me, you'll be put down by the guards?"

Jacob stood and wiped the blood from his lip. "Where are your precious guards then?"

No sooner than the word left his lips than four guards stepped out of the shadows. "Is everything all right, Princess?"

"Yes, Kyne, I can handle this," Rilla commented to the captain of the guard.

"Very well, Princess," he replied, bowing to her. He and the other three stepped back into the shadows and seemed to vanish.

Rilla turned her attention back to Jacob just in time to see him charging at her. She dove out of the way, and he ran straight into the wall. "I think you need to cool off." Rilla brought her hands together and formed a large blue orb between them. "Why don't you take a shower?" She threw the orb at him, and upon impact, it exploded, knocking him to the floor and soaking him with ice water. With a wave of her hand, the water puddled up and suddenly wrapped around Jacob's arms, preventing him from moving. "Don't bother getting up," she said as she turned to the shadows. "Kyne, I think my husband needs to sleep off the alcohol. Could you escort him to his room for the night?"

The guards reappeared and stepped toward Jacob. "Of course, Your Highness," Kyne answered as the other three picked Jacob up with a blue force field surrounding him.

Rilla sighed as they carried him off. He screamed about how they couldn't do this to him. As she turned to head back inside, she stopped when she heard laughter. "How long have you been there, Mother?"

"Long enough to strengthen our case to have this marriage annulled. Is that the first time he's tried to hit you?" Queen Amirilla asked.

"No," Rilla replied. "It's only when he's drunk. He doesn't have the balls to try it otherwise."

"He never was a very good fighter," the queen commented.

Rilla nodded. "Can you really do it, Mother?"

"I believe so," her mother said as she walked over to Rilla. "Between the drinking, his temper, and the infidelity, we can claim he's not a fit husband for the heir to a kingdom, and his attempts to abuse you will support that."

"And Risa?"

"I believe an arrangement can be made with Lord and Lady Vinusian to let her live here and visit them on occasion. When the marriage agreement was written, you weren't the next in line for the throne, so there was no need to have her here prepping to be a ruler, but now she's heir to the throne and should be living here. I mentioned changing the marriage agreement to your father when she was born, and he just kept putting it off. But now he'll have no choice but to deal with it, and I think he'll actually be quite relieved that it's done."

"How long do you think it'll take, Mother?"

Sighing the queen hugged her daughter. "No idea, my dear. But anyway, how did things go with Nathaniel?"

"Not good," Rilla said as she leaned against the balcony railing. "He was very angry and wouldn't listen to me at all."

"Maybe this was for the best then, Rilla-chan."

Rilla sighed. "Maybe. I still can't believe he tried to blame me for his own stupidity."

"Oh?" the queen inquired.

"Mahogany told me to ignore him and have fun without him, so I did. I met a man and danced with him a few times. The idiot challenged him to a duel and got himself beaten by an unarmed man."

"Unarmed?"

"The doctor that was with Nathaniel when we found him, I think he said his name was Shade, said his opponent was unarmed and had beaten him with his own sword." Queen Amirilla's eyes went wide when she heard the name Shade. "Neither would name his opponent, but Nathaniel said it was to protect my honor from the devil I was with, so I'm certain it was Shadow."

"Shadow?" the queen asked, sounding very alarmed, but Rilla failed to notice her panicked tone.

"Yeah, that was the name he gave me, at least. He was very mysterious." Rilla shook her head. "I think I've met him before, but he didn't look familiar. It's strange. I knew I'd never seen him before the party, but I felt like I'd known him for years, but I don't know why."

"Did he say anything?"

"Like what, Mother?" Rilla inquired, suddenly noticing her mother's worried expression.

"Oh…uh…where he's from, his rank or title, something that could help you locate him?"

"Oh, no, he didn't say much about himself." Rilla smiled. "He's one hell of a dancer, though." Queen Amirilla gave a sigh of relief. "The empress does know him, though, and she seemed very concerned about him leaving the party."

"Sounds right," the queen said without thinking.

"Oh?" Rilla asked, raising an eyebrow. "Mother, do you know Shadow?"

"What? No. Of course not. I just meant that sounds like the empress," her mother said quickly.

Rilla eyed her suspiciously. She was certain there was more to this than her mother was saying. "If you say so, Mother." She sighed. "Mother, there are a couple of things that have been bothering me."

"What is it, dear?"

"Mother, about my crystal," Rilla started as she played with the crystal around her neck. "The enchantment on it won't work if the other person isn't wearing the crystal, correct?"

"As I understand it, that is correct. The spell uses a little of your own life force to create the glow. Why?" the queen asked curiously.

"I've woken up from a couple dreams, and my crystal was glowing, but I'm not sure how or why it was glowing." She sighed. "I mean, without Di-chan's life force, the spell is incomplete."

The queen placed her hand on Rilla's shoulder. "Could have been from you. If you were focused on something, you might have caused it to glow."

Rilla shrugged. "Perhaps."

"What were you dreaming about?"

"Di-chan. It was more like a memory than a dream. I've had several of them," Rilla explained. "I saw the time big brother gave me Vixie and my crystal."

"You haven't dreamt of Amdis in years. When did this start?"

"The night Tora left." Rilla looked up at the stars and sighed. "Mother, who is Mister?"

"Mister who?" the queen asked, hoping it wasn't who she was thinking of.

"I don't know," Rilla said, feeling frustrated. "Vixie said he was a friend of yours. She also told me Di-chan challenged him to a duel, and apparently he beat big brother. I heard from Maurice that I used to play with him and called him Mister, but I don't remember him at all. And in the dreams I keep having, I mention Mister not coming back." Rilla looked her mother in the eyes. "Mother, who is Mister, and why didn't he come back?"

"I believe you're talking about the ambassador that was here for a while when you were little. He played with you a few times." The queen ran her fingers through her light teal hair. "What else did you dream about?" she asked, hoping to change the subject.

"Mostly memories of big brother and a couple odd visions." Rilla told her mother the details of her visions, the weird white trees, the man with the silver hair, and the feeling of darkness and danger she felt each time. "The man with the silver hair said I was in danger and that he needed to get me home. I felt so warm and safe in his arms. I have no idea who he was, though. Do you know, Mother?"

Shadows of the Past

The queen looked around nervously, unsure of what to say. "Come with me, Rilla. There's something I should tell you." Rilla followed her mother nervously to her chambers. "Have a seat, my dear," the queen requested as she motioned to the bed. Queen Amirilla sat beside her daughter and sighed. "Rilla, when you were very little an ambassador from another system came to visit us a couple times. His name was Lord Merlonas. He stayed here for a week or two at a time, and yes he played with you. He also taught you about illusion magic."

"Taught me? I studied that at the academy," Rilla interrupted.

"Yes, you did, but where do you think the interest in it came from?" Standing, the queen paced the floor. "Rilla, he was teaching you magic. He told me you have a very special gift, and he wanted to help you learn to control it."

"Gift? You mean my oracle blood?" Rilla inquired.

"Perhaps, but I can't be sure." The queen placed her hands on her daughter's shoulders and smiled. "You've always been gifted in many aspects, my dear. Your intelligence is undeniable; your gift of sight is stronger than mine or your cousin Michael's, and your ability to see things that others often cannot is outstanding. He saw great potential in you the first time you tugged on his cloak."

Rilla smiled as a fuzzy memory came to her. She reached her hand out and tugged on an invisible cloak.

"Hey, Mister."

Smiling, the queen nodded. "He often complained to me about you always finding him and tugging on his cloak, but I think he actually enjoyed it."

"Why didn't he come back? If he saw such potential in me and wanted to teach me, why leave and never come back?" Rilla almost demanded.

Sitting down, the queen took her daughter's hands in hers and sighed. "He couldn't come back. When you were almost four, he was killed in battle. You adored him so much we couldn't bring ourselves to tell you because we knew it would break your heart."

"So you simply let me forget about him?" Rilla's head was down, and her dark hair had fallen forward and was covering her eyes.

"I'm sorry. We thought it was best at the time. You were so young, and we weren't prepared to try and explain death to you. I see now we were wrong to keep it from you, but please believe me when I say we were only looking out for you." The queen released Rilla's hands and stood.

"Were you ever going to tell me?" Rilla asked as she looked up to meet her mother's gaze.

"At first we planned on explaining it once you were old enough to understand, but as you grew, it seemed better to let you forget him altogether. I never thought you'd suddenly remember him after all these years," Queen Amirilla explained.

"Merlonas…" Rilla said the name, but it just didn't sound right to her. "Does he have a grave anywhere? I'd like to visit him if possible."

Her mother smiled. "I'll see if I can find out for you, and I know he'd be thrilled to have you visit his grave. He was a good man." Rilla nodded and sat silently, in deep thought, for several moments. "Anyway you should tell your father what's going on," the queen spoke up, breaking the silence and quickly changing the subject.

"You didn't tell Father about trying to annul my marriage?" Rilla questioned without looking up.

"I believe that's your duty. He was responsible for this arranged marriage, and you did it to please him; therefore you need to be the one to tell him you wish to end it," the queen informed her.

Rilla nodded, letting the subject of Mister drop for now. She wasn't sure if she should be hurt that her parents had hidden it from her, but she knew there was nothing she could do to change it now. As for her marriage annulment, she knew her mother was right, though it wouldn't make the conversation any easier for her. "Where is Father?"

"In his study, last time I checked."

"Guess I'd better go talk to him."

"I think that's a good idea."

Rilla hugged her mother and headed to the study to talk to her father.

* * *

Rilla found her father in the study like her mother said. He was busy reading over reports from the outer rim of the system. Taking a deep breath, she entered the study and approached the king. Nervously, Rilla explained everything to her father, leaving out only the intimate personal details. When she was finished, she waited for her father to say something. She wasn't sure if he was upset or just in deep thought. "Father, I'm sorry. I…"

The king held up his hand, interrupting his daughter's apology. "No, it is I who should apologize, my dear. I pushed you into this marriage for my own selfish reasons. Things between our kingdom and the Venusians weren't bad enough that a royal wedding was needed. I simply wanted to be sure you were taken care of. Amdis objected and I should have listened to him. His protests were the only thing that postponed your marriage for so long. I should have listened to my son from the beginning. Instead his death made me rush you into a marriage that never should have happened. I should have thought of your happiness above all else." King Arkanthius stood and walked around the desk to embrace Rilla. "Can you forgive an old fool?"

A tear made its way down Rilla's cheek as she hugged her father. "Of course, I can, Father. Of course, I can."

The two stood embracing each other for several silent minutes. Neither wanted to let go or was sure of what to say next. When they finally did move, both sat, and they discussed the queen's plan to have the marriage annulled. The king agreed that the marriage should be annulled, but he worried about the political ramifications involved with his wife's plan.

"I don't know about this, Rilla. While I want to do what is necessary to make you happy, I don't want to start a war with Venus."

"Father, I'll talk with Rena. Jacob is her cousin. I'm sure she'll understand and help things go smoothly."

The king smiled and yawned. He hugged Rilla and said good night. Rilla went to bed feeling relieved.

* * *

The next day Jacob left, claiming he had important business on Venus. He left Marisa on Mercury to spend time with her mother and grandparents. Rilla enjoyed the rest of her stay at home with her family. She sent word to Princess Rena of Venus that she needed to speak to her after the initiation ceremony and hoped that Rena truly would understand.

* * *

In no time at all, the week passed by, and it was time for Rilla to head to Neptune, where she would meet up with Michael and Rukia and, from there, travel to Central Palace for the ceremony.

When it was time to leave, Queen Amirilla, King Arkanthius, and little Marisa accompanied Rilla to the station. "Give my love to your aunt," the queen said as she hugged Rilla.

"I will, Mother. Are you sure you can't come with me? Auntie Miriella would be thrilled to see you."

"No, no. This is your day, Rilla-chan. Our time has come and gone. Go and enjoy the ceremony and the party the empress throws for you all afterward. Besides I have to make preparations for the dinner we will be having when you return. I have an announcement to make to the court. So you go and have fun. The empress throws marvelous parties."

The king nodded as he scooped up his granddaughter. "Your mother is right. Go and enjoy yourself. We'll be here when you get back."

Rilla took her child from her father and hugged her tight. "Risa, you listen to your grandparents and do as they say."

"But, Mama, I want to go with you."

Rilla smiled. "Not this time, honey. One day, you'll get to visit Central Palace."

"Promise?"

"I promise." Rilla placed Marisa down and hugged her father. "I'll see you when I get back." She grabbed her small travel bag and boarded the shuttle for Neptune.

Chapter Twelve

When Rilla arrived on Neptune four days later, Michael, Rukia and Saedi met her at the station, which didn't surprise her. She was, however, surprised to see two bodyguards there.

"Everything all right?" she asked as she hugged Michael.

"Worried parents is all," he replied.

Rilla nodded and greeted the others. The two bodyguards, whom Rilla knew as Sir Vexian and Sir Magnus, bowed and grabbed her bags.

"Thank you," Rilla said, bowing her head slightly.

"Our pleasure, Princess," Vexian responded.

"We live to serve," Magnus added.

Rukia tried to contain her laughter but failed miserably.

"Rukia…" Michael started to scold.

"More like live to make trouble," she said before bursting out in hysterical laughter.

"That's not nice, big sister," Saedi said.

"Saedi's right," Michael agreed. "Vexian and Magnus may do some interesting things in their free time, but when they are on duty, they are completely professional."

"Interesting? Yeah, I guess you could call it that," Rukia said, still laughing.

Rilla shook her head. "What did you two do this time?"

Vexian and Magnus grinned. "We just helped the garden crew with a bug problem," Magnus replied.

"That was three weeks ago, and there hasn't been a bug in the garden since then," Vexian added.

"Really?" Rilla asked, surprised.

"Yeah, that's great, except it smells horrible, and the bugs, snakes, birds, dogs, and anything else that was in the garden at the time that you did whatever it was you did ran straight for the palace," Rukia explained.

Michael sighed. "Yes, Mother was quite distraught to have the council room filled with animals during a meeting."

"And what about the time they glued that stable boy to a saddle and sent him riding the horse upside down across the field?" Saedi said, giggling.

"He deserved it," Magnus said quickly.

"Yeah, he kicked Demon," Vexian added.

Rilla shook her head smiling. "Well, one thing is certain; with you two around, it's never boring."

Vexian and Magnus grinned and loaded the bags onto the carriage.

Shadows of the Past

The trip to the castle was filled with stories and laughter as Vexian and Magnus recounted their numerous adventures. Once they arrived, the two guards exited first, helped the ladies out, and unloaded Rilla's bags. As they walked up the front stairs, they were greeted by one of the royal hounds.

"There's Demon," Magnus warned them. The pup rushed over, bouncing all over the place, barking very loudly. "That's enough, Demon," Magnus scolded. The pup just growled at him and continued to bark at the others happily.

"Sit," Vexian instructed.

"Still only listens to you, I see," Rilla commented as she walked by the pup, who was trying very hard to remain sitting.

"Yeah, it was nice at first, but sometimes he does get annoying with constant barking and wanting to play all the time," Vexian explained. "Stay, Demon. We'll be back," he said before walking in behind the prince and princesses. "We'll take your bags to your room, Princess."

"Thank you," Rilla said with a smile as she turned to follow Michael, Rukia, and Saedi into the dining hall for lunch, where they found the king and queen already enjoying a meal.

"Rilla!" Queen Miriella exclaimed happily as she stood to greet her.

"Hello, Aunt Miriella," Rilla said as she hugged her.

"So glad to have you here. How is my sister?"

"Mother's fine, and she sends her love," Rilla answered.

"And your father?"

"Busy as always," Rilla said, smiling as the king walked over. "Hello, Uncle Aldwyn."

The king hugged Rilla tightly. "You certainly have grown, Rilla. Sorry I wasn't here to see you the last few times you visited, but the safety of the kingdom must come first."

"It's fine. I understand completely, Uncle. I'm just glad I get to see you this time," Rilla responded.

"Come. Sit, my dear," Queen Miriella said as she led Rilla to the table. "I'm sure you must be hungry after your long trip." Rilla nodded and took a seat by her aunt.

Lunch and the rest of the day passed without incident. Rilla actually started to forget about her worries of seeing Nathaniel and the stress of dealing with Jacob. That all changed after dinner, though. Rilla was walking silently through the garden, looking up at the stars, when her thoughts were interrupted. "Time to spill it, Mi-chan."

Rilla turned to see Michael and Rukia walking toward her. "What are you talking about?"

"You're keeping secrets, Rilla," Rukia scolded. "That's not nice at all."

"Come on, little cousin. Tell us what's been going on. What did you do to Nathaniel, and why is your husband on the warpath?" Michael asked.

Rilla sighed. She knew they would find out sooner or later. "It's a long story. I'll tell you on the shuttle ride to Central Palace in the morning. I promise."

Michael and Rukia gave her a look that said she had better keep that promise. "All right. Keep your secret for another night. Just be warned that Nathaniel is at the castle. So if you wish to avoid him, the garden isn't the best place to be," Michael advised.

"Thanks, Michael. I'll be heading back inside soon," Rilla said with a smile.

Michael nodded and asked Rukia to give them a moment. Rukia nodded and said "good night" to Rilla before heading back inside. Once she was out of sight, Michael turned back to Rilla. "Any more visions?"

Rilla nodded and told him about the dreams and visions she had had since she last saw him. He listened quietly as she told him all the details she could remember. She also told him about her crystal glowing and her conversation with her mother. When she was done, she waited for Michael to say something. He simply sat with his hand rubbing his chin, deep in thought.

"Michael?"

Looking up, he nodded. "I'm sorry, Rilla. I don't understand it either. I wish I could be of more help."

Rilla studied her cousin carefully. He was hiding something, she knew it. "Is everything all right, Michael?"

"Yeah, everything's fine." He stood and hugged her. "Don't worry, Rilla. We'll figure this out, and no matter what I'll keep you safe." He held her tight for a few moments. "Anyway, we should head to bed. I'll see you in morning, Mi-chan. Don't stay out too late." He kissed her forehead and headed back inside.

Rilla sighed and looked up at the stars once more. "So much for a relaxing night," she said to herself out loud. As she turned to head back to the castle, she heard a rustling in the shrubs behind her. "Who's there?" She slowly reached to her side and pulled out her sword. "Show yourself!" she demanded.

Before she could react, she was tackled from behind by an unknown figure. "Shh…lie very still," a familiar voice said. Glancing over her shoulder, she saw the last person she wanted to see at that moment.

"Let go," she ordered as she tried to pull free of his grip.

"Stop moving before he spots us," Nathaniel demanded.

"Who?"

Before Nathaniel could answer a blue hound with red eyes jumped out of the bushes, growling and baring its teeth. Rilla and Nathaniel froze. Rilla looked closely at the dog and started laughing. "It's just Demon." She pulled away from Nathaniel and stood. She brushed herself off and walked slowly toward the hound.

"Rilla, don't!" Nathaniel yelled as he reached to grab her.

Seeing him go for Rilla, Demon lunged at his hand and barked furiously at him. Nathaniel backed away and drew his sword. "Stay back!"

"Demon, it's all right," Rilla said calmly. Demon looked at Rilla then back at Nathaniel. He growled ferociously and stepped closer to him.

"Demon!" Sir Vexian yelled as he rushed over. "Demon, sit!" The dog sat but continued to growl. "Enough!" Vexian said firmly before slipping a chain leash over his neck. He looked at Rilla and bowed his head. "Sorry, Princess. He didn't hurt you, did he? Sometimes he gets a little too hyper."

"I'm all right, Vexian. Demon didn't do any harm. Just scared poor Nathaniel." She chuckled.

"I was only afraid for your safety," Nathaniel protested. "That dog is crazy. He needs to be put down."

Demon lunged at Nathaniel and was yanked back by Vexian. "That's enough out of you. Time to go in the cage." Vexian pulled the leash and headed toward the stables. Demon followed Vexian with his head down, whimpering quietly.

Rilla watched Vexian lead the hound away and started to walk back to the castle, not wanting to talk to Nathaniel.

"Rilla, wait!" he called after her.

Sighing, she stopped and turned to face him. "Nathaniel, there's nothing to say. You refused to listen to me before, so why should I listen to you now?" Nathaniel walked over to her without saying a word.

He reached for her hands, but she pulled away and turned her back to him. "Rilla…I…" He sighed. "I don't know what to say. I don't want things to be like this. I want…"

"I know what you want, and it can't happen." Rilla debated telling him about the marriage being annulled but decided not to. After all, she wasn't sure how long that would take or how she really felt about Nathaniel. "Friendship is all I can give you right now, Nathaniel. If you can't accept that, maybe it's best if you just leave me alone."

Rilla walked back to the castle with no further protests from Nathaniel. Once inside, she headed to bed. As she drifted to sleep, she wondered if she had done the right thing.

* * *

The next morning, she had a pleasant breakfast with the others. Her thoughts kept wandering to the events of the night before and finally she decided to forget about it. Nothing could change until the marriage was annulled, so no point lingering on it till then. After breakfast Vexian and Magnus loaded their things into the carriage, and they prepared for the trip to Central Palace. On the ride to the station, Rilla's nerves finally got the best of her.

"Michael," she said.

"Hmm?" Michael looked up from the book he was reading.

"Is the empress really as cruel as people say? I've met her a few times, and she seemed pleasant, but what should I expect once I'm a member of the court?"

Michael couldn't help but chuckle. "You'll be fine, Mi-chan. The empress is going to love you. She's already expressed her excitement in getting to know you personally after all she's heard about you."

"Really?" Rilla asked, unbelieving.

"Yes, and you have nothing to fear from her. She does have a temper, but I've rarely seen it, and when I have, it wasn't aimed at any of us. She's a good and fair person. A little demanding at times, but not unreasonable."

"And she throws the best parties," Rukia added sleepily from Michael's shoulder.

Chapter Thirteen

The rest of the trip was relatively silent. They boarded their shuttle, and Rilla spent most of the trip reading, or attempting to read. Her thoughts jumped from one topic to another, which made reading rather difficult. She thought of her mother and the strings she was having to pull to annul her marriage to Jacob. Her mind wandered to thoughts of Nathaniel. Had she made a mistake not trying to tell him about the annulment again? Would he take her offer of friendship for now or would he avoid her all together? She wondered about the empress and the court. What stories had the empress heard, and who had told them to her? Was she ready to be general? Her thoughts were interrupted when Rukia tossed a balled-up handkerchief at her. "Rilla, stop daydreaming!"

"What?" Rilla asked, confused, as she looked around.

"I've been trying to get your attention for five minutes," Rukia informed her. "What's got you so preoccupied? And when do we get details on what's going on with you and Nathaniel? You promised to tell us on the shuttle."

Rilla sighed. She had promised to explain everything, but she really wasn't in the mood to talk about it, but a promise was a promise. So she told Rukia and Michael everything. She told them about the affair, the annulment, the stranger that Nathaniel had fought, her decision to not attempt telling him about the annulment again, and her current feelings of uncertainty. They listened intently, not interrupting her. When she was done, they looked at each other and sighed.

"No wonder you were so distracted," Rukia said. "Sounds like things are looking up, though."

"Rukia's right, if Auntie gets the marriage annulled, you can do what you like. Don't worry about it till then. Once you're free, then deal with Nathaniel. He's an idiot, but I doubt he'll blame you for waiting to talk to him, especially with how he's acted," Michael offered. "Besides, this should be a happy time for you. You're having your induction ceremony, and then there's the ball to celebrate. So don't worry, Rilla. Everything will work out."

Nodding, Rilla hugged them both. They chatted quietly the rest of the trip to Central.

* * *

Once they arrived, they were taken to a large room to change and prepare. Rilla looked around for her friends and spotted them lining up by the main hall. She rushed over, and a servant asked her to stand at the front. The empress wanted them lined up for the ceremony. She nodded and took her place at the front of the line, which did nothing to help her nerves. Rena of Venus soon joined the group and was asked to stand behind Rilla. Smiling, Rilla faced her friend. "Rena, I need to talk to you."

"Hi, Rilla. I got your message. What's going on?" Rena asked with a huge smile on her face as she brushed her long red hair behind her shoulder. Before Rilla could respond, they were told to head down the hall as the ceremony was about to begin.

As Rilla walked down the dark hallway with the others, she nervously recited the pledge in her head. She knew it by heart; she had for years. This ceremony was what she had worked for more than anything. When she was told she would be joining the court, she dedicated her life to getting ready for this day, because before that she had been destined to just be a diplomat, as her brother was heir to the throne. With his death, that had all changed and now she just wished Amdis could have been there to see it. Her thoughts were interrupted by the sounding of trumpets.

"This is it," she whispered to herself as she took a deep breath. She smiled as she felt Rena squeeze her hand from behind.

They entered the throne room and knelt along the wall. "All hail the empress!" the herald called as Galactica entered the room.

Rilla bowed her head until the empress was seated on her golden throne.

"Friends, we are gathered here today to welcome the next generation into the inner court. Those of you joining the court will step forward when called and recite the oath," Galactica said. "Once all of you have recited the oath, you'll receive a gift, along with your new uniform." She waved her hand, and everyone stood. "Let the ceremony begin!"

The young princesses and prince walked to the throne and knelt. Rilla's palms were sweaty as she approached the empress. She bowed and waited. "Mercury."

Rising from her position in line, Rilla stepped forward before kneeling in front of the empress. "I am Amirilla VI, Princess of Mercury, daughter of Arkanthius and Amirilla V, descendant of Mercuria. I have traveled here to pledge my loyalty to the Intergalactic Court. I give my heart, body, and soul to the service of the court. I shall be virtuous. I will aid only the truth. My sword and power is to defend and protect the innocent and weak. Never shall I use my skills for selfish or wrong reasons. Enemies of the court and the empress will know my wrath. This is my pledge and vow. In the name of Mercury, I pledge my life." The words came out clear and full of confidence, even though Rilla was so nervous she was almost shaking.

Galactica smiled. "Rise, daughter of Arkanthius and Amirilla."

Rilla stood with her head bowed, and Galactica tapped her on her right shoulder with her golden rapier. She lifted the sword over Rilla's head, and before tapping her left shoulder, the empress said, "From this day forward, you are General Amirilla. You speak for your people and will serve this court in their name. Should they enter battle, it is you who will lead them."

"Thank you, Empress." Rilla bowed again and walked over to take her seat in the place marked with her family's royal seal. She relaxed a bit and watched as the others said their oaths. Right behind Rilla was Rena of Venus, followed by a slender, dark-skinned girl named Anya from Mars, and Mahogany of Jupiter. Behind Mahogany was a girl Rilla had never met before, but she knew she was Rebecca of Saturn, the younger sister of Juno. Rebecca's brother had been killed in a duel a week before the ceremony, and she had been prepped at the last minute to take his place on the court. She hadn't yet graduated the academy, and Rilla wondered if the young brunette was ready for this.

Sighing, Rilla thought of her own brother as Rebecca said her oath. Amdis had sat there before as the new general of Mercury, but he wasn't the only general being replaced. Anya was replacing her big brother as well. Anya's older brother, Akito, had died a year earlier of an unknown disease that even the empress's healers were clueless about. Rilla's heart ached for Anya. The loss of her brother had been really hard on her. She had locked herself in her castle for almost half a year before she agreed to come out and begin the training required to take her brother's place. Rena and Mahogany were replacing their mothers now that they were of age, so for them, this was a simple rite of passage as the eldest child in the family. As for Rukia, Michael, and Sazuka of Pluto, this was a simple formality for them. They had already had their induction ceremony at the same time as Amdis, Juno, and Akito. They were saying their oaths again to be there and support the new members of the court. Now that the next generation had stepped forward to join the court, the kings and queens could deal more closely with the affairs of their own kingdoms. Rilla smiled, realizing that one day Marisa would take her place.

As Sazuka finished her oath, Rilla looked around the room. She recognized a handful of people, but most were strangers to her.

"Friends and family, I give you the new inner court of our system," Galactica said once Sazuka had taken her seat. She stood and sheathed her sword. "Now for your presents." She motioned for her servants, and they stepped forward and placed two boxes in front of each of them. The larger of the two boxes contained their new uniform, which they would wear to official court meetings and when requested to by the empress.

Rilla opened the smaller box in front of her to find a framed photo of herself sitting on her brother's knee. Before she could stop it, a tear ran down her cheek. She glanced to her right and found Rena's eyes were glossy as she stared at the red hair pin made from rubies that she held in her hand. Rena looked at Rilla and smiled. "I made this for Mama when I was little." Rilla reached over and squeezed Rena's hand. She understood the gifts now. They were items that were precious to the previous generals.

"I'm sure each of you recognize the item in front of you and understand its importance. Let them be a reminder of what you're fighting for and why the court exists. Now a servant will show you to your rooms. Please change into your uniforms and then join the rest of us in the ballroom to celebrate." Galactica nodded to the servants and exited the room.

Once the empress was gone, those who had been watching the ceremony slowly followed and the eight generals followed the servants to their own rooms. When Rilla reached her room, the servant unlocked the door and handed the key to her. "Your Highness, the empress wanted me to tell you that the trunk at the end of your bed is full. The items are now yours, and she asks that you wait until after the party to go through it." He bowed and walked away.

Rilla walked in to find the room decorated very much like her room at home. She quickly spotted the large trunk, and though she was tempted to open it and look inside, she left it alone. There was a large four-poster bed with a blue bedspread and lots of fluffy pillows. A couch sat a few feet away, along with a large rocking chair. Opening the door to her left, she found a large bathroom with a huge tub. Amdis told her that the rooms at the palace were lavish, but she hadn't expected this.

Once she had changed into her uniform, she admired herself in the mirror. The uniform fit perfectly and the blue matched her eyes. Rilla had seen her brother wear this uniform many times, and now it was her turn. Rilla placed the photo of her and Amdis on the table by the bed and made her way to the ballroom.

* * *

As she entered the ballroom, the herald announced her: "Announcing General Amirilla of Mercury."

It sounded weird to Rilla to be addressed as a general instead of a princess, but she knew it was something she could get used to. She looked around and didn't see anyone she knew, which made her feel out of place.

"Rilla! Over here!" Rilla looked to see Mahogany calling and waving at her. Smiling, she rushed over. "Rilla, you look amazing in your uniform!" Mahogany said before hugging her.

"So do you, Mahogany," Rilla replied, smiling, "Where's everyone else?"

"Probably still getting dressed or admiring themselves in the mirror," Mahogany said, chuckling. "But come on. Let's get something to eat. Have you seen all the food?"

"Yeah, I noticed the table. The empress went all out, didn't she?"

"I hear this is normal for her. The party for her niece's wedding will be the grandest we've ever seen," Mahogany said excitedly. Rilla nodded and followed her friend to the food table. "I don't know what to have first," Mahogany complained. "It all looks so delicious!"

Rilla laughed and fixed a plate for her friend then one for herself. "There's a little of each, so we can try it all."

"Great idea, Rilla!" They walked arm in arm to a table. Once they were seated, Mahogany looked around. "I have no idea who most of these people are."

"Me either." Rilla ate slowly and watched the strangers dance.

"There you are," a voice said from behind them. Rilla and Mahogany turned to see Michael, Rukia, and Sazuka. "We wondered where you disappeared to, Mi-chan," Michael said as he pulled out a chair for Rukia and then one for Sazuka.

"Should have known she'd be with Mahogany. Where you find one, you usually find the other," Rukia said, chuckling.

"Where's Rena?" Sazuka asked. "She's usually with you two as well." She looked from side to side for the Venus princess, her long pale-violet hair swaying back and forth.

"Probably still admiring herself in the mirror," Mahogany stated. "You know how Rena is about her looks." Everyone chuckled and nodded in agreement.

"Michael, do you know any of these people?" Rilla asked her cousin.

"Most. There's a few I don't recognize. You'll meet them all soon," Michael answered.

"Most are foreign diplomats from other systems," Sazuka explained.

"See the blonde lady surrounded by the seven young girls?" Michael asked as he pointed to the lady in a long, flowing white gown. Rilla looked and nodded. "That's Lady Pleiades and her maidens."

"From left to right it's Maia, Electra, Taygete, Alcyone, Celaeno, Sterope, and Merope. They're her personal bodyguards," Rukia explained.

"Seven bodyguards?" Mahogany inquired.

"She must be really important." Rilla added.

"Most of them are equally ranked with the empress."

"What?" Rilla and Mahogany asked together.

The older three chuckled, and Sazuka explained, "The empress is the member of a higher court made of close to a hundred different systems. Most of the people here are leaders of other systems."

"So there's someone the Empress answers to?" Mahogany asked.

"Not really." Michael hesitated, trying to think of the best way to explain it. "The Stellar Court isn't like the Intergalactic Court. We have eight kingdoms that make up our systems, and we all answer to the empress. Each kingdom is independent, but we all work together. The Stellar Court really doesn't work that way. They meet, and each ruler represents their system, and there is no supreme leader. The empress is usually the one that leads the meetings and keeps order, but she's not a higher rank than the others."

"She just likes taking charge, and they voted her to be the one that runs the meetings. Most of them really don't want anything to do with the others," Rukia added.

"In fact, the only time they meet is if there's a war, something that threatens multiple systems, or someone calls for a meeting to request aid from the others. For example, a few years ago, Lady Orion requested aid for her system as they were at war with a system that refused to even join the Stellar Court," Sazuka informed them.

"Did anyone help her?" Rilla asked.

"Of course," Michael said. "The empress sent us immediately."

"Lady Orion is very close to the empress," Rukia stated.

"Is she here tonight?" Mahogany asked.

Michael looked around. "Yes, she's the one in the green dress by the empress."

Rilla looked and soon spotted the empress, who had changed out of her golden armor and into a very slinky silver dress. Her hair was now up in a loose bun, and she appeared to be much taller. Probably because she was wearing high heels, was Rilla's guess. Beside her stood a very beautiful woman in a long flowing green dress. Her long brown hair was braided, and her smile seemed to light up the room. "She's beautiful."

"Don't let her looks fool you, though. She may look and act like a beautiful, spoiled princess, but she's the toughest fighter in any system--well, other than the Draco System, but I hear they are dirty fighters that don't care about honor," Rukia said.

"Oh, no, Lady Orion can handle even Draco himself. I've seen it firsthand," Sazuka corrected.

"Oh?" Michael inquired.

"I was asked to accompany the empress and Lady

Orion to a party on Draco once. Lord Draco got a little fresh and wound up starting a fight with Lady Orion."

"How'd that go?" Rukia asked.

"Let's just say, it was quite a while before Lord Draco was able to dance," Sazuka said with a smirk.

"Who's the other woman with the empress?" Mahogany asked.

The group looked over again to see a tall brunette in a lavender dress laughing with the empress and Lady Orion. "Oh, that's Lady Kathrine from the Sirius Sector. She's here a lot," Rukia replied.

"Rumor is she's too rebellious for her family," Michael added. "I've also heard she's hiding out here to avoid marrying the suitor her parents chose for her."

The group chatted and enjoyed the food and drinks, though this time Rilla stayed away from the alcohol. She didn't want a repeat of last time. She looked around, wondering if Shadow was there and if he was a diplomat like the others. The empress made a speech thanking everyone for coming and then disappeared for a bit. No one noticed, though. They were too busy partying. Rilla kept trying to talk to Rena, but she was too busy flirting with all the guys. The night seemed to go by so quickly. When it was all over, the generals were told they were welcome to stay in their rooms for the night.

"Please see my home as yours," Galactica said. "You are all welcome here anytime. Those wishing to stay can join me in the main dining hall for breakfast in the morning.

Those leaving first thing, have a safe trip, and I look forward to seeing you all very soon." With a smile, she left the ballroom with Lady Orion.

Rilla said "good night" to everyone, and they parted ways.

* * *

Inside her room, she finally opened the trunk and tears poured out of her eyes when she saw the contents. It was filled with her brother's armor, personal belongings, and every letter she had ever written to him. At the very bottom, wrapped carefully, was a blue rose with a ribbon on it. Rilla recognized it as the flower she'd made for him to wear to his induction ceremony. The flower was old and a little faded, but it was still beautiful. Rilla placed it beside the framed picture of her and Amdis and cried herself to sleep.

* * *

The next morning, Rilla woke early and dressed. She wanted to talk to Rena before she left. Knocking on the door to the room she had been assigned, Rilla waited nervously. While she was certain her friend would understand, she didn't want to cause any unneeded drama between Jacob and his cousin. Slowly the door opened and Rena peered out groggily. "Morning, Rilla," she mumbled before letting out a large yawn. "Is it time for breakfast already?"

Rilla shook her head. "Sorry, Rena. I need to talk to you about something rather important. I didn't mean to wake you so early though, but I wanted to make sure I didn't miss you."

Rena opened the door and invited the Mercury in.

"Let me wake up a little, Rilla," she requested as she covered her mouth to hide another yawn. Rilla nodded and waited for her friend to get ready. After stretching and yawning for a few minutes, Rena sat on the bed and hugged one of the pillows. She motioned for Rilla to join her and slowly she sat beside Rena on the bed. "So what's going on, Rilla?" the Venus princess asked as she rubbed the sleep out of her eyes. "Must be big to get you to wake me up this early."

Sighing, Rilla looked at the floor. "It's not easy to tell you this, but Mother is trying to have my marriage to your cousin annulled. She's doing so at my request."

Rena sighed. "That idiot." Rilla looked at her, surprised. She hadn't expected that. "I'm sorry, hun. I told that idiot he'd better change his ways and take good care of you. I'm guessing he's still partying and doing whatever he likes all over the system?" Rilla nodded, and Rena clenched her fist. "I told him not to disgrace the kingdom. He'll know what he's lost soon enough, and then it'll be too late." Rena hugged her friend and apologized again for her idiot cousin.

"Do you think your aunt and uncle will have an issue with the request, especially since Marisa would be living on Mercury full time?"

Rena released her friend and smiled. "You just leave Uncle and Auntie to me. I'll make sure things go smoothly, and if my idiot cousin gives you a hard time, you let me know. I'll make sure he does as is expected of him, and he will learn the hard way what happens when you don't follow the wishes of the Kingdom." Rena took Rilla's hands in hers and held them tight. "Look on the bright side, now you can flirt with all the cute guys without feeling guilty, and who knows, you might find a much better candidate to marry."

Rilla tried to smile, but Nathaniel came to mind. "Rena, there's more and I beg you to please keep this between us. Jacob isn't the only one that was unfaithful. I…"

"Did what any lonely unhappy woman would do. I don't nor would any other woman blame you. Jacob was never there and from what I've seen and heard he was usually drunk when he was with you. I told him over and over to clean up his act or another guy was going to sweep you off your feet. So don't sweat it, Rilla. I won't say a word. On one condition." Rena paused and the smirk on her face had Rilla a little worried. "I want to hear all the juicy details. Who is he? Where did it happen? How long has it been going on? Can I join in next time?"

Rilla couldn't help but laugh at her friend's request. Rena smiled, happy to see Rilla being more cheerful. Over the next couple hours Rilla filled her friend in on the details of her brief affair. Rena was extremely surprised that it was Nathaniel of all people who had swept Rilla off her feet. She was also extremely disappointed that it was just a one-night fling. She had hoped it was a steamy affair that had been going on for months and was still keeping the shy Mercury happy during the cold nights.

When Rilla joined Michael and Rukia on the shuttle to Mercury they were surprised to find her in much better spirits than she had been the day before. They were all even more surprised when Mahogany joined them. "Well, the shuttle does stop on Jupiter as well," she informed them.

"Why don't you just go with us to Mercury?" Rilla asked. "Mother would love to see you again. Plus you can be there for mother's announcement."

"Announcement?" Rukia asked.

"Yes, she plans to make an important announcement at dinner," Rilla explained. She had a feeling she knew what the announcement was but she would wait and see.

"I'd love to, but I'm heading to the Alpha Quadrant. Perhaps I can meet you afterwards and ride to Earth with you."

"Sounds great, Mahogany," Rilla said happily.

Chapter Fourteen

Rilla, Michael, and Rukia arrived safely on Mercury after parting with Mahogany at the transfer station on Jupiter. She was off to visit her father in the Alpha quadrant before meeting the others for the trip to Earth. By the time Rilla and the other two arrived at the palace, it was well after dark. Queen Amirilla met them at the front gate.

"Welcome home, Rilla-chan," the queen greeted her daughter as she exited the coach.

"Hello, Mother." Rilla hugged the queen and looked around "Where's Risa?"

"The shuttle from Venus was delayed due to a severe electrical storm. Jacob and Risa should be here in the morning."

Rilla nodded and waited for the others.

"Hello, Auntie," Michael said after he helped Rukia out of the coach.

"Welcome back. It's good to have you both here again," the queen replied as she hugged each in turn.

As they entered the main hall, they saw Vixie was sitting by a large box, waiting for them. "Welcome home, Rilla-chan!" she exclaimed as she wagged her tail happily.

"Hi, Vixie," Rilla said before catching the fox in mid-jump.

Vixie wrapped her paws around Rilla's neck and hugged her tightly. "Congratulations on becoming a general!"

"Thanks, Vixie," Rilla replied, chuckling slightly.

"So what's in the box?" Rukia asked.

Vixie jumped down and ran over to the box. "A present for Rilla-chan."

"Go on and open it, Mi-chan, before curiosity gets the better of Rukia," Michael said teasingly. Rukia made a face at him that caused everyone to laugh.

Rilla walked over and slowly untied the blue ribbon and lifted the lid off the box. "Mother, isn't this—"

"Yes, and now it's yours," the queen interrupted.

"What is it?" Rukia asked, standing on her tiptoes, trying to see inside the box.

Rilla reached in and carefully pulled out a small blue harp. "It's Mother's harp."

"I didn't know you played the harp, Auntie," Michael stated, sounding very surprised.

"I used to. I haven't touched it in years. So now it's Rilla's turn to use it."

"Use it?" Rukia chuckled. "Never heard anyone refer to playing an instrument in that way."

"Well, I used it for certain spells," the queen informed her. "There are some very powerful healing spells that require music. I found the harp to be the best instrument for those spells. I used it all the time when the children were sick."

Rilla smiled and plucked a couple of strings. "I remember you playing this every night when you tucked me into bed."

Smiling, the queen replied, "Helping little ones fall asleep was an added reason to have it."

"Do you know how to play anything on it, Rilla?" Michael asked as he wrapped his arms around Rukia.

"Mother taught me how to play a few songs. I think I still remember how to play them," Rilla replied as she sat on the bottom of the staircase and placed the harp on her lap. She thought for a moment and then slowly started plucking strings. In no time, it all came back to her, and she started playing the old lullaby from her childhood. The queen smiled as she watched her daughter play. The song was an ancient ballad about three legendary guardians. She sang along in her head as Rilla continued to play. Rukia and Michael watched in amazement. They had no idea Rilla could play an instrument, much less play one so beautifully.

When Rilla was finished, her mother, Michael, and Rukia applauded. Rilla turned when she heard clapping coming from behind her. "Bravo, Rilla," the king said, smiling. "I thought it was your mother until I saw you at the bottom of the stairs."

Rilla stood and placed the harp down. "Hello, Father."

"Welcome home, Rilla-chan," he exclaimed as he hugged her. "So good to have you home. Your mother and I are so proud of you, General Amirilla."

Smiling, Rilla thanked her father and picked up the harp. "It's good to be home. Sadly it'll be a short visit. We need to leave for Earth in a couple of days."

Arkanthius nodded. "Duty calls. We understand, but enough of that. Maurice has dinner ready. He's prepared all your favorites, so we better not keep him waiting."

***

As they entered the dining hall, Rilla was hit by the aroma of the wonderful spread of food on the table. There was enough food to feed half of the Mercurian army. Smiling, she took her seat and folded her napkin in her lap. Once the glasses where filled with ale, her father lifted his to make a toast. "To Rilla, Michael, and Rukia. Let their days of service to the empress be peaceful, and their reigns as rulers be successful." Everyone cheered and drank their ale.

"How is the empress?" Queen Amirilla asked.

"She's fine, Auntie," Michael answered. "Still throwing a party every chance she can."

The queen chuckled. "Some things will never change."

They ate and talked of the ceremony and the upcoming trip to Earth. Rilla's thoughts were elsewhere, though. She wondered about her mother's announcement and if it was indeed that she was successful in annulling her marriage to Jacob. She sighed as she thought of what was to come. While she was looking forward to seeing her daughter, Rilla dreaded dealing with Jacob, especially if he was drunk.

"Everything okay, Mi-chan?" Rukia asked, startling her from her thoughts.

"Yeah, I was just thinking," Rilla responded.

"Well, no more thinking about whatever it was," Arkanthius said. "Tonight you should be happy and celebrating."

Rilla smiled. "Yes, Father."

* * *

After dinner they all gathered in the study, where Rilla was asked to play the harp again. She played the few songs she could remember and then her mother took over and taught her the healing songs she knew, including one that she said was powerful enough to heal any wound. They all laughed and joked late into the night.

When Rilla finally retired to her room, she found Vixie fast asleep on her pillow. Smiling, she changed and climbed into bed. Gently moving the sleeping fox, she lay back on the pillow and pulled the covers over herself and Vixie.

* * *

The next morning, Rilla woke bright and early to head to the station. Her mother and Vixie accompanied her. The trip to the station was filled with awkward silence. Finally Rilla spoke up. "Mother, were you successful?"

Queen Amirilla smiled. "So far I have been. I've made arrangements with Jacob's family, and Risa will live here full time, no matter what. Seeing as how she's now heir to the throne, she needs to be raised as a Mercurian, not a Venusian. As for the marriage…I still have to make a formal request to the empress. First I have to inform Jacob so that he can be prepared to make a statement to the empress about his behavior. Once you leave for Earth, I'll prepare and send in the request," she explained.

Rilla nodded. "Do you think the empress will grant your request?"

"That all depends on you."

"Me?"

The queen nodded. "She'll want to hear your side of this. If she believes that Jacob is unfit and your reasons for the annulment are valid, then she'll grant it. If not, you'll be forced to remain married, and if you're caught cheating or doing anything inappropriate, you could lose Risa."

Rilla stared out the window of the carriage. Were her reasons valid, or was she just being selfish? Was being free of Jacob and free to choose whom she was with worth all the hassle and the risk? She had slipped up once and if she was forced to remain married, it could mean losing her daughter if she slipped again.

"It'll be okay, Rilla-chan," Vixie said, seeing her worried expression. "That idiot is a dirty cheater who is unfit to be a father or husband. I'm sure there are a lot of people who could testify to that, and the empress is fair and understanding from what I've heard."

"Thanks, Vixie." Rilla hugged her guardian and scratched behind her ears.

They rode the rest of the way to the station in silence. Rilla thought long and hard about what she would say to the empress when the time came. Then she thought about how to explain things to little Marisa. She didn't understand love and marriage at her age and might get upset at her if the annulment happened, but would things really be that different? She'd be living on Mercury and would visit Venus to see her father and grandparents, if Jacob even bothered with her at all. At the moment, he seemed inconvenienced by her and dumped her with his parents, Rilla or her parents, or a nanny whenever he could. No, this was the best choice; Rilla was certain of it. She would have more time with her daughter, and her mother would see to it that Risa was properly trained for her future as a ruler, not just a lady of the court, as she was being raised to be on Venus.

When they arrived at the station, the shuttle had already landed, and soon the passengers would be allowed to exit and collect their luggage. Rilla paced nervously. Never had she been so excited to see her daughter but so nervous about it at the same time.

"Mama!" Rilla turned when she heard the excited cry of her daughter. Marisa rushed over to her.

Rilla scooped up the girl and hugged her tight. "Risa! Oh, how I've missed you!"

"I missed you, too, Mama," Marisa said as she hugged her mother tightly. "Did you get job?"

Rilla chuckled. "Yes, dear, I got my promotion."

"That's right, Risa," the queen spoke up. "Your mama is now a general and represents our planet in the court."

"Wow!" the girl exclaimed with wide eyes. "That sound varry impotant."

Rilla nodded as she sat the girl down. "It is, and it's a great honor to hold this position, and you know what else?"

"What, Mama?"

Rilla knelt down, so she could look her daughter in the eyes. "One day you'll take my place as general, and eventually you'll be crowned queen, as well."

"Me?"

"That's right. You're the heir to a great kingdom," Rilla said, smiling.

Marisa turned to her grandmother, "But Grandma's queen."

The queen laughed and held out her hand to the observant little one. "Yes, but I won't be forever. Your mother will take my place one day, and then you'll take hers when the times come, but you've got a while before you have to worry about that. I don't plan on going anywhere for a long, long while."

"Well, can we go somewhere now?" came a voice behind Rilla. They all looked to see a very unhappy Jacob.

"Or do you plan to stay here all day?"

They had completely forgotten about him in the excitement of seeing Marisa again. Rushing to her father, Marisa excitedly called to him, "Papa, Papa! I going to be queen one day, but after Grandma and Mama are done."

"Yeah, yeah. So I've heard," Jacob said almost in a disgusted tone as he pushed the child aside and walked toward the exit. "I'll be at the carriage."

Losing her balance, Marisa took a step to try and steady herself after the push from her father, but fell and scraped her knee on the corner of a bench as she fell. She cried out in pain, but Jacob never even looked back. Rilla rushed over to her and scooped her up quickly. "Shh…it's all right, love. Let Mama see." Marisa held her knee up and sniffed and sobbed softly as her mother examined it. "Not that bad. I'll have you patched up in no time." Rilla formed a water orb in one hand and held her daughter with the other. She chanted softly, and the water left her hand and covered Marisa's knee.

"Use the harp, Rilla," her mother suggested.

Nodding, Rilla sat Marisa on the bench and pulled the harp from her bottomless bag. "Wha…what dat?" the teary-eyed girl asked.

"It's called a harp, and its going to make you feel better," Rilla replied before she slowly plucked the strings. As she played softly, she continued chanting, and Marisa watched in amazement as her knee healed. When Rilla was done, she sat the harp down and pulled the water back into an orb in her hand. "Feel better?"

Marisa nodded and wiped her eyes on her sleeve. "Tanks, Mama."

"You're welcome, honey," Rilla said, smiling. She put the harp away, then picked up Marisa, and headed out to the carriage.

As they approached the carriage, they rushed over when they heard loud shouts. "Get out of my way, you mangy mutt!" Hearing growling, Rilla quickly handed Marisa to her mother and rushed over, grabbing Jacob's hand as he went to swing at the open door of the carriage. "Let go, or I'll..." he stopped mid-sentence when he realized who had grabbed his arm.

"Or you'll what?" Rilla demanded.

"Nothing." Jacob lowered his arm and stepped aside. "About time you got here. Maybe the guard dog will listen to you," he spat.

"I'm not a dog!" Vixie protested.

Rilla looked to Vixie, ignoring Jacob for the moment. "What happened, Vix?"

"What happened was I tried to get in the carriage and that damn mutt tried to bite me!" Jacob blurted out before Vixie could speak.

"Is that true?" Rilla asked her guardian.

"Yes, but what this idiot forgot the mention is he told the driver to take him to the castle. He tried to leave without you," Vixie explained.

"Not that I would have left without you and the queen," the driver spoke up quickly.

"Of course, you wouldn't, Manuel," the queen said softly as she placed Marisa in the carriage. Vixie quickly made herself comfortable in the child's lap and enjoyed having her ears scratched. Rilla and her mother climbed into the carriage, and as Jacob started to get in, Queen Amirilla prevented it. "You can find your own way home," she stated firmly and closed the door.

Jacob stood there with a dumbfounded expression on his face as he watched the carriage drive off without him.

Chapter Fifteen

As they exited the carriage at the palace, Queen Amirilla told Manuel to return to the station once all the bags were unloaded. When he gave her a questioning look, she explained that he was to make sure Jacob had gotten a ride; if not he was to find him and offer him one. "After all, we can't have him causing trouble all over the place."

Manuel nodded. "Understood, Your Highness."

When the bags were unloaded, he left to do as the queen had asked. Meanwhile the servants carried the bags inside and the queen, Rilla, and Marisa went in search of the king.

They found him in his study, nose in a book. Marisa ran over as soon as her mother put her down. "Grandpa! Grandpa!"

Looking up, the king smiled. "Hey! There's my girl." He pushed his chair away from the desk in time for the energetic girl to jump on his lap for a big hug. "Easy on your old grandpa." He laughed. "I'm not as young as I used to be."

"Silly Grandpa!" Marisa laughed and hugged him again. "You neva be old!"

""Tell that to my gray hair," Arkanthius said as he tickled his granddaughter. "So how was your trip?"

"Okay. Papa in bad mood, so I stay quiet," Marisa answered.

"I see. Have you seen your cousin Michael yet?" The king asked as he stood and placed Marisa on his chair.

"Mike here?" she cried as she bounced on the chair.

"Yes, and so is Rukia," Rilla said, smiling as she watched Marisa get even more excited.

"Rilla, why don't you take Risa to see Michael and Rukia while your mother and I discuss some things."

"Gladly, Father." Rilla held out her hand. "Come along, Risa."

"Okay!" She jumped down and ran to her mother.

* * *

Rilla led her down the hall to the room her cousin and his fiancée were staying in. Knocking on the door, Rilla hoped they were up. She knew it had been a long week for them, and Rukia especially was known for sleeping in.

Soon the door opened, and a sleepy Rukia poked her head out. "Is breakfast ready? If not, I'm going back to bed."

"Ruk Ruk!"

Rukia's eyes got wide hearing the excited cry, and she looked down, smiling when she saw the girl jumping up and down.

"Well, what do we have here?" Rukia teased as she knelt.

"Is that little Risa?" Rukia placed her hand on the child's head. "No, it can't be. Rilla, who is this tall girl? I know it's not Risa because our little Risa isn't this big."

"It me!" Risa shouted with a huge grin on her face. She knew Rukia was teasing her.

"It is?" Rukia looked her over. "Well, I'll be…it is Risa!" She grabbed her and pulled her into a tight hug. "You're getting so big!"

Marisa giggled as Rukia scooped her up and swung her around. Rilla smiled as she watched her friend play with her daughter. "Sorry if we woke you."

"Don't worry about it. What better way to wake up than to this adorable girl?" Rukia gave her a kiss and put her down. "But your cousin is still asleep." Rilla's eyes got wide at her comment. Rukia up before Michael? "Why don't we go wake him up?" Rukia said with a mischievous grin.

"Flying sumsalt?" Marisa asked, grinning from ear to ear.

"Flying somersault," Rukia said, nodding. She quickly grabbed the girl's hands and lifted her off the floor as she ran toward the bed. She tossed her in the air, and Marisa spread her arms and legs out wide as she prepared to land on the middle of the large lump on the bed. As the girl landed, the bed cushioned her fall and she bounced a time or two before she stopped. Rukia noticed the large lump flattened under the girl, and she turned her head, confused. "Wait a minute…" She pulled the covers away and found that she had thrown Marisa onto a pile of pillows.

"Boo!"

Rukia jumped as two arms grabbed her from behind. "Michael!" she cried as he tickled her.

"Thought you'd get me with a flying somersault, huh? Did you forget who taught her that one?" he asked.

"Mike!"

"Morning, Risa." He smiled. "I see you're full of energy as usual." He let go of Rukia and stepped over to the bed and held out his arms for a hug. Marisa happily jumped into his embrace and wrapped her arms around his neck. "Have you been a good girl?" Marisa nodded and looked at him with hopeful eyes. He placed her on the bed and walked over to his bag. "I guess you can have this then." He pulled out a large light blue stuffed dog and tossed it to Marisa.

The dog was as big as the girl it was thrown at, but Marisa caught it and hugged it tightly. "Tanks, Mike!"

Rilla smiled, remembering the day she got her stuffed dog. "Look familiar, Rilla?" Rukia asked, interrupting her thoughts.

"Yeah, looks just like mine."

"What did you name yours again?" Michael asked.

"Ruu," Rilla responded.

"Mama has puppy, too?" Marisa asked as she looked the stuffed animal over, examining every detail.

"Yeah, I do Risa." Rilla smiled. "Mine was a gift from my big brother Di-chan."

"Di-chan?" Risa looked at her mother, confused.

"He was your uncle. He passed before you were born," Rilla explained. "You would have loved him though, and he would have adored you."

"Inkle Di-chan was fun?"

Rilla chuckled. "Yeah, he was my best friend when I was your age. He taught me a lot of things." She paused, feeling her eyes get watery. "I miss him a lot."

Marisa dropped the dog on the bed and ran over to her mother. "Don't cry, Mama. I here." She hugged her mother's leg tightly.

Rilla smiled and patted her head. "Yes, you are here now, and now it's my turn to be the teacher. I get to teach you all the wonderful things that Di-chan taught me."

"Uh oh," Michael said with a big grin. "You know what that means, Risa?"

"Wat?" she asked, looking up from her mother's leg, which she was still hugging tightly.

"One day, you'll be able to beat up Rukia." A pillow hit the back of his head as soon as the comment was out of his mouth.

"Why I beat up Ruk Ruk?"

Rilla laughed and picked up her daughter. "What your cousin means is that one day you may be able to win a duel against her because I can."

"Fine, fine. I'll admit it. Rilla is a better fighter than me, but it doesn't leave this room. I have a reputation to maintain after all," Rukia said defiantly.

"Wat a repotasson?"

"Rukia means she doesn't want people to think Rilla deserves all her trophies," Michael said. "See, Rukia fights in competitions to prove she's the best. Your mother is too modest for that. So if people knew your mother could beat Rukia, they might question if she gets to keep her title and award."

"I would never take those from Rukia. Besides, if everyone knows how well I can fight, then I'd never get a duel partner other than those wanting to take titles and trophies," Rilla informed them. "Di-chan always said the element of surprise is your best weapon when it comes to battle. If your opponent doesn't know what to expect, he won't be prepared for your strategy."

Rukia nodded. "But sometimes brute force is the best way."

Michael hugged Rukia and ruffled her brown hair. "Which is why we don't tell anyone that Rilla is better than Rukia. Your mother is our secret weapon." Michael winked at Marisa and pushed Rukia on the bed. "Now why don't you and your mother head down to the dining hall. I'll get lazy bones cleaned up and dressed, and we'll meet you there for breakfast."

"Okaaay!" Marisa said excitedly as she climbed out of her mother's arms and pulled her toward the door.

Rilla followed her daughter to the dining hall, where they found the king and queen already waiting. She informed them that Michael and Rukia would be joining them shortly, and then she helped Marisa into her chair and took a seat beside her. Her mother informed her that Manuel had returned a few moments ago with a furious Jacob, and last she had heard, he was in the garden. Rilla nodded and decided she would let him cool off and then talk to him.

When Michael and Rukia finally arrived, the table was covered with hot meats, cheeses, breads, and a large selection of fruit spreads to put on the bread. Rilla was already devouring her bun covered in sweet cream with berries on top. Breakfast was relatively quiet, other than Marisa going on about her trip and what she had been learning from her tutor on Venus.

Once the meal was done, Rilla asked Michael and Rukia to take care of Marisa for a little while. Rukia accepted gladly, offering to give the girl her first fencing lesson. Rilla smiled as she watched them head for the courtyard. Sighing, Rilla nodded to her parents and headed for the gardens.

As she entered the gardens, she could hear Jacob still ranting and raving to himself or whomever would listen. Approaching slowly, she looked to see if he was actually talking to someone, and if so she wanted to find out who so that she could ask them to leave, but as she had figured, there was no one there. She waited for him to take a breath and then she spoke, "Hello, Jacob."

Slightly startled, Jacob turned to face Rilla. He sighed and shook his head. "How long have you been there?"

Rilla stepped forward and sat down on the fountain that Jacob had been pacing in front of. "Not long. Marisa missed you at breakfast," she said calmly, trying to avoid a fight.

"Only Marisa?"

"She's used to eating meals with you, and she's worried you're angry with her about something," Rilla said, trying to dodge his question.

"I have no reason to be angry with my daughter," Jacob said plainly as he rubbed the reddish scruff that covered his chin. "Though I think that I have reason to be upset with my wife. That is, if you're still my wife." He ran a hand through his deep red locks. "Damn it, Rilla! Is it true? Is your mother going to summit a request to the empress to have our marriage annulled?"

Rilla hesitated, unsure of what to say. Sighing, she nodded and looked at the fountain. "Yes, Mother is going to send in that request. You'll still get to see Marisa and attend events with her, but we would no longer be husband and wife. I'm sorry, Jacob, but this is what's best for both of us."

"Best for both of us? Don't I get a say in what's best for me?" Rilla was shocked to see his eyes get glossy. "Don't you love me at all, Rilla?"

Rilla looked him dead in the eyes; she wanted there to be no confusion. "No, Jacob. I'm sorry, but I do not love you. We never should have gotten married to begin with. I'm certain we'll both be much happier this way."

"You heartless bitch! Who is he?" Jacob demanded.

"What are you talking about?" Rilla was caught off guard by his sudden change in demeanor and stood quickly, in case he got stupid in his rage.

"Who is the boy toy that you would rather have by your side? Is it Nathaniel? I've never liked the way he looks at you. Or is it that stranger from the ball at Central? That's right. I heard all about your fun at the empress's ball while I was away. Now tell me which one it is, and I'll kill him!"

"This is exactly why I want out of this marriage," Rilla stated firmly. "You don't love me; don't even try to act like you do. I'm property to you. You want to run my life the way you see fit and Mercuria help anyone that tries to touch what's yours. I'm not a mare you can saddle when you feel like taking a ride and then throw back into a stable to stay there and be alone when you're done. I have friends, family, and duties that require my attention. But then you've got your little mares all over the system, don't you?" Rilla glared as she moved to the other side of him. "I wouldn't cower to your every whim and so you satisfy your desires when and how you see fit."

Jacob pulled his hand back as if he intended to take a swing at her. Rilla watched and prepared to counter if he attempted it. "Then why did you agree to the marriage, if you felt nothing for me. Were you naïve enough to believe I'd change? Surely Rena told you about my reputation. She certainly lectured me enough about giving up my wild ways once you and I were wed."

"I married you because it's my duty to do as my father wishes, but he acknowledges that pushing me into this was wrong. He was too concerned with making sure I was taken care of, especially after my brother was killed by raiders."

"Raiders?" Jacob asked, suddenly starting to laugh. "Is that what Arkanthius told you?"

"Are you calling my father a liar?" Rilla demanded with clenched fists.

"If he told you that Amdis was killed in a raider attack, then I guess I am." He smirked. "Very well then. Have it your way. You were always too independent and strong-willed for me," he said as he turned his back on her. "But I don't think you'll like what it'll take to get your annulment." He walked away before Rilla could stop him or ask what he meant.

* * *

Returning to the castle, Rilla sat in her room, pondering her conversation with Jacob. Had something else been the cause of her brother's death? She had never seen a body and only had her father's word to go on. He had told her that Amdis was accompanying him on a routine scouting mission to the outer rim. There had been reports of raiders attacking Mercurian trade ships en route

Shadows of the Past

to Neptune. Instead of requesting help from the empress, her father had insisted on checking it out himself. "If we can't defend our own, how can we defend the empress?" It was the last thing her father had said before leaving that day.

Rilla pushed it from her mind. Jacob was pissed and lashing out at her in any way he could. She didn't put it past him to make up a lie to try and cause more drama. Sighing, she looked out her window and spotted Rukia and Michael in the courtyard with Marisa. They had given the girl a stick to use as her first sword. Deciding to have a little fun, Rilla hurried down to challenge Rukia to a duel.

Rukia gladly accepted the challenge, and they dueled for hours as Marisa watched from Michael's lap, while he gave the girl a play by play of the particular moves being performed. Rilla was harder on Rukia than normal, and she knew it. She was frustrated and needed to let off steam. Rukia was aware of that and encouraged her to continue by taunting her. They were so focused on their duels that they didn't realize how late it was getting until a servant came to inform them that the queen wanted them to clean up for dinner. By that time, Marisa had gotten bored and fallen asleep. Michael handed her over to the servant, who took the child up to Rilla's room and put her to bed.

Rilla thanked Rukia for the exercise, and the three returned to their rooms to prepare for dinner. Upon entering her room, Rilla took a moment to watch her daughter sleep with Vixie curled up next to her, also fast asleep. After pulling a blanket over them, Rilla quietly showered and dressed for dinner. She debated waking Marisa for dinner, but given the announcement her mother was going to make at dinner, Rilla decide it was best to let the little one sleep. She would explain the situation to Marisa when the time was right. Before leaving she woke Vixie and told her she planned to leave Marisa sleeping and asked her to stay and look after her. Sleepily, Vixie nodded and agreed to stay with her. Rilla was certain Vixie was asleep again before she made it down the hall.

* * *

In the dining hall, the table was quickly being covered with exotic dishes that had been prepared for the night's feast. Smelling the delightful aromas, Rilla thought back to the last feast held in that room. Secretly Rilla wished that Lord Abraxis would make an appearance, if for nothing other than to prepare the delicious soup and dessert again. She found her mother by the kitchen, talking with Maurice.

"Mother, are you giving Maurice a hard time again?" Rilla asked with a smile.

Maurice laughed and gave the princess a gentle hug. "Oh, no, my dear. Your mother was just telling me what to include on young Miss Risa's plate."

"Then, it's a good thing I came along," Rilla stated. "Don't bother making a plate for my daughter. She's sound asleep, and I've left Vixie to look after her."

"She's not coming for dinner?" Maurice sounded rather disappointed.

"Not tonight, but don't worry, she'll be looking forward to leftovers, so be sure to save a plate of her favorites for her."

"Is Risa feeling ill?" the queen asked.

"No, I just thought it best for her not be at dinner, given the announcement you intend to make. I'll explain it all to her in private when the time is right," Rilla explained.

Queen Amirilla nodded and gave Maurice a few final instructions before walking with her daughter to the table. King Arkanthius was already seated, talking with Duke Louis. The duke stood when he saw the ladies approaching.

"There they are. Now the room is complete. For surely no greater beauty is going to walk through that door."

Rilla smiled and gave him a big hug before taking her seat. The queen nodded to him and sat beside Arkanthius. The room slowly filled with dukes, duchesses, lords, and ladies of the court. Rilla wasn't sure why, but she was a little disappointed that Lord Abraxis wasn't among them. All but three seats at the table were filled — the one beside the king, which was reserved for Prince Amdis, and two beside Rilla, which were intended for Marisa and Jacob. Normally at a dinner with all the members of the court present, Rilla felt at home, as they were all like family to her, but tonight she worried about their reaction to the queen's announcement.

As plates and cups were filled, the room filled with idle conversation. Many congratulated Rilla on her promotion to general, others commented on the weather, raider attacks, or any other subject that allowed them to gossip. Michael and Rukia, who were seated across the table from Rilla, knew why Rilla was nervous and tried to pull her into several conversations, but Rilla ate quietly, only speaking when spoken to.

Finally, the time arrived. Queen Amirilla stood and tapped against her glass to get everyone's attention. "First I want to thank everyone for being here tonight. I have two important things to say to all of you. The main reason we're here is of course to congratulate my daughter Rilla, my nephew Michael of Neptune, and his fiancée Rukia of Uranus on being promoted to generals in the Intergalactic Court." Everyone lifted their glasses and applauded and cheered for the new generals. "The second is a sensitive matter. I will be sending a petition to the empress asking that she annul the marriage between Rilla and Jacob of Venus." She paused as the room filled with comments and nods and head shakes. Raising her hand, she silenced them and continued, "In recent weeks, we've determined that Jacob is not a fit husband for my daughter, and certainly would not be suited for taking the throne when the time comes. While he is the father to the future heiress Marisa, he won't be allowed to take the throne with Rilla, but we will allow him to keep his current title of Prince and all the luxuries he received since his marriage to my daughter, along with unlimited visitations with his daughter. Nothing is certain yet, but as members of this court, I felt you all needed to know of my intentions."

"Rilla, what do you think of all this?" Lady Veronica asked.

Rilla blushed slightly. "Honestly, I hope the empress agrees to mother's petition. Jacob is a good man, but I don't love him, and his behavior is not what I expect or want from my husband, the father of my child, and certainly not for your future king."

"So your hand will be free once more?" Duke Marcos questioned.

"If the empress agrees, yes."

Before Rilla could continue, Duke Louis piped up, "There's always my son Antony. He's always been fond of you."

Rilla laughed. "I thank you for the offer but, if the empress annuls the marriage, I plan to stay single for a while. I rushed into this marriage and made a mistake in doing so. I don't want to make another mistake. Whomever becomes my husband, if I do marry again, will be a suitable husband, father, and king when the time comes."

"And what does your current husband think of all this?" Lady Rosalina inquired.

"That I will willingly agree to it all on one condition." Everyone turned to see Jacob in the doorway. "You can have your annulment and Marisa if King Arkanthius tells everyone the truth. Tell them how Amdis really died. I want you to tell Rilla the real reason she lost her brother and why you rushed her into this marriage, a marriage Amdis never wanted to happen."

Chapter Sixteen

The room was filled with angry, outraged shouts.

"How dare you?"

"Are you calling the king a liar?"

"This is an outrage!"

"Amdis died fighting raiders!"

King Arkanthius looked at his wife and sighed. "It's time she knew the truth anyway." Standing, the king motioned for everyone to quiet down. "Very well, Jacob. If that is what it'll take to make this process easier, then so be it. I will tell them the truth."

"Father, what are you saying?" Rilla asked, astonished.

"Rilla, I lied to you. I lied to everyone here, including your mother." The queen reached over and squeezed his hand. "While your mother does know the truth now, I made her swear to me that she would never tell you." He paused and closed his eyes, trying to summon forth a memory he had buried in the back of his mind and hoped would never resurface. "We were told by our scouting party that something weird was going on near what used to be called Darerius. The area is quarantined, but some trade ships still have to go by that area. So we went to investigate. Our ship was getting strange readings from the planet below, and even though we knew the risks, we took a shuttle down to the surface. The planet was dead. Not a living thing in sight. The buildings that remained from the once great Darerius Empire were almost completely demolished. I told Amdis to check out the source of the energy readings we were picking up while I checked out what was left of the palace." Arkanthius paused to wipe a tear from his eye. "It's all my fault. I never should have gone down to the surface, and I never should have let Amdis out of my sight."

"Father," Rilla stood and looked her father in the eyes. "What happened to Di-chan?"

Sighing, the king looked around at all the eyes staring at him, all but Rilla's. Her eyes were the ones he couldn't look at. "I wish I knew exactly what happened to him. All I know is I was in what used to be the throne room, when I heard him scream. I ran faster than I've ever run before, but when I got there, it was too late." The king leaned against the table for support as tears ran down his face. "All I found when I got there was my son's lifeless body. I tried every healing spell I knew and a few I had only heard of, but I couldn't save him. I couldn't…" Rilla reached for her father, but he pushed her hand away. "I wish that was all." He took a deep breath and wiped his eyes, trying to regain some form of composure. "I left him for a moment to search for who or what killed him. I was just outside the door when I heard a noise behind me. I turned with my sword in hand and…"

The queen rubbed her husband's shoulders. "Want me to tell the rest?" she whispered to him.

"No, this is my duty. I kept it from her. I have to tell her everything." He patted the queen's hand and looked at Rilla, his eyes red and puffy. "I turned and he was there. He lunged at me, and I defended myself. Rilla, you have to believe me when I say I had no choice."

"What do you mean? No choice about what?" Rilla's hands were clenched so tight she almost cut her own skin with her nails. She was filled with a mix of emotions—fear, hatred, anger, and sorrow.

The king sighed and closed his eyes, too afraid to look his daughter in the eyes as he revealed the secret that had haunted him for five years. "It was Amdis. He was up on his feet and attacking me. I tried talking to him, but it wasn't my son, at least, not his soul. It was as if some demon had possessed his body. He groaned and made sounds like a wild beast and kept attacking." The king paused as the members of the court started to mumble among themselves.

Rilla motioned to them to keep quiet and closed her own eyes as she asked a question she was almost positive she didn't want to hear the answer to. "Father, what did you do?"

"I fought back…I…" The king broke down and cried like he had the day his son died. "I killed him!" he cried through his tears. "I killed my boy!"

"Shhh…" Queen Amirilla hugged him and rubbed his back as he leaned over the table, crying.

Rilla and her mother helped him to a chair and comforted him the best they could. She was upset that her father had lied about Amdis's death, but she was pissed at Jacob. Rushing to the doorway, she drew her sword from her bag and slashed at his face, cutting him from his ear down to his chin. "Get out!"

"Rilla, I…"

"Get out now! I don't care if you agree to this annulment or not. I will make sure you lose everything that you gained from marrying me. No more parties, no more title, and no unsupervised visits with my daughter. If I ever see your face in this palace when you're not supposed to be, I will run you through."

"I get your father to tell you what really happened to your beloved Amdis and I get thrown out? What the hell is wrong with you?" Jacob demanded.

"My father may have lied, but you've embarrassed him in front of the entire court. This could and should have been done in private. Now get out of my sight," Rilla hissed. Jacob quickly left, and Rilla turned back to her father, who had his head buried in his hands.

"Your Highness, you shouldn't blame yourself. You said yourself it wasn't your son. Prince Amdis was killed by whatever used him to attack you." Rilla looked to see Count Greyior, standing and speaking calmly to her father. While Rilla watched Count Greyior, she couldn't help feeling like she knew him from somewhere else, other than on Mercury. "I'm sure your daughter knows that, and no one here blames you for his death. If you hadn't defended yourself, we would have also lost our king that day."

Rilla smiled slightly, glad that someone was speaking up for her father. The count was right, her father didn't kill him. He simply stopped something from defiling her brother's body. "He's right, Father, and I dare anyone to argue otherwise. And now that I know the truth, I vow that one day I will find out who or what really killed my brother, and I will avenge his death."

"No!" the king said, looking up. "You have to stay away from that place."

"Dear, let it go for the moment. We'll talk about this in private." Rilla's mother jumped in. She nodded to Rilla and motioned for her to leave the dining hall.

Nodding back, Rilla turned to the members of the court. "I'm sorry you all had to see this. This was supposed to be a joyous occasion, and now it's become a day of mourning. Please enjoy the rest of your meals and feel free to help yourselves to the ale." Walking over to her father, she placed her hands on his shoulders. "If you'll excuse us, I believe we need to have a family meeting. Michael, would you and Rukia please see to our guests?"

Michael nodded and stood to help the ladies get the king to his feet. Giving Rilla a quick hug, he turned back to the guests and tried to brighten things up. "A toast, to Prince Amdis and his undying bravery."

Rilla looked back to see everyone toasting her brother. She mouthed a silent "thank you" to Rukia, who was watching them leave. Rukia nodded and bowed her head silently, saying, "You're welcome."

As Rilla and the queen led the king to his study, he continued to cry, and all he said over and over again was, "I'm sorry. I'm so sorry…"

* * *

The next morning, Rilla explained everything to Marisa, who wasn't sure she understood, but she agreed to do as she was told and help out in any way she could. After a long talk with her father, she understood better why he had pushed the marriage. He felt so helpless and guilty about losing Amdis that he wanted to make sure Rilla and the queen wouldn't be alone. She wasn't able to completely forgive him for lying to her, but she understood his reasons. When Rilla asked her parents how Jacob knew that her father had lied about Amdis's death, the only explanation her father could come up with was that he had read the king's personal journal. Arkanthius explained that he had caught Jacob snooping around in his study a year or so previous. He didn't think much of it, but he remembered that the drawer the journal was hidden in was unlocked that day. Jacob could have easily read it and learned the truth about what happened.

Michael and Rukia did an excellent job caring for the guests, and Rilla hoped no one would think less of her father for the events of the night before. Later that day, the king left for Venus with Marisa. He felt time away would be good, and he wanted to spend more time with his granddaughter. The queen had also suggested he visit Lord and Lady Vinusian to try and smooth things out, especially after Rilla's threat to Jacob.

* * *

The next night, after dinner, Michael asked to speak with Queen Amirilla in private. Rukia kept Rilla busy in the study with conversation and a horrible attempt at chess, while they slipped out to find a quiet place to talk. Once they were out in the garden, away from everyone else, Queen Amirilla turned to Michael. "What's wrong? You never ask to speak to me in private like this."

Michael sighed. "I've had a few disturbing visions, Auntie. Rilla tells me she's been having strange dreams and odd visions, as well. I was wondering if it was true for you, too."

"No, I haven't had a vision in months. What about your mother?"

"Same. Mother says I may be stressed and that what I've seen might not even be anything more than a nightmare," Michael explained.

"What did you see, Michael?" Amirilla asked, her stomach in knots.

"I keep seeing a black arrow flying through the air. I hear screams and see blood everywhere."

Pacing, the queen looked to the sky. "That's not very detailed. That could happen to anyone at anytime. Not easy to avoid it."

"There's one more thing," Michael stated. The queen turned to face him. "I see who the arrow hits, and I promise you I will do everything in my power to see that it doesn't happen."

Michael and the queen continued to talk for an hour or so and finally decided to head back before Rilla came looking for them. They found Rukia throwing chess pieces and shouting about how the game was not a good way to practice battle strategies and that every piece should have free movement like the queen. Michael shook his head and proceeded to remove all throwable objects from her reach.

* * *

The day they had to leave for Earth came all too soon, and Rilla paced the room. Her bags were packed, the carriage would be ready soon, and Mahogany would meet them at the station. Everything was going according to plan. So why did she feel like something was horribly wrong?

"Mi-chan." Rilla turned to see Michael at the door. "The carriage is ready, and our bags are loaded. It's time to go."

She nodded. "I'll be right there." Michael nodded and walked away, and Rilla turned back to her bed. She grabbed Ruu, her Mercurite dagger, her harp, and her bottomless bag that she'd had since she was little. Placing the last minute items in the bag, she took one last look around before heading out.

At the main gate, her mother, Rukia, and Michael were waiting for her. "Have a safe trip, Rilla-chan," her mother said as she hugged her.

Rilla found that she didn't want to let go and was certain that her mother felt the same way. Did her mother have the same feeling that she was having? Finally letting go, Rilla smiled and said, "I'll see you at the ball." Even as she said it, she had trouble believing it to be true.

Her mother nodded and helped her into the carriage. "Until then, Rilla-chan." The queen signaled the driver and waved until the carriage was out of sight.

As Rilla watched the palace vanish into the distance, she couldn't help but feel that she would never see her home again. As the carriage pulled into the station, Rilla looked out the window for Mahogany. As they came to a stop, she spotted her friend.

"Mahogany!" she called as she climbed out.

"Rilla!" Mahogany called, rushing over. "Oh, I thought you guys would never get here."

"How long have you been here?" Rukia asked.

"I lost track, but long enough for me to hit on every single guy on the last three shuttles."

"And probably hit on a few not-so-single guys," Michael said as he smiled at Mahogany.

"Ha! Ha! Very funny," the Jupiter replied in an annoyed tone. She turned her attention back to Rilla and asked, "So,

Rilla, how was the banquet? What about your mother's announcement? Did Tora even bother to show up?"

Rilla laughed. "Easy, Mahogany. I'll give you all the details on the way there."

They all chatted casually as they waited for the luggage to be loaded and for the announcement that they could board the shuttle to Earth. Rilla nodded and half-listened to the conversation. She tried to focus her thoughts, but was unable to.

Once they boarded the shuttle, Mahogany and Rilla made themselves comfortable in the room they were going to share. It was a three-day trip to Earth because of the type of shuttle they had to take. With Earth not being a member of the court, they didn't have access to the more advanced shuttles used by the other kingdoms, and none of them bothered using their shuttles for transport to Earth, but that would soon be changing, if Earth joined the court. Michael and Rukia naturally wanted to room together, and it wasn't a new thing for Rilla and Mahogany to share a room. After all, they had lived together every year at the academy.

"Rilla!" Mahogany called.

Rilla looked up from the paper she'd been staring at. "Hmmm?"

"You okay? You seem very distracted lately. Everything okay?"

Rilla sighed, "I have this feeling."

"What kind of feeling?"

"Like something horrible is going to happen. I can't explain it, but I get the feeling that I'll never see my family again."

"Don't talk like that," Mahogany said firmly. "Nothing bad is going to happen…is it?" she asked, rethinking her statement. "Have you had a vision?"

"No, no vision, just the feeling. I think Mother felt it, too. She seemed hesitant to let me leave."

Mahogany shook her head. "Sometimes I envy you for being able to see the future, but at times like this, I thank the empress it isn't me, and I wish you didn't have to go through this either."

Rilla nodded. "So what is our mission? Rena said it was a waste of time that doesn't require the full planetary guard."

Mahogany nodded, "And she's right. We're flying all the way to Earth just to escort the prince and his brother to the ball at Central Palace."

"What?" Rilla protested. "Earth can provide guards to escort their princes, so why send us? What about—"

"I know," Mahogany interrupted, "but Lucydion insists on this as a formal sign of friendship. We escort the princes and accompany his guards to the ball. It's rumored that Lucydion plans to try and arrange marriages between us and members of his court once his son is married to the princess."

"Which son?" Rilla asked with a smirk.

"What do you mean?" Mahogany asked. "The eldest prince, of course. Eldest prince or princess gets married first, and the next oldest serves as the captain of their guard or royal diplomat. That's how it always works."

"Apparently, you don't know the princess or her family very well," Rilla replied, still smirking, "They're not ones for following tradition, and she has a crush on the younger brother, Chocheese or whatever his name is."

"Really? And just how do you know this?" Mahogany asked.

"The same way I know…" She stopped mid-sentence as images flooded her mind.

Rilla saw her home in flames and heard screams all around her. She ran toward the palace, hoping she wasn't too late. As she pushed her way through the front gate, the scene changed, and she was suddenly standing before the empress. "I'm going to raise an army."

She tried to look around, but the room started spinning, and she heard voices from all around. "Where are the generals?"

"How could this happen?"

"So many dead. And for what?"

The voices grew louder and louder as the room continued to spin. Rilla was filled with feelings of fear, hatred, and sorrow. When the room stopped spinning, she saw the flags of all the kingdoms. They were torn and tattered and some were on fire.

Mahogany watched as her friend sat there, just staring straight ahead. She knew she was having a vision, but she was confused as to why her crystal was glowing again. "Rilla? Rilla?" Getting no response, Mahogany grabbed her by the arms. "Amirilla!"

Rilla shook as she snapped out of her vision. "Mahogany?" Rilla looked around, feeling disoriented.

"You were having a vision and your crystal was glowing again." Mahogany brushed the hair back from Rilla's face. "Are you all right?"

"There's going to be a war," Rilla said calmly as she grabbed her mercurite crystal, which stopped glowing the minute she snapped out of the vision.

"A war? With who?" Mahogany asked.

"I don't know, but we have to stop it. If we don't, it could mean the end of the kingdoms and the destruction of our homes."

* * *

Back at the palace, Queen Amirilla was taking a stroll through the garden, thinking over things. So much had happened in the last few weeks, and she had barely had a moment to relax. Finally having a little time to herself, she decided a long bath was in order, so she turned to go back in the castle, but nearly fell as a vision hit her.

She saw her daughter dueling a dark figure. Rilla was obviously angry. Suddenly she saw a black arrow fly through the air and heard Michael scream. The scene then changed to the royal tombs. She watched Michael, Jacob, Nathaniel, and

Triston place a coffin in the empty slot. When it was sealed, the marker on the front read: "Here lies Princess Amirilla VI, beloved daughter, sister, wife, and mother."

The queen snapped out of her vision to find herself kneeling by the stairs with Vixie at her side. "Are you all right, Your Majesty?"

"Get me Count Greyior immediately!" the queen ordered before running inside.

Vixie jumped up and took off as fast as her legs, which were growing in size along with the rest of her, would carry her. By the time she reached the main gate, she was the size of a horse. The guards quickly opened the gates to let her out, knowing she must be on an urgent errand to take such a size.

Vixie hurried down the path through the woods, not stopping for anything. She hurried through the first village, and just before she reached the second, she dashed up the winding path that led to a large mansion on a hill. Reaching the door, Vixie returned to her normal size and banged on the door. "Count Greyior! Count Greyior! The queen needs you at the castle immediately!"

The door opened, and a tall man dressed in black, with black spikey hair and a very pale complexion opened the door. "Whoa! Easy, little fox. What's the emergency?"

"Her Highness had a vision and demanded me to get Count Greyior. Something must be dreadfully wrong. Please, is the count in?"

He nodded. "I'll send him right away. Please go see to the queen."

Vixie bowed and said, "Thank you," and hurried back to the castle.

The man closed the door and grabbed the coat by the door. "I better see if Ami-chan is all right."

Dashing out the back door, he took his true form and spread his wings. Cloaking himself with an invisibility spell, he took to the sky, and in no time, the black dragon arrived in the courtyard. Finding a dark, secluded corner, he took the form of an old man with gray hair. Running up the stairs to the main entrance, he opened the door and called, "Queen Amirilla!"

The queen came out of the study and rushed to the top of the stairs. "Thank Mercuria. I prayed you were still on planet." Taking two stairs at a time, he made his way up the stairs, much faster than a man of his apparent age should have been able to. "We need to talk in private. I've prepared the silencing circle." Amirilla turned to lead him to the study.

"Your Highness!" Vixie called the moment she entered the castle. "Count Greyior…"

"Is already here," Amirilla stated, cutting the fox off. "Thank you, Vixie. Please see that we are not disturbed."

"Yes, Your Highness." Vixie sat at the bottom of the stairs to stand guard, feeling slightly confused as to how the Count had beat her to the castle.

Count Greyior followed the queen to the study and stood in the circle of crystals. Once Amirilla was done casting the spell, the man known as Count Greyior changed back to the tall man with spikey hair. "So what's wrong, Ami?"

"I need you to call him," Amirilla said urgently.

"Whoa! Hold on a minute. Just tell me what's wrong. Maybe I can fix it," he said with a smile.

"Shade, please," she begged. "My baby is in danger."

Shade sighed and rubbed his neck. "I don't know if he'll answer." Reaching into his pocket, he pulled out a porcelain bell. "Stand in front of a mirror and say 'I call to the shadows. Summon thy lord, so I might see his face.' Then ring the bell three times."

Amirilla carefully took the bell from Shade. "Thank you."

"If he doesn't answer at first, wait a while and try again," Shade explained. "Now where is Mi-chan?"

Chapter Seventeen

At the Earth space dock, Princess Rena sat with Princess Emi of Pluto, Princess Rebecca of Saturn, and Princess Anya of Mars. Their shuttles had arrived at various times in the last three hours, but everyone agreed to wait at the station, so they could leave together.

Things were tense on Earth. Even though they were joining the Intergalactic Court, anyone from another kingdom was still looked at with suspicion and distrust by most of the Earthers. No one was sure who they could and couldn't trust, especially under the rule of Lucydion. His father had overthrown the previous ruler and established a male-dominant court. Those who disliked Lucydion's rule kept it to themselves out of fear. While it was officially denied, rumors of the ruthless acts of Lucydion and his court had reached even the outer kingdoms of Uranus and Pluto. So while Earth claimed to be peaceful and said that they wished to ally with the other kingdoms, many suspected ulterior motives.

"How long do we have to wait here?" the young blonde complained. Emi was Sazuka's younger sister and often she was sent in her sister's place. Like Rebecca, Emi was still attending classes at the academy and was not very good at using magic yet.

"Until Rilla, Michael, Rukia, and Mahogany arrive," Anya replied in an annoyed tone. The dark-skinned Mars princess hated to wait for anything. She preferred to charge in, do the job, and leave.

"Take it easy, you two," Rebecca replied as she took a seat by the window.

"Don't worry, Emi. The others will be here soon, and then we can head to the palace and meet the prince," Rena said cheerfully.

"You make it sound like meeting him is a big deal, Rena," Anya stated.

"Rena just wants to meet any cute guy she can, and being a prince certainly doesn't hurt," Emi commented.

"Sorry, Rena," Anya started, "but this prince already has his princess."

"Doesn't mean I can't try though," Rena replied with a smirk as she took a brush from her bag and started brushing her red hair.

Their conversation was interrupted by an announcement on the overhead speaker. "Flight 976 from Mercury now arriving at space dock 3. Passengers leaving for Mercury on Flight 976, please head to Bay 3 to board your shuttle at this time."

"Yay! They'll be here soon," Emi said excitedly.

"Good," Anya stated. "Sooner we get this all over with, the sooner we can get off this planet."

"What's with you, Anya?" Rena asked as she tossed a snack bag she'd gotten from her flight at the Mars princess.

"I don't like being here," she replied. "I don't trust Earthers. They follow the orders of a man who is not the rightful king. His father killed the true queen and her daughter. The daughter would have been the same age as my older brother. She might have even gone to the academy with him."

"That's the way of politics, Anya," Rena said.

"That's why we must look after our people and rule the best we can. Our lives belong to our subjects," Rebecca added.

Emi nodded, "Besides this planet is beautiful and has some of the strangest and most unique creatures."

Anya sighed. "Still I don't like any of this. I'm sure you've all heard the rumors."

"What rumors, Anya?" Emi asked.

"Once his son is married, Lucydion intends to propose more arranged marriages to supposedly prove his commitment to the court and strengthen relations," Anya said as she stood to stretch her legs.

"But isn't that a good idea? I mean, all the kingdoms have been doing that for years," Rena said as she pulled her makeup kit from her purse. "Just look at Rilla, she's married to my cousin Jacob, and that was an arranged marriage to strengthen relations between Venus and Mercury. Our kingdoms are working together and Rilla and Jacob are happily married," she said as she touched up her makeup. While she knew the truth about Rilla's marriage she knew it wasn't her place to say anything to the others.

"Happily?" Anya questioned. "Happy in the fact that they never see each other maybe. Every time I see them together, all they ever do is fight."

"Every couple has their quarrels, though. Look at Michael and Rukia. Last big fight they had, they almost destroyed the room they were staying in," Emi said.

"Room? Don't you mean castle?" Rebecca asked.

Ignoring Rebecca's question, Anya glared and added, "Fighting is one thing, but it's something else altogether to have intimate relations with other people."

"Surely you're not implying Rilla is unfaithful?" Rebecca asked, horrified at the thought.

"I wouldn't blame her if she is. No offense, Rena, but your cousin is a cheating bastard. I've seen him with half a dozen different girls while on 'diplomatic' trips to Mars." Anya held her hands up, making air quotes when she said the word *diplomatic*. "I'm sure he does it everywhere he goes…well, other than Mercury. If he's that dumb, I want to be there when Rilla catches him," Anya said with a smug grin on her face.

"What? Aren't you going to tell Rilla?" Emi asked.

"Emi's right. If you know this, why haven't you told her?" Rebecca added.

"Same reason I haven't," Rena piped in. "Politics. I didn't lie. They are happy, as happy as most arranged marriages are. Rilla knows her duty to her kingdom and the Intergalactic Court. Telling her would only upset her and cause a scandal and embarrass her and both Mercury and Venus. If she finds out, it needs to be on her own, and she'll handle it privately. Although if my idiot cousin is that obvious about his affairs, I'm sure she is already aware of it and dealing with it in her own way."

"I don't get it," Emi said. "How can you marry someone you don't love?"

"You do as you're told, Emi. It's part of who we are," Anya replied. "You're still young. One day, you'll understand."

"Anya's right," Rena stated as she closed her makeup kit. "Our lives are devoted to the service of our people. So we marry who is in the best interest of our kingdoms, but that doesn't mean we can't have a little fun on the side, as long as we're discreet about it," she added with a smile.

"So wait…Anya, if you agree to this arranged marriage idea to serve your kingdom, what is wrong with Lucydion's arranged marriages to strengthen relations?" Rebecca asked, confused.

"I'm against it because he wants to marry a member of his court to a member of every royal family. It's completely unheard of and would give Earth too much influence in the affairs of the other kingdoms," Anya explained.

Before she could continue, a voice behind them said, "None of it will matter if we don't stop the war."

The group turned to see that their companions had finally arrived.

"Rilla!" Rena exclaimed, jumping up to greet her.

"Yay! Everyone's here!" Emi exclaimed, jumping up to hug Rukia.

"It's good to see you, too, Emi," Rukia said as she tried to pry the young Pluto off her. "Where's your sister? I expected to see her here."

"Big sister couldn't get away from her duties, so she sent me in her place," Emi explained as she hugged Michael.

"About time you guys got here," Anya teased as she hugged each in turn. "Thought we'd have to sleep here."

"Nice to see you, too, Anya," Mahogany chuckled.

"Now what is this about a war, Rilla?" Rebecca asked as she hugged the Mercury princess.

"I'll explain later. Let's get out of here. There are far too many eyes and ears around here," Rilla explained. The others nodded and grabbed their bags, and the group made their way to the exit where a grand carriage was waiting to carry them to the palace.

* * *

It was a long, silent trip to the palace. After Rilla's warning about not talking around so many people, no one dared to open their mouths until she said it was safe. They all trusted her with their lives, and if she was worried, then so were they. Once they arrived at Lucydion's castle, they were met by the royal advisor, Azurite.

"Welcome to Earth, Your Majesties. You honor us deeply with your presence. I'm sure the trip was exhausting. The rooms have been prepared as each of your kingdoms requested. Please follow me, and I'll show you the way. Your bags will be unloaded and delivered to you rooms shortly, once they go through a customs check."

"Customs check?" Anya questioned. "What do you mean? We went through customs when we arrived on the planet!"

"Anya's right," Rena agreed. "Why another check?"

"Please relax, Your Graces. There is no need for concern. It's protocol. I assure you," Azurite stated. "Now if you will please, follow me. I'm sure all of you could use a rest before tonight's banquet."

Reluctantly the princesses and prince followed Azurite. Rilla looked back to see the guards unloading the carriage. She sighed, happy that all her valuables and weapons were packed in her bottomless bag, which hung by her side unseen by the Earthers, thanks to its glamour. They were all escorted to their rooms and told dinner was at seven. Rilla was the last to be shown to her room.

"Here we are, Princess Amirilla. The room was decorated according to your mother's request to make your stay here more comfortable. Dinner will be served at seven. A guard will come to escort you to the dining hall at the appropriate time."

"So I'm a prisoner until then?'

"Oh, no, Your Highness. You're free to come and go as you wish, but for your safety, we ask that you have a guard accompany you at all times," Azurite explained before leaving and closing the door behind him.

Walking over and checking the door, Rilla was surprised to find it unlocked. She slowly opened the door and peered out. There was a guard right outside. Not wanting to draw his attention, she slowly closed the door. She hurried over to the window and looked out. She was several stories up, and everywhere she looked, there were guards. Luckily for her, her room had a balcony that connected to the room next door, which she was certain was Rena's room. She stepped outside and knocked on the door. She was happy to see it was Rena and not a guard who opened the door. "Rilla!"

"Shh!" Rilla said, putting a hand over Rena's mouth. "We don't want to draw any unwanted attention."

Rena nodded and grinned from ear to ear. "So what's the plan, Rilla?" she whispered.

Hurrying over to the door, she peered out. Rilla was glad that they had assigned one guard for both rooms, and he was the only one in the hall. As he paced back and forth, looking up out the windows across the hall that over looked the main courtyard, Rilla slowly closed the door and turned back to Rena. "We've got to get to the others without alerting the guards.

Nodding, Rena looked out the window. "How about a distraction? I could push that statue over the balcony. That would definitely make a lot of noise when it hit the ground."

Rilla shook her head. "We can't guarantee the right guards will investigate the sound. No, we need something better. Plus, we don't know how many guards are around the corner." She sat and thought hard.

"You've got a plan, don't you?" Rena asked, seeing the grin on Rilla's face.

"Rena, I need you to do what you do best."

Chapter Eighteen

Rena raised a curious eyebrow and listened intently as Rilla explained the plan in detail. "All right. I'll go back to my room. You go out and keep him busy till I give the signal." Rena nodded and watched Rilla head back to her room.

Once she was there, Rena closed the door to the balcony and opened the door to the hall. As Rilla predicted, the guard met her at the door the minute she stepped into the hall. "Is there a problem, Princess?"

"Not anymore," Rena said with a seductive grin.

As Rena continued to flirt with the guard, Rilla quietly slipped out of her room and focused on the guard's uniform. Quietly, she cast a glamour spell and took on the appearance of another palace guard. Rilla took a minute to listen to their conversation, hoping to learn enough to make convincing the guard to leave a little easier. After hearing him tell Rena his name, Rilla smirked and called out to him. "Richard!" she said in a very masculine-sounding voice, thanks to the voice-altering spell she cast. The guard talking to Rena turned to face her. "His lordship sent me to relieve you."

"You're early," Richard replied. "I'm on duty for another hour."

"I'm just following orders," Rilla fibbed.

Richard looked at her suspiciously, but sighed and walked away. "Very well. Guess I'll take an early dinner."

Rilla watched him walk around the corner and then turned to Rena. "One down." She smiled, and they slowly walked toward the hall where Anya's room was located. She peered around each corner carefully, and Rena stayed close behind her. As she peered around the last corner, Rilla found herself staring at the back of a guard's head. She quickly ducked back and leaned against the wall.

"What now?" Rena whispered.

Before Rilla could reply, they heard a familiar voice. "I refuse to be treated this way!"

Rilla peeped around the corner to see the guard walking toward a very pissed off Anya, who was storming down the hall toward them.

"What seems to be the problem, Princess?" the guard asked.

"The trouble is we're being treated like prisoners. We can't leave our rooms without a guard to escort us, and we aren't allowed to see each other. I won't stand for this. As a member of the Intergalactic Court and future ruler of Mars, I demand to see my friends!"

Rilla smiled as she got an idea. "Rena, follow my lead."

Rena nodded and followed as Rilla walked calmly around the corner. "Is there a problem?"

Anya and the guard turned to see another guard and Rena walking toward them.

"Great! More guards," Anya said.

"What are you doing here?" the guard asked.

"Princess Rena wanted a tour of the castle. I was asked to escort her."

"Where's Richard? I thought he was assigned to Princess Rena."

"He's guarding Princess Amirilla."

"We don't need guards!" Anya exclaimed. "You have no right…"

Rilla cut her off by saying, "You're right, Princess. You are quite capable of taking care of yourself. We are merely here to assist you. Princess Rena asked for a tour, and I'm happily accompanying her. Perhaps you would like to join us."

"I would not," Anya replied, crossing her arms.

"Come on, Anya!" Rena piped in. "Come with us." Rilla hoped Anya would agree and play along. It would make things so much easier.

Anya gave Rilla a skeptical look. "I guess, but we go where we want, and you tell us about it. I don't want the tourist-guided tour."

"Very well, Princess," Rilla replied, bowing to her.

Rena grabbed Anya's arm and pulled her down the hall.

"This way, Anya!" she exclaimed cheerfully. Rilla followed them down the hall and around the corner. When they were a safe distance away, Rena turned to Rilla. "Now what, Rilla?"

"Rilla?" Anya asked, unbelieving.

Rilla smiled. "So my glamour even fooled you, Anya?"

Anya looked Rilla over. "Wow. I knew you were good, Rilla, but I never knew you were that good."

"Can't give you all my secrets, Anya," Rilla replied with a smile. "But back to business. Luckily for us the others are all on the same hall downstairs. Trouble is, we don't know how many guards are between here and there."

Rena nodded and looked around. "Rilla, do you remember where the rooms are exactly?"

"Yeah, I do. It's the next hall over, two floors down. Why?"

"Could we sneak into a room on this floor and climb down?"

Rilla smiled. "Wonderful idea, Rena!" she exclaimed. She went ahead of the other two and glanced around the corner. Seeing it was all clear, she motioned the others to follow and headed for the middle room, which should be two floors above Rukia and Michael's room. She turned the knob and sighed. "Locked."

"Not for long." Anya stated. She pulled a pin from her hair and quickly and quietly picked the lock.

"Nice," Rilla said as they entered the room.

"Anya, where'd you learn to do that?" Rena asked.

"Just something my big brother taught me. He said little things like that could come in handy sometimes."

"And he was right," Rilla noted as she canceled her glamour.

The three entered the room to find it was much larger and more ornate than they had expected. It had to be the most elegant of the rooms they had seen so far. "Wow," Rena said in awe. "Wonder whose room this is?"

"Let's not stick around to find out," Anya replied.

Rilla nodded and walked over to the door that led to the balcony. Opening them slowly, she walked out and peered down below. She was glad to see there was no balcony on the floor below them and smiled when she saw five familiar figures on the balcony two floors down. She walked back in to join Anya and Rena. "Well, looks like the others are plotting."

"Why do you say that, Rilla?" Anya asked.

"They're all out on the balcony, talking." Reaching in her bottomless bag, she pulled out a rope and tied one end to the bed post and walked out and tossed the other end over the balcony, scaring the group below her. She waved to them and turned back to Anya and Rena. "All right, girls! You go first, and I'll follow behind." She said as she gestured to the rope.

Nodding, they made their way to the balcony and climbed down the rope. Rena went first, with Anya right behind her. As they made their way down, Rilla reached in her bag and pulled out a small vial of liquid. She checked to see that Rena and Anya were safely down on the balcony with the others, and then she walked over and poured a bit on the rope's knot. As soon as the liquid hit, the rope it started bubbling as it ate through the rope. Rilla rushed out and hurried down the rope. Once she made it to the balcony below, she gave the rope a hard tug. Not getting the result she wanted, she waited a moment then tugged again. This time the rope gave a little. She gave it another good tug, and the rope came over the balcony and almost landed on her head.

"Rilla, don't we need to go back up there?" Anya questioned as she watched Rilla wind the rope around her arm and place it back in her bag.

"Eventually, but I think it's best to find another way. We don't want the owner of that room coming back and finding a rope tied to their bed," Rilla explained.

The others nodded, and they followed Michael inside to his and Rukia's room. "So, Rilla," Michael said once they were all inside. "I think you should tell the others of your vision."

Rilla nodded. She pulled crystals of different shapes and colors out of her bag and placed them in a circle around the room.

"A silencing circle?" Anya asked. "This must be serious."

Once she was done, everyone entered the circle and joined hands. Rilla nodded, and together they said, "We devote our lives to our planets and hold their secrets in our hearts. In the service of our planets, we form this circle. Let it hold our secrets from all not in its heart."

Then, one by one, they released their hands and called out their home planet, starting with Rilla.

"Mercury."

"Venus," Rena followed.

"Mars," Anya said next.

Then Mahogany. "Jupiter."

"Saturn," Rebecca said.

"Uranus," Rukia stated as she let go of Rebecca's and Michael's hands.

"Neptune," Michael said, looking at Emi, nodding slightly.

"Pluto," Emi said quietly, finishing the spell. Michael patted her on the head, knowing it was her first time using spells outside of the academy.

With the ritual complete, Rilla nodded to the others, and they all took a seat on anything in the circle, including the floor. "On the way here, I had a vision. I saw my home in flames and saw the flags for all our kingdoms in ruin. I heard voices asking, 'How could this happen?' and 'Where are the generals?' I saw the empress in full battle gear and heard her say she was going to raise an army. I believe there are forces conspiring, even as we speak. They plan to overthrow and destroy the Intergalactic Court."

"Who would do such a thing?" Emi asked.

"I'm not sure," Rilla replied, "But if we don't stop them, there will be a great war and thousands of our people will be killed, and our homes will be destroyed."

"Rilla, what you're talking about has to be a very well thought-out plan with hundreds of supporters to overthrow the empress. Surely someone would have heard of this," Anya stated.

"Maybe, maybe not," Michael added. "As you said, it would have to be very well thought-out. Whoever is behind this has no intention of the empress or anyone knowing of the plan before it's too late."

"Any idea when this is all supposed to take place, Rilla?" Rukia inquired.

Rilla shook her head. "No, but it wouldn't surprise me if it's during or right after this whole marriage thing."

"What makes your think that?" asked Rebecca.

"Right now, things are tense. Earth is joining the court, but many don't approve of it. And while the situation here on Earth is out of our hands, many don't want to deal with Earth's internal problems, which is exactly what will happen if Lucydion gets his way. His son is about to marry a princess from a very influential family. Selen is the empress's niece, and then he's planning to propose marriages between members of his court and members of every royal family. That would give Earth too much influence in the Intergalactic Court."

"Surely, the empress wouldn't allow such a thing to happen?" Rukia questioned as she leaned back against Michael.

"I'm not sure she could do anything to stop it," Rilla stated. "Marriages between the kingdoms are for relations between the individual kingdoms. That falls under kingdom affairs. Under the laws of the court, the empress cannot directly interfere in the affairs of the kingdoms. If Mars agrees to an arranged marriage with Earth to strengthen their diplomatic relations, then the empress really can't do much to stop it."

"But all marriages have to be approved by the empress," Anya stated in a very annoyed tone.

"True," Rena added. "But Rilla is right. The empress has no authority to do anything in this situation. Without a legitimate reason for denying the marriages, she has to approve all of them or risk a rebellion from the kingdoms for interfering in their affairs, and some may even see it as her trying to become a supreme dictator of the whole system. That isn't why she set up the Intergalactic Court. The job of the court is to provide support to each kingdom and help ensure there are no more wars between the planets. Each kingdom is required to provide a chosen warrior to be a part of the empress's royal guard, and in a time of need, we act as generals for the armies of kingdoms." She looked around and saw shocked and confused looks from her comrades and smiled. "What? I did pay some attention to the lectures at the academy."

Everyone chuckled, and Rena was glad to see everyone smile, but it didn't last long.

"So what do we do now, Rilla?" Michael asked.

"All we can do at the moment is keep our eyes and ears open and watch what we say while on Earth," Rilla replied.

"And then once we get home, do all we can to prevent these marriages. My hand is taken for now, but I wouldn't be surprised if Lucydion tried to marry my sister and the rest of you to members of his court."

"He can take his marriages and shove them where the sun doesn't shine," Anya said, crossing her arms. Rilla tried not to chuckle at Anya's indelicate suggestion. Leave it to a Mars to be completely honest and blunt.

"I agree. If we go back home after this, we can prevent these marriages. Surely our parents will agree marrying into all the families is too much," Rebecca spoke up.

Emi nodded. "Big sister is already engaged, and I refuse to marry someone I don't know."

"Wait, what? Since when is Sazuka engaged?" Rukia almost shouted.

Emi shrugged. "That's what I heard her telling Mother last week."

Michael laughed. "I think it's similar to Starfire being engaged. She wants him and thinks he'll marry her one way or another. Remember, things do work a bit different in the outer kingdoms."

"Oh, yeah." Rukia shook her head. "They'll learn the hard way you can't force someone to love you."

"Any idea who the unwilling groom is?" Mahogany asked, chuckling.

Michael shrugged. "Starfire's I know, but no clue about Sazuka."

"Doesn't Starfire want to marry that weird lord that's usually at Central Palace?" Rukia asked. "The one that the empress and Lady Orion keep trying to get to dance."

"Yeah, that's him," Michael said, nodding. "I've seen him several times but never got a name."

"Okay, first off, who is Starfire?" Anya butted in.

"Lady Orion's little sister," Emi answered. "She stayed with me once while my big sister went with Lady Orion on a mission."

"You girls know her bodyguards very well?" Michael said with a sly grin.

"Oh, yeah! I forgot about that." Rukia chuckled.

"Anyway," Rilla interrupted. "We should get back to our rooms. We'll discuss these things more at a later time. For now, keep your ears and eyes open. Think of this as an intelligence gathering operation. The more we know, the better prepared we'll be."

"Yes, General Amirilla," Rena replied as she stood and saluted, gaining another chuckle from the group.

"How are we getting back?" Anya asked.

"I'll think of something," Rilla said as she looked through her bag.

Before she could come up with something, there was a knock on the door.

"Shit!" Michael and Rukia cried out together.

"Hurry! Gather the crystals and hide," Rilla instructed. The others nodded and helped her gather the crystals and place them in her bag before hiding.

"Princess Rukia!" came a voice from the door. "Please open up."

Rilla grabbed Rukia's arm before she reached the door and pulled her to the bed. Confused, she mouthed, "What are you doing?"

Rilla tossed her the robe at the end of the bed and motioned for her to put it on. As she did Rilla formed a water orb between her hands and quickly soaked Rukia's hair. Finally getting the plan, Rukia pulled off her pants and pulled the robe tightly around her to hide her shirt. Hurrying to the door, she looked to see everyone was as out of sight as they could be before opening the door slowly and peering out. "What do you want?"

"Forgive me, Princess. I didn't mean to disturb you, but His Royal Highness Prince Daymion wishes for you to join him in the courtyard," the servant answered as he bowed his head.

"And why does he want to see me?" Rukia inquired.

"He would like to spar with you, Princess. He's heard of your fighting skill and wishes to see how he compares to you."

"Will this be a private match or are we to be entertainment?" Rukia asked as she crossed her arms.

"He is alone," the servant answered. "Your companions may watch if they wish to do so."

Rukia rubbed her chin. "Very well. Give me a few moments to get dressed."

Shadows of the Past

The servant bowed and handed Rukia a violet rose. "His Majesty is glad you accepted his request. He shall be waiting in the courtyard."

When the servant was gone, Rukia looked out in the hall to find that the guards had also left. Closing the door, she hurried to get dressed. "Coast is clear. The guards are even gone."

"Shall we accompany you to your duel?" Michael asked.

Rukia shrugged. "I kind of think they're expecting it."

"Well, guess that solves the issue of sneaking out of here," Anya said almost cheerfully.

"Yeah, it does," Rilla replied as she played with the crystal around her neck.

"What's wrong, Rilla?" Mahogany asked, knowing that she only played with her crystal when she was worried or upset.

"It just seems a little too easy," Rilla said. "Just as we start to plan our exit, a servant shows up with an invite for a duel, and we're all allowed to be there. Then the guards at the door just disappear." Rilla paused. "I just don't like it. I have a bad feeling about this duel."

Rukia smiled and walked over and ruffled Rilla's dark blue hair. "Good thing my healer will be with me."

"Rukia's right," Michael agreed. "If we're all there, what could happen?"

Rilla sighed. "I guess, but still something feels off."

"It'll be all right, Rilla," Mahogany said as she hugged her arm. "Rukia's the best in the system."

"Almost," Michael said with a smirk.

A pillow flew across the room and smacked Michael in the face. "Shut your mouth!"

Rilla and Michael chuckled and shared a knowing grin. "Well, let's get going," Michael said as he handed Rukia her pants. "We shouldn't keep His Highness waiting."

Rukia snorted as she pulled on her pants and removed the robe. "Ha! Let him wait. The more he waits, the more agitated he'll be, and the worse he'll fight."

"Worried you can't beat him?" Anya teased.

"Hell no! Just want to make as big of a fool out of him as I can," Rukia answered with a grin.

Chapter Nineteen

As the group entered the courtyard, they found a tall, slender boy with dark hair, whom they assumed was Prince Daymion, stretching and swinging his rapier around. He was accompanied by a younger boy with dirty blond hair and two servants. Looking around at the empty windows and dark balconies that surrounded the courtyard, Rilla's stomach clenched. She gripped her crystal, and Mahogany grabbed her left hand and squeezed it tight while Rena rubbed her right arm. "It'll be all right, Rilla," Rena whispered.

"I hope you're right," Rilla mumbled.

"Ah! Welcome, ladies," the boy in fencing gear greeted them when he realized they had entered the courtyard. "And gentleman," he added when he saw Michael. "I am Prince Daymion of Earth. Thank you all for making the journey to my humble little kingdom.

"Thank you, Your Highness," Michael said, bowing.

"We thank you for your gracious invitation."

"Come, friend, no need to be so formal. Daymion will do, although I'm afraid I don't know which of you is which other than you being Michael of Neptune, obviously," the Earth prince said as he looked at the group.

Smiling, Michael nodded. "Then allow me to introduce my friends." He placed his hands on Rukia's shoulders. "This is my fiancée and your dueling partner, Princess Rukia of Uranus."

Daymion bowed. "An honor to meet you at last. I've heard so much about you, but the rumors never mentioned your beauty. I look forward to our duel."

"Flattery won't get me to go easy on you," Rukia said with her arms crossed on her chest.

"I would be greatly disappointed if you didn't give it your best," the Earth prince said with a smile.

Ignoring the competitive glares between the two, Michael grabbed Rilla's arm and pulled her close. "This is my cousin, Princess Amirilla of Mercury."

"Pleased to meet you," Rilla said shyly.

"Surely not the same Amirilla that Prince Amdis spoke of?" Daymion said quizzically.

"Yes, this is Amdis's little sister," Rukia answered. "What of it?"

"I understand now why he was so protective." He took Rilla's hand in his and placed a kiss on it. Rilla tried hard not to gag from his sickening display of affection toward her. "You have my deepest sympathies on the loss of your brother," he said as he released her hand. "I only met him once, but he earned my respect that day. He was a good man."

Rilla nodded and Michael squeezed her arm before moving on. "I guess you can say this one is Rilla's cousin, seeing that Rilla is married to her cousin Jacob." Rilla started to protest Michael telling so much information about her, but Michael winked at her and gave a smirk that told her why he was doing it. It was the same reason he had emphasized that Rukia was his fiancé. He wanted to make sure the Earther knew they were off limits. "This is Princess Rena of Venus."

Rena, being her usual flirty self, held out her hand and gave a seductive grin. "The pleasure is all mine, Prince Daymion."

He smiled and kissed her hand. "An honor, my dear."

"Next is Princess Mahogany of Jupiter."

"Don't introduce us as if you're selling us off!" Mahogany scolded.

Michael chuckled. "Wouldn't dream of it."

When Daymion reached for her hand, Mahogany pulled away. "Nice to meet you."

Anya shook her head and sighed. "Enough already. I'm Anya of Mars; this is Rebecca of Saturn, and Emi of Pluto. There. We've all been introduced. Now can we get on with this?"

Daymion stood shocked for a moment. "Uh, certainly."

"Wait," Rena called as Daymion turned to walk away.

When he was facing her, she continued, "Who is that handsome lad over there?" She pointed to the younger boy, sitting by the dueling field. He was smaller than Daymion and looked frail, almost as if he wasn't eating enough. Rilla studied him closely and got the distinct impression he may have been abused.

Daymion looked behind him. "Oh, Koacho? He's just my younger brother. I told him he could watch the duel as long as he doesn't bother you lovely ladies."

"Oh, he's no bother," Rena said as she rushed over to greet the young prince.

Daymion sent a glare in his brother's direction as the group followed Rena to where Prince Koacho was sitting. He gave a gentle smile and greeted them. "Welcome to Earth. You all honor us with your presence." They returned his greeting and took the seats around him while Daymion and Rukia prepared to start their duel.

"First tap or first blood?" Daymion asked as he took his stance.

"I thought this was a friendly duel?" Anya protested.

"And it is, but surely you aren't fighting at your best if you're trying not to hit your opponent," Daymion replied with an evil grin.

"First blood it is," Rukia said defiantly. "Best two out of three. That way it's not just luck."

"Very well." Daymion nodded and looked to Rilla. "Amirilla, would you give the signal and call point?"

As Rilla started to stand, Koacho leaned over and

whispered, "Warn her that my brother cheats. He doesn't wait for the flag to hit the ground."

Rilla nodded and walked over to the two with the duel flag in hand. She told them to take their spots, and she stood in the middle. Facing Daymion, she asked, "Ready?" He nodded and said he was. She faced Rukia and again asked, "Ready?" Before Rukia could answer, Rilla mouthed Koacho's warning. Rukia nodded that she understood and answered that she was ready as well. Nodding, Rilla tossed the flag up. "Then begin!"

Instead of watching the flag, Rukia kept a close eye on Daymion. Just as Rilla warned, he lunged just before the flag hit the ground. Rukia dodged and caught him off guard.

"He attacked before the flag landed!" Mahogany cried.

"Good thing Rukia noticed," Emi commented.

"You mean, good thing Rilla warned her? Thanks to Koacho's advice," Michael corrected.

Everyone looked at the young prince. "Big brother fights dirty, and he hates to lose," Koacho explained. "I hope Princess Rukia can handle him. I've only seen him lose to one person."

"And who was that?" Rilla asked.

"Your brother, Princess," Koacho replied.

Rilla wasn't really surprised, but wondered about Daymion's fight with her brother. When was it? Why were they fighting? Was it a friendly duel like now or something else? She and the others turned their attention back to the duel. Rukia was smirking, which only pissed Daymion off. For every lunge or swing of the sword he made, she had a counter move. Deciding she had played around enough, Rukia went on the offensive. She moved in and attacked up close, forcing him to back away. It was obvious that he was a range fighter. His height and long arms combined with his unusually long blade gave him the advantage until his opponent got too close, and then his movements became slow and awkward. Rukia, who was similar in height, on the other hand, was an expert at close-range fighting. Her movements were swift and controlled. Daymion was barely able to block them. With one final movement, Rukia pushed him back and sliced his left arm. Rilla jumped up. "First blood! Point to Rukia!"

The two stopped fighting, and Daymion examined the cut. It wasn't deep, but his shirt was already staining red. "You're as good as they say. Guess I'll just have to do better."

Koacho shook his head. "He's angry now."

"Think he'll try more dirty tricks?" Rebecca asked.

"I know he will."

Nervously Rilla approached the ring again; this time Koacho accompanied her to wrap his brother's arm. "Don't hurt her, big brother," he begged as he wrapped Daymion's arm with a bandage.

"Stay out of it, brat," Daymion hissed. "I'll show her."

Rilla handed Rukia a towel and formed a water orb in her hand for her to drink from. "I think you should end this now. You've drawn first blood. You don't have to prove anything to him or anyone else."

"No." Rukia shook her head and sipped cold water from the orb in Rilla's palm. "I said two out of three; to back out now would be cowardly. I have to finish this."

Sighing, Rilla nodded. "Just be careful. Koacho says the more you piss him off, the more he'll cheat."

Rukia smiled. "Don't worry, Mi-chan," she said as she ruffled the Mercurian's hair. "I just have to nick him, and it's all over. I won't play around this time. I'll jump in, cut him, and end this."

Rilla nodded and dispersed the water orb. She glanced over at Daymion, who was pushing his brother away forcefully.

"Ready?" Rilla asked him.

He nodded as he glared at Rukia. Turning to the Uranian, she asked the same to her. Rukia nodded and replied that she was ready. Rilla held up the flag and exclaimed, "Begin!" as she tossed it up in the air.

Rukia watched Daymion closely, expecting him to rush in before the flag landed again, but he didn't. This time he waited, and even after the flag fell to the ground, he didn't move. He stood perfectly still. Rukia stepped side to side, watching and trying to anticipate his attack, but he didn't attack. He just stood there, glaring at her, not moving a muscle. Confused, Rukia lowered her sword. "You all right?"

Rilla and the others watched from the sidelines, just as confused as Rukia was.

"What's he doing?" Emi asked.

"Why doesn't he attack?" questioned Rebecca.

"What dirty trick is he up to now?" inquired Anya.

"Just hit him, Rukia!" Rena yelled.

Rukia glanced over at the group and nodded. Rilla looked to Koacho, but he was staring down at the ground, his hands gripping each other on his lap. She was certain Daymion had threatened to hurt him if he warned them again. Looking back to the duel, Rilla stared at Daymion. Just as Rukia charged, she noticed it.

"Rukia, wait!" Rilla screamed as she jumped up, but it was too late. Rukia charged straight into his trap. He was slowly and quietly saying a spell. His lips barely moved, which was why no one noticed. Daymion had created a large, solid stone wall across the field that came up to Rukia's knees. As he created it, he had also glamoured it. There was no way she could avoid it if she couldn't see it. Rukia slammed into it at full speed and toppled over headfirst. She slid across the ground after landing hard on her left shoulder. Her sword fell from her hand, and then he made his move. As she stopped sliding, he quickly dashed forward and cut her right shoulder.

"I believe that's a point for me." He beamed as he looked at the ladies sitting on the sideline.

"What just happened?" Emi asked, looking around confused.

"Rukia tripped over something," replied Anya.

Rilla formed a water orb in her hand and threw it at the wall. When it hit, the water ran down, revealing the shape. "He made a wall and glamoured it," Rilla explained before she rushed over to Rukia.

"How did Rilla see that?" Rebecca asked.

"Rilla studied illusion magic," Rena answered. "She started learning about it when she was little."

"She even took extra classes at the academy and specialized in glamours," Mahogany added.

"Wow!" said Emi, wide-eyed. "That's amazing."

Rilla glared at Daymion as she helped Rukia stand. "You all right?" she asked her friend as she limped to her side of the ring.

"Yeah, I'll be all right," she replied. As Rilla knelt to examine her leg, Rukia whispered, "Wrap it." Looking up, Rilla gave her a questioning look, but before she could ask, Rukia answered the question. "Two can play this sneak game. He doesn't know you're a healer. Heal my leg, but bandage it as if it's still hurt. He'll expect me to be slow with a hurt leg."

Rilla nodded and went to work. "Watch out for glamoured traps," Rilla warned.

"How did you see that wall anyway?" Rukia asked as she faked a limp on her now bandaged leg.

"I noticed the odd coloration. If the glamor is rushed or poorly done, the color is different," Rilla explained.

"Also he forgot to glamour the shadow. He was good until the sun came out of the clouds." She put a light bandage on Rukia's shoulder, letting a little blood soak into it before she healed it. "There. Now he'll think your shoulder is hurt, too. Just watch him carefully. Who knows what other dirty tricks he may try."

Rukia nodded. "I won't be fooled again." She continued to fake a limp as Rilla looked her over for other injuries. "I'm fine, Rilla. Let's just get this over with."

Nodding, Rilla stepped back. She glared at Daymion once again before asking if he was ready. When he nodded that he was, Rilla started the final round of the duel and then took her seat. Rukia watched Daymion cautiously as she limped toward him. Daymion approached slowly, his sword raised and ready to strike. The two circled each other, each waiting for the other to make their move. Seeing Rukia limp made him smile. Deciding to take his chances, Daymion charged at her full force. Rukia waited until the last minute to dodge. As she sidestepped to avoid him, he grabbed her arm, pulled her toward him, spun around, and thrust his sword straight back into her stomach. The blade went all the way through, and Rukia dropped her sword as he pulled away and yanked the blade out. She looked down at the blood pouring from the wound and fell to the ground.

Chapter Twenty

"Rukia!" Michael yelled as he rushed to her. He pushed Daymion so hard he nearly hit the ground, but he didn't care. He picked up Rukia and cradled her in his arms, one hand against her stomach, trying to stop the bleeding. "I'm here, sweetheart. You'll be all right." He looked around frantically. "Rilla!"

"I'm here, Michael," she said calmly as she knelt beside him. Pulling the harp from her bag, she placed it beside her and formed a water orb in her right hand as she moved Michael's hand with her left. As she chanted the healing spell in ancient Mercurian, the water from the orb left her hand and surrounded the stab wound. When the orb had completely left Rilla's hand, she picked up the harp. "Hold her still," she instructed Michael.

The others stood in a circle around Rukia, watching Rilla work. Gently Rilla plucked the strings and focused her energy. She played the healing song her mother had taught her and continued to chant the healing spell. Rukia groaned as she was surrounded in a blue light. As she wound closed itself, Michael held her hand and whispered words of comfort. When Rilla was finished, she drew the water back to her hand, reforming the orb, which was now a dark red.

"How do you feel?" she asked Rukia.

Rukia opened her eyes and sat up slowly and examined her stomach. "Good as new. Not even a scar to show off," she said with a smile. "See, I told you everything would be fine. As long as you're with me, I know I'll be fine." She reached over and ruffled Rilla's dark hair affectionately.

Everyone had been so concerned with Rukia's injury that they had almost forgotten about the man that had inflicted it to begin with, but Rilla hadn't. She stood and looked over to where Daymion was standing. She quickly drew her sword from her bag and charged at him, the red orb still in her hand. "How dare you!"

Daymion barely had time to draw his sword and block Rilla's attack. Not expecting her, or anyone else for that matter, to retaliate against him, he had sheathed his sword and taken off his gloves. Now he held the rapier with sweaty hands while being backed against the wall he'd been leaning on.

"Rilla?" Michael called questioningly from behind her as she continued her assault. Michael didn't deny that Daymion deserved this and needed to be taught a lesson, but he felt it was his place to do it, not Rilla.

"I'm going to teach this arrogant prick a lesson!" Rilla exclaimed as she threw the water orb at him. The orb exploded on contact, drenching Daymion, turning his white shirt red.

"Rilla, be fair," Emi pleaded.

"Fair?" Rilla stopped her attack and backed off to look at her companions. "He challenged her to a friendly duel and then not only cheats but critically wounds her, and you want me to be fair?" While she was distracted, Daymion took the time to quickly put his gloves back on to improve his grip on his sword.

"Rilla, we all feel the same, but don't attack in anger," Mahogany cautioned.

"Go for it, Rilla," Rukia said as she stood. Everyone turned to her with shocked expressions. "Show him what you can do."

Seeing that everyone, including Rilla, was focused on Rukia, Daymion thought it was his chance. He charged at Rilla, intending to put her down quickly for her sudden assault on him.

"Rilla, look—"

Before Michael could finish his warning, Daymion had attacked, and failed. Rilla blocked his attack without ever looking at him. She held her sword in one hand, not even seeming to make much of an effort to push against his sword. Daymion, on the other hand, had swung with all his might and was struggling to try and force her sword down. Rilla rotated her sword around his, trying to disarm him, and nearly succeeded.

Daymion jumped back, trying to put space between them. He only had a moment before Rilla was on him again. He didn't have time to think; he had to go on instinct to keep up with her attacks, and he wasn't very good at that. Every time he blocked one attack, she was already starting her next. Feeling cornered, he blocked her next attack by pushing as hard as he could. This forced her back a little. Then he dove forward, into a roll, hoping he could get behind her. Before he came out of his forward roll, Rilla was at his back, sword at his neck.

"Do you yield?" Daymion stayed motionless. "Do you yield?" she repeated as she pressed the blade of her sword against his throat.

"He yields." Everyone turned to see a six-foot-tall gentleman with white hair and a thick white beard approaching.

"Father, I—"

"You should know when to yield to someone who is better than you," Lucydion interrupted.

Rilla pulled her sword away and bowed. "King Lucydion."

Smiling, Lucydion reached out and took her hand. "You must be Amirilla of Mercury. I see you have your father's dark hair, your mother's eyes, and your brother's fighting skill." Rilla opened her mouth to speak, but Lucydion cut her off. "I'd know that fighting spirit anywhere. I'll never forget it, especially seeing as how it was your brother who gave me this." He pulled the collar of his shirt aside to show a large faded scar. "I had hoped that my son would have learned the lesson that your brother taught me by now, but hopefully you've shown him the error of his ways," Lucydion added.

Rilla glanced at Daymion, who simply glared at her. "If not, I will gladly teach it to him," she said firmly.

"Uh, well, this has certainly been an interesting time," Michael said, rushing in to try and prevent another fight. "King Lucydion, we're honored by your invitation to visit your beautiful kingdom, and we assure you that your sons will be safe on their trip to the outer part of the system."

Lucydion looked at Michael and nodded, "Yes, of course." Turning to Koacho, he ordered, "Get your brother cleaned up for dinner and clean up this mess. Once that is done, you may join us for dinner." Koacho bowed and rushed over to help Daymion up. "I look forward to speaking with all of you at dinner," Lucydion said with a nod of his head. Then he turned and left.

When his father was gone, Daymion pushed his brother away. "I can fend for myself." He pushed him a second time, knocking him to the ground.

Rilla's sword quickly found its way back to Daymion's throat. "Is that how you treat your own brother?" she seethed.

"Half-brother," he growled.

"Half-brother, full-brother, or servant you will treat him with some respect. Or have you forgotten how you became a prince?" Rilla stated, her voice full of venom.

"Rilla…" Michael warned as he moved her sword.

"And what is that supposed to mean?" Daymion demanded.

"It means you could be overthrown, just like your grandfather overthrew the previous ruler. Being royalty means you serve your people, not the other way around," Rilla explained.

"That's enough, Rilla," Michael said as he led her away.

Rukia helped Koacho up and dusted him off. "Come on, Prince Koacho," she said, making sure to emphasize the word *prince*. "Since your brother doesn't want your help, you can entertain us until dinner." Rena happily grabbed Koacho's arm and led him away before anyone could protest.

Once the group was away from the courtyard, Emi spoke up, "So what now? It's still a couple of hours until dinner."

The group stopped and looked at one another. "Good question, Emi," Rebecca said.

"Well, we could take a look around and see what there is to see," Mahogany suggested.

"You're not supposed to wander around the castle," Koacho said nervously.

"We won't be wandering," Rena said seductively as she hugged his arm.

"Yeah, we'll be with you, so it'll be like a guided tour," Emi said cheerfully.

"Sounds like a great idea," Michael said, smiling.

"Yeah, since this is our first trip to Earth, and with your kingdom joining the court soon, it would be great if you gave us a tour and told us a little about your world and your family," Rebecca added.

"Oh, okay," the young prince replied. Starting to feel better about himself, he smiled. "Where should we start?"

As Koacho took the group on a tour of his home, he told them the brief history, as he had been taught, of his family's rise to power. Rilla was certain that he was quoting the history written by his grandfather or father about the previous queen and why she needed to be overthrown because Koacho didn't sound like he truly believed what he was telling them. Anya started to speak against what he was saying several times, but Rilla grabbed her arm and shook her head, silently telling her it was best to keep quiet.

When Koacho had concluded his tour, he showed each of them back to their rooms and returned to the courtyard to clean up the mess, as his father had ordered. Meanwhile Michael and the princesses relaxed in their rooms and started to get cleaned up for dinner.

* * *

At seven sharp, a guard arrived at each door to escort them to the dining hall. They were greeted by Queen

Delecia, who stood and hugged them all in turn. "Welcome to Earth. So sorry I wasn't here to greet you earlier, but there were several last-minute arrangements for the wedding I had to attend to. I do hope my husband and sons were good hosts in my absence." They just smiled and held their tongues about the conflict in the courtyard.

As they took their seats, Rilla looked around at the strange decorations on the wall. She was slightly disgusted that they used the heads of wild animals for ornaments. Deciding to ignore the walls before it upset her, she focused on the table and the massive spread of food before them. There were, at least, twenty different dishes surrounding the main course, which was a large animal with a red fruit stuffed in its mouth. Sighing, Rilla realized that animals weren't given a lot of respect on this world. As the servants walked around filling plates and glasses, the group was quiet. No one really knew what to say, and all hoped to avoid conflict, all but Daymion, that is.

"So, Father, when do we join the court? I'm looking forward to competing in their fencing tournaments. I'm sure they'll be thrilled to have a new champion," he said with a smug grin.

"Right after your wedding, my boy. I'm meeting with Galactica the next day," Lucydion responded.

The king started to continue, but Rukia cut him off. "Empress."

"Excuse me?" Lucydion seemed almost astounded that anyone would interrupt him.

"She is our empress, and you will address her as such," Rukia said firmly.

Lucydion made a disapproving face. "Very well. I will be meeting with the empress." He paused to glare at Rukia. "Once Daymion is wed, I hope he can take his place as a general in the court like the rest of you."

Seeing the tension, Rena spoke up and changed the subject. "Daymion, how did you meet Princess Selen?"

"I haven't," he said plainly. "Father thought it was a good way to establish a relationship with the Intergalactic Court. I've heard she's very lovely, though. Have any of you met her?"

Rukia nodded. "She visited my home with the empress when I was little."

"She's been at a few of the balls at Central Palace," Michael added.

"Didn't your father or mother meet her? Surely the empress asked Selen about a marriage first," Mahogany questioned.

"Koacho and I have met her a few times in our travels, but they were brief encounters," Queen Delecia said. "She seems to be a lovely girl, though. I'm sure she'll make a fine wife for Daymion."

Rilla noticed Koacho's distracted expression and the way he played with his food when they were talking about Selen. While the encounters may have been brief, they were long enough for an attraction to form. Sighing, Rilla thought of her own marriage and prayed Selen wouldn't have a similar or worse life. She listened as the queen gave them details about the wedding and their roles in it. When Delecia commented on it being a historic event, Rilla thought she saw Koacho smirk. Before she could decide if she had actually seen that, Rena asked something that made him blush, "So once your brother is married, are you going to start looking for a bride of your own?"

"I…uh…"

"Who would want to marry him?" Daymion said, before laughing. "Honestly, what would be gained from him marrying?"

"He is next in line for the throne," Anya spoke up. "It's only right he marry and have children as well."

"I'm next in line, and my children will inherit from me," Daymion spat.

"If you live that long," Rukia spoke calmly.

"What?" Lucydion nearly jumped out of his chair.

"Nothing is certain," Rilla jumped in. "I wasn't supposed to become a general and be the next queen, but that all changed with the death of my brother. So don't be so cocky as to think you'll live forever. Koacho may very well find himself being crowned king someday." She spoke calmly and clearly, making sure her point was made, and then turned to Koacho. "And should that day come, I think he'll make a fine king."

"Thank you, Princess," Koacho whispered.

"Spoken like a true diplomat, Amirilla," the queen said with a smile.

"Yes, you certainly have a way with words, Princess. Gifted scholar and fighter. If your hand weren't already taken, I'd arrange a marriage between you and Daymion, instead of Selen," Lucydion said with a smirk, trying to get a rise from Rilla.

"You'd try, but in the end, it would be my call. While my current marriage was arranged, I was the one who chose to go through with it," Rilla informed him. "While Jacob isn't the sweetest or most charming man I know, he is preferable to some," she added, glaring in Daymion's direction.

Daymion returned the glare but kept quiet. As did everyone else. The rest of dinner was silent, other than an occasional request to pass something or a whispered comment between Lucydion and his son.

Chapter Twenty-one

That night after dinner, Rilla's sleep was anything but peaceful. She kept having visions and nightmares and was overwhelmed with feelings of doom and despair. The final vision she had that night was the most terrifying of them all.

Rilla was running through a dark forest. The only light she had to go by was the dim glow of the moon, which was blood red. She was filled with fear and didn't dare look behind her. She stopped for a moment and leaned against a tree to catch her breath. As she looked around, the shadows of the trees seemed to move on their own. "Too slow," a voice whispered as Rilla felt a hot breath on the back of her neck.

Jumping, she took off running again as she heard a deep voice that sent chills down her spine laugh. When she turned to the left to try and get away, she stepped into a shadow and felt her feet fall into a giant hole. As she stood there, her entire lower body hidden in a dark invisible hole, Rilla heard the sound of horses' hooves approaching fast. Glancing back, she saw a dark figure, riding a flaming horse, racing toward her. Struggling to pull herself out of the hole, she quickly realized the hole was filled with mud. She barely managed to get out and on her feet before the horse and rider were on top of her.

Racing down the path again, Rilla heard him laugh again. "Foolish girl! You'll never escape me. Death will find you, and you shall know fear, and you shall know pain, and then you will die!"

Faster and faster, she ran, trying to get away. Stepping into a second shadow, Rilla felt as if her feet had just run over hot coals. Stumbling slightly, she managed to catch herself, just to step in a third shadow. This time, her whole left side felt like it was wrapped in thorns. "The shadows hide danger." She heard the voice, but didn't recognize it as her own. Rilla tried to run again but found herself feeling weak.

Hearing noise behind her, she turned and screamed when she saw the deformed face of her pursuer. "Got you!"

"Take these shadows from my sight and fill the room with light!" a voice called from behind her. There was a bright light that filled the room and Rilla's mind, and then she passed out.

* * *

When Rilla awoke the next morning, the sun was shining and her dreams from the night before were one giant blur. She started to sit up and quickly realized she wasn't alone. There was a weight on her chest, and glancing down, she saw bright red hair surrounding a round face with cherry red lips. The redhead's arm was wrapped around Rilla, and she was fast asleep. Smiling, Rilla sat up slowly and moved Rena to the pillow beside her. Rena snuggled up to the pillow and continued to sleep. Carefully, Rilla climbed out of bed and started to get dressed. Once dressed, she sat on the edge of the bed, and finally Rena started to wake up. She sat up and looked sleepily at Rilla, who smiled and said, "Good morning, Rena."

"Morning," she said before yawning and stretching her arms over her head. "Is it really morning already?"

"Yes." Rilla chuckled. "How long have you been in here?"

"I don't know. You were screaming in your sleep," Rena explained as she climbed out of bed. "I came in through the balcony door and tried to wake you. You grabbed me, and your eyes were all weird looking. Then you yelled at me, something about watching the shadows because danger is in the shadows and that you were going to die." Rena grabbed Rilla's hand and squeezed it. "Oh, Rilla! I was so scared. I didn't know what to do. You kept screaming, so I used a light spell to banish the shadows. You called out for your sister and passed out. I didn't want to leave you alone in case it happened again, so I climbed in bed with you."

"And you had to use my chest as a pillow?" Rilla asked with a smirk.

Rena grinned and released Rilla's hand. "Well…you started tossing and groaning, so I hugged you to keep you still."

"Did I say anything else?" Rilla asked in a serious tone as she stood.

"Not that I recall. You don't remember?" Rena questioned, concern obvious in her voice.

Rilla shook her head. "Not really. It's all a big blur. Blood, death, all of you crying..." She tried to remember. "I don't know. It's weird. I usually remember visions perfectly, but this one I can't recall other than a few images. It's been happening a lot lately. I don't know why my visions are so blurred lately."

"Do you think it was my spell? Did I mess up your vision? I was scared and I panicked, and..."

"It's all right, Rena," Rilla said, cutting her off. "You were just trying to help. I'm sure it'll come to me in time," she assured her. "But now we should get downstairs. I'm sure the others are waiting for us." Rena nodded and hurried to her room to get dressed.

* * *

Once they were downstairs, they found everyone in the dining hall having breakfast.

"About time you two got up," Rukia teased as they sat down.

"Yeah, went to check on you, and your door was locked and Rena's room was empty," Mahogany said with a raised eyebrow.

"Not what you're thinking, Mahogany," Rilla said, almost scolding. She wasn't in the mood for the teasing. Her stomach was in knots, and it was driving her crazy that she couldn't remember her vision. "Rena was in my room because I was screaming in my sleep."

"Nightmares?" Rukia asked.

Rilla nodded.

"Same here, cousin," Michael spoke up.

"Visions?" Anya inquired.

"I believe so," Rilla answered. "Rena said my eyes were weird looking."

Putting his fork down, Michael asked, "What did you see, Rilla?"

"A forest filled with shadows, feelings of fear and despair, and the rest is a blur."

Michael and Rukia looked at each other and then her. It was unlike Rilla to have a blurry vision or forget it. "I think it's my fault," Rena blurted out, seeing their confused looks. "I was scared, and she told me there was danger in the shadows, so I cast a spell to fill the room with light. She called out for Tora and then passed out."

"Tora?" Rebecca wondered out loud.

"Rilla's younger sister," Mahogany told her.

"What does she have to do with this?" Anya almost demanded.

"No clue," Rilla said as she buttered a slice of toast. "What did you see, Michael?"

"Me?" Michael looked around absently. "Uh...about the same as you, just a bunch of jumbled images and strong feelings of dread."

Rilla knew when he avoided eye contact with her that he was lying. He had seen something he didn't want to tell her, something about Tora perhaps. Rilla decided not to push him. She knew he'd tell her in time. The group ate the rest of their meal in silence as they all thought about the events of late. So many things were happening so fast. Things were changing, and no one was sure if they were for the best.

As the servants cleared the table, the group looked around and wondered what to do next. The king and his sons were nowhere in sight. Queen Delecia had made a brief appearance to say "good morning" and then she, too, disappeared. Walking up and down the halls of the castle, they couldn't help but notice how deserted it was.

"Where is everyone?" Emi said, voicing the question everyone was thinking.

"I don't know, but I don't like this," Anya stated.

"What gives?" Mahogany crossed her arms over her chest. "Yesterday we were treated like prisoners, and today they can't be bothered with us?"

Rilla peered out a window and spotted Koacho racing across the courtyard. "There's Koacho. Looks like he's headed to the stables. Let's see if we can catch him."

Before anyone could say a word, Rilla took off at a dead run, heading for the stables. Seeing Koacho had filled her with a feeling of sadness, and she saw a flash of a crossbow firing and a pool of blood. She didn't know why, but she knew she had to catch Koacho because something bad was going to happen. When Rilla raced into the stables, the young prince was saddling a horse.

"Koacho!" she called as she panted, trying to catch her breath.

"Princess Amirilla, is everything all right?"

"I was about to ask you the same thing," Rilla said with a smile. "We haven't seen anyone other than your mother all morning."

"Father and my brother are out collecting taxes and checking on the villages," Koacho explained. "I was about to ride out and join them."

"Mind if I come along?"

"Uh…I'm not sure if Father would like that," Koacho said nervously.

"Rilla!" Michael called as he rushed into the stables with the others right behind them.

"It's all right, Michael. I caught him before he left," Rilla said.

"I was about to go join my father and brother in the villages," Koacho explained.

"Then we're all going with you," Rukia said in a tone that told Koacho not to argue.

"Well, Father did tell me to take care of our guests, so he can't be mad if I give you a tour of the kingdom, right?" Koacho said, smiling. He quickly prepared the carriage and saddled a second horse. Seeing the carriage only held six plus a driver, two would have to ride on horseback alongside the carriage. Rilla and Michael volunteered to take the horses, which greatly surprised her, seeing as Michael disliked horseback riding. She figured he was just being a gentleman in letting the ladies have the cushioned seats of the carriage.

Koacho was true to his word about a tour; he showed them every village, historic site, and even the best places for a picnic or to just lie back and watch the clouds. Rilla smiled at how happy he seemed to be when he was sharing these peaceful spots. At the same time, she felt very sad for him. She got the feeling he spent a lot of his time in these places, where he could be free from his father and brother. Life for him seemed to be more like that of a servant than that of a prince. Thinking about it made Rilla's blood boil. If her vision had been a warning of something terrible that was to happen on Earth, she planned to do all in her power to see that it wasn't to this young prince.

* * *

By late afternoon, they caught up with the king and Daymion, who were at their last stop before returning to the castle. No one was surprised to see the king barking orders or Daymion flirting with every farm girl. They were, however, shocked to see three men tied to posts being given lashes with a whip.

"What's going on?" Anya cried, outraged.

The king and Daymion turned to see Koacho driving the carriage filled with their visitors.

"Ah, it's nice of you to join us, boy. I was expecting you sooner, but I see now what delayed you." The man with the whip gave another round of lashes, but Lucydion didn't seem to notice their screams of agony as he continued, "I hope my son hasn't been a bore to you, ladies."

"Lucydion, what is the meaning of this?" Michael demanded as he got off his horse and rushed to put an end to the lashes.

Grabbing Michael's arm, Lucydion stopped him from interfering. "It's nothing you need concern yourself with my boy, just making an example out of some lawbreakers."

"And what crime have they committed?" Rilla asked as she dismounted her horse.

"Not paying taxes, of course," Lucydion said casually.

"You must be joking?" Mahogany interjected.

"No, he's not. Don't your kingdoms enforce the payment of taxes?" Daymion jumped in, coming to his father's aid.

"Yes, but not by brutally whipping them," Rena stated.

"If you honestly want to join the Intergalactic Court," Michael started, "then I suggest you cut those men loose and find a more suitable means of punishment."

Rilla didn't wait for the king to reply. She pulled out her dagger, causing the king's two guards to draw their swords. She ignored the guards and went to the men tied to the posts and started cutting the ropes binding the first man.

"Now see here!" Lucydion barked. "You have no right. Even if we were members of the court, each kingdom is free to rule as they see fit. Or was that a lie?"

"Not a lie, but there are certain rules and principals we all must follow. One of them being no cruel or unusual punishments," Michael explained.

Daymion and the guards went to stop Rilla, but all three found swords pointing at them. Rukia had climbed off the carriage when the guards drew their swords and now had a sword pointed at each of them. Daymion found himself, once again, facing Rilla's rapier. Thinking he could take her because her back was slightly turned as she continued to cut the prisoner free, Daymion started to move, but stopped dead in his tracks when she turned her head to glare at him.

"Go ahead and try it," Rilla dared. "Your father won't save you this time."

Daymion backed off and sheathed his sword. "Let…let them go," he stammered.

"Daymion!" his father bellowed.

"Sorry, Father, but it was you who told me to know when to surrender to someone better than myself. If you want, you can take her on," Daymion stated as he backed up further.

Rilla turned to face the king and pointed her sword at him, daring him to try it. Lucydion stared at the Mercury princess, trying to determine if she was bluffing or not. When he glanced over at the others, who were watching to see what he would do, he decided against it.

"Guards, release them," he ordered, even though it pained him to say it.

The guards nodded, sheathed their swords, and cut the other two prisoners down as Rilla finished freeing the first. Once the ropes were all cut, the men fell to the ground. Rilla did her best to catch the first man, while the guards let the other two men fall to the ground without offering to help.

Easing the man to the ground, Rilla told him to lie on his stomach and that it was going to be all right. Rena and Mahogany jumped from the carriage and hurried over to the other two men. Rilla formed a water orb and began healing the first man's injuries, just as she had done for Rukia. Meanwhile Rena formed a ball of bright white light in her left hand and chanted in ancient Venusian as she moved the ball over the second man's back. A beam of light shone from the orb in her hand on to the man's back. Slowly the second man's injuries began to heal.

Mahogany, on the other hand, used a different method of healing. She pulled various herbs from a bag she kept tied at her waist, and mixed them in her hand. By the time her dry mixture was done, Rilla had already completely healed the first man and was at her side. Knowing what her friend needed, Rilla formed a new water orb and slowly poured water into her hand as Mahogany continued to mix.

"Together?" Rilla asked.

Mahogany had chosen to learn the art of herbal healing at the academy. She told Rilla she felt bad about always having others healing her injuries and not being able to return the favor, so she learned how to use herbs.

Shadows of the Past

Mahogany's way may have taken a bit longer, but it was no less effective. Nodding, the Jupiter princess began to spread the paste over the man's back. Rilla slowly surrounded the area with water, being careful not to wash away the paste. Together they chanted in their respective planet's language. When the men were fully healed, they thanked the princesses and ran off before Lucydion could change his mind about letting them go.

While Lucydion was not pleased with their interference, he didn't do or say anything else against them. He did make a mental note to come back once his visitors were gone. The guards loaded the tax money onto the wagon and prepared for the trip back to the castle. Michael drove the carriage and gave Koacho his horse, as the king ordered his son to ride up front with him and Daymion. Rilla was certain it was so he could scold him. At first they rode back silently; the king and his sons led the way, followed by the wagon, and Rilla and the carriage brought up the rear. About halfway there, Rilla could hear the king's angry voice but couldn't make out what was being said.

The path they took back was more direct and less scenic than the way that Koacho had taken them. The road was dark and deserted with dense forest surrounding them. Suddenly it got quiet, too quiet. The king was no longer yelling. There were no sounds, except those of the horses' hooves and the creak of the wheels of the wagons.

When the horses started trying to back up or stop, Rilla steered hers closer to the carriage.

"Something's wrong," she whispered to Michael. Nodding, he stopped the carriage, and Rilla allowed her horse to stop and gently patted his neck. "Shh…it's all right."

"Move, you stupid horse!" Rilla looked up, hearing Daymion yell at the horse. He and his father were kicking their horses, trying to force them to keep going.

"Something's not right!" Rilla called to them. "The horses are spooked; we should take another way back!"

"Nonsense! We go on!" barked Lucydion.

"What do we do, Rilla?" Rena asked.

"We have to stay with them. I have a bad feeling, but I'm not going to let Koacho get hurt if I can help it," she answered. The others nodded, and slowly they followed the king, keeping their eyes open for signs of trouble. Rilla continued rubbing her horse's neck and whispered comforting words to keep him calm.

"What's going on?" inquired Emi when the king stopped suddenly.

When the wagon carrying the tax money stopped and the guards climbed down, Rilla's stomach turned.

"I don't know, but I'll find out." Slowly she rode forward to see what was wrong. When she saw the reason they stopped, she looked around frantically. The road ahead was blocked by large trees and brush. Rilla was certain someone had done it on purpose. Hearing the snap of a branch, Rilla looked and spotted it. Someone was in the tree with a large crossbow pointed at the king and his sons.

"Koacho, get down!" Rilla yelled as she kicked her horse, getting him to sprint forward.

The king and princes turned to see Rilla charging toward them.

Seeing her take off, Michael panicked and dove off the carriage.

"Rilla, wait!"

He took off running after her, trying to avoid what he knew was coming. Rilla's dash to save the young prince was putting her in the line of fire. As she reached the prince, there was a bright flash that blinded Michael and the others for a moment. When he opened his eyes, Michael saw Rilla falling from the back of her horse, an arrow sticking out of her back.

"NOOOOOO!" Michael heard his own scream echoed by the voices of his friends. He ran as fast as he could until he made it to his cousin. The others hurried to join him, none noticing Rukia race toward the woods in pursuit of the shooter.

Rilla was face down with the black arrow sticking straight up when Michael reached her. He picked her up and held her sideways to give the others access to the arrow, which he prayed wasn't poisoned.

"Hold on, Mi-chan," he whispered with tears in his eyes. "Just hold on."

Rilla looked up at him, opened her mouth as if to say something, and then her eyes closed and her body went limp.

Acknowledgments

First, a big thank you to everyone who purchased a copy of this book. I hope you enjoyed it and are looking forward to the rest of the series. Second, a huge thank you to my dear friend Jeremy who made my dream of being a published author happen a lot sooner than I could have on my own. I owe you more than I can ever repay. Third I'd like to give my love and great appreciation to Miriam and Dee Jay at GenkiGoth Studios for the beautiful cover art they provided for this book. I'd also like to thank my mother and all friends who read the early drafts and offered feedback and advice, as well as some editing for me. Finally an enormous thank you to my loving husband for supporting me and putting up with me while I struggled to write, edit, and publish this book. I wouldn't have made it this far without you.

-Lannie 9/15

Made in the USA
San Bernardino, CA
19 June 2016